THE SOUTHLAND

THE SOUTHLAND

Johnny Shaw

Copyright © 2020 by Johnny Shaw
Cover and jacket design by Georgia Morrissey

ISBN 978-1-947993-96-9
eISBN: 978-1-951709-22-8
Library of Congress Control Number: available upon request

First trade paperback edition August 2021 by Agora Books
An imprint of Polis Books, LLC
44 Brookview Lane
Aberdeen, NJ
PolisBooks.com

For Joaquín

PART ONE

ONE

The madman on the bus hated Mexicans. He had been barking the same nonsense from the moment he had boarded at Whittier Boulevard.

Since Luz Delgado's arrival in Los Angeles years earlier, she had heard all the names Americans had for Mexicans, spoken both to her face and behind her back. The names no longer bothered her, but the man's shouting interfered with her nap. The pinche chiflado could call her whatever he wanted, so long as he kept his voice down. Luz counted on the twenty minutes of sleep on the commute to her day job. It had been wishful to think that she could enjoy such an extravagance.

The man reminded her of Hector Dávila from her pueblo. Tia Ramona joked that Hector's father had hit him so many times that his head had become soft like a sponge. Hector would spend mornings yelling at the street dogs—and the rest of the day trying to find the same dogs to apologize. He was harmless, but his softest tone was a falling man's scream.

Luz was annoyed, but she couldn't raise much anger toward a lost soul who stank of sour liquor and mierda. With his wild hair and unkempt beard, the man was a wounded animal, beaten down by his surroundings, his circumstances, and his own mind. He lived in a reality that only he understood, pieced together from voices, both real and imagined.

In the madman's reality, Mexicans were destroying America. He was a patriot and they were invaders. The word *scourge* was uttered more than once. Mexicans were the problem. All the kinds of Mexicans. The madman hated Guatemalan Mexicans, Salvadoran Mexicans, Colombian Mexicans, even Puerto Rican Mexicans. But he especially hated Mexican Mexicans.

Luz avoided eye contact, glancing at the man's reflection in the big round mirror at the front of the bus. When he looked in her direction, she immediately turned away. She tolerated the show, but didn't want to be dragged onto the stage.

The rest of the passengers—Mexicans, Central Americans, and African-Americans—employed similar tactics. The tops of shoes, graffitied-over bus ads, and the predawn glow of Los Angeles out the window became fascinating. Eyes focused anywhere but on the yelling man.

Luz's seventeen-year-old son, Eliseo, was the exception. Young men lived without caution or sense. Eliseo sat with his legs in the aisle, staring directly at him. He leaned forward, taut as a spring.

Luz put a hand on her son's arm. "Don't do anything. It'll only make trouble."

Eliseo shook off her hand, neither answering nor looking away from the man.

"He is not right in the head," Luz said.

The madman's voice grew piercingly high, upset with the lack of attention from his captive audience. "*You come to America. My America! The greatest country in the world. You bring your drugs. And your gangs. And your crime. You steal our jobs and our women. You collect welfare and food stamps and illegally vote Democrat. You're lazy.*"

Before Luz could suppress it, a small laugh escaped. The thought of lecturing a group of people on their way to work at five in the morning about laziness amused her. Without looking, she knew the man had turned in her direction.

The madman's voice grew. "*You are all weeds in the American garden. Ugly. Strangling the native roots. Using precious resources. Unwanted. You need to be removed before you destroy the natural beauty.*"

Eliseo stood in the aisle and pointed at the man. "Cállate."

"Eliseo," Luz hissed, reaching for him.

"He makes my head hurt," Eliseo said.

"He doesn't speak Spanish," Luz said. "He is crazy in the head."

The madman looked Eliseo up and down. He staggered slightly, but remained upright on the moving bus. A deranged sea captain, alone and battered by the raging storm.

"*Shut up,*" Eliseo said, his accent thick and his words unsure. One of the few English phrases that he had picked up.

The bus driver turned in her seat and looked at Eliseo. "*Sir, I need you to sit down.*"

"What did she say?" Eliseo asked Luz.

"You need to sit down. You're causing trouble."

"What about him*?*" Eliseo said to Luz.

"There are privileges to being mad."

"*Sir, I need you to sit down,*" the driver repeated. "*Now.*"

"*It's okay,*" Luz said. "*He's young. He has no patience.*"

"What are you saying to her?" Eliseo asked. "Tell her that people stand on buses all the time. I don't have to sit."

The madman joined the conversation. His face glowed red. The veins on his forehead bulged. Trying to regain the center of attention, the man uttered a loud and insistent string of rapid-fire gibberish. It sounded like he was saying "magamagamaga."

"*That's it.*" The driver pulled to the curb. "*It's too damn early for this bullshit. I'm calling the police.*"

A communal groan rose from the other passengers. When the bus came to a stop and the doors opened, everyone rose from their seats and gathered their belongings. No loud protests. Simple resolve. They shook their heads and quietly muttered, glaring in Luz and Eliseo's direction. Even the madman left. Today's performance had come to a close.

"Let's go," Luz said to Eliseo. "Unless you want to talk to the police?"

"The police don't scare me."

"Such a macho."

"This isn't over."

"What happens next?" Luz asked. "How does this end?"

"I don't know."

"I'll tell you. It ends with me walking to work, praying I arrive on time. It ends with you at the underpass hopefully finding work today."

"I should have stayed in México."

Luz and Eliseo walked the mile and a half in silence. When they reached the hotel where Luz worked as a housekeeper, Eliseo didn't break stride or say goodbye.

Seven years had been too long apart. Luz couldn't reconnect with her son. She didn't know Eliseo at all, and he didn't want to know her.

Luz took one last breath of the cool morning air, walked around the building to the employee entrance, and went to work.

TWO

Nadia placed the brick onto the wet mortar, tapped it down with the handle of the trowel, scraped off any excess, then repeated the actions. Brick by brick. One by one. In time, the bricks would form a wall.

At first it had been difficult for Nadia to get day work as a bricklayer. It had taken a particularly hot day, low worker turnout, and Miguel Hernández's recommendation to get the contractor to hire a woman. It hadn't been charity. It came as no surprise when he had demanded Nadia return the favor by drinking with him at his apartment. When she refused, he called her a tortillera and bluffed violence.

She hadn't needed his recommendation after that day. The other bricklayers had seen her work, matching their speed and endurance, if not always their finesse. Her work ethic and skill earned their respect enough to get her more work the next day. In the months since, she had become more confident and practiced, her movements more fluid. The return of a dormant skill from her youth, temporarily lost but embedded deep in muscle memory.

Nadia's father had been a bricklayer. As a child, she had watched Papá perform the same motion for hours. A dancer's grace in the calloused hands of a laborer. Nadia had inherited his ability and his patience.

She had assisted him, but nobody in Cualicán would hire a female mason. It seemed strange now to think about how crushing that disappointment had been at fifteen, the day she realized that she would never work alongside her father.

Even the simplest dreams could shatter.

Nadia had enough youthful ambition to set herself on a new path away from the family trade. One that had led to opportunity and happiness, then tragedy, then right back to the future that she had desired as a teenager. Her childhood dream had become a reality only when it no longer mattered to her. Nadia found no humor in the irony.

She was careful in her reminiscences. Her youth remained friendly territory, safe to unearth. The distant past lived safely in faded photographs and almost-forgotten nostalgia. It was a toothless animal, benign and approachable. Unlike the more recent past that needed to remain in its lair. That was the monster that could eat her whole.

On the days that she held off the bottle until dark, Nadia's survival depended on repeated action and mundanity. Day by day. Moment by moment. Brick by brick. To let the bricks slowly form a wall.

"All right, Pacos. And Paco-ette," Dan Schauer bellowed. "Finito. Terminado. *That's it.* No más. *All done.* Todo listo."

Nadia wanted to tell him that his Spanglish and horrible pronunciation only made his communication worse, but everyone got the gist. The workday was done.

Schauer walked along the brickwork, giving the wall an overly dramatic eyeball inspection. It wouldn't have surprised Nadia to see him run his finger along the bricks and taste it. All a show for the client who watched from the kitchen window. The woman was Nadia's age, at least forty—no matter how much she attempted to stop time with plastic surgery—and had spent the day walking among the working men. She appeared to only own a bikini.

Nadia's back seized when she tried to stand. She crouched until the cramp subsided. Her joints slowly creaked into motion. While the blisters on her hands had hardened, the twelve-hour days took a toll on her joints. Her ego insisted she could do the physical things she had done in her youth, but reality had a way of punishing the delusional.

"*Clean up the tools. Chop, chop. I want to get home. It's Taco Tuesday at my house. I suppose it's always Taco Tuesday for you fellas.*"

Moving slower than at the beginning of the day, the men gathered the equipment. Nadia found loose tools along the perimeter and placed them in the cleanest wheelbarrow. They all worked together, efficient and practiced. A few jokes and laughs arose, but halfhearted after an exhausting day.

"*All of you that need a ride back to the lot—*" Schauer mimed turning a steering wheel. "*Meet me at my truck. El truck-o. We'll square up after I take a shit.* Dinero después caca.*"

Nadia walked to the truck and lined up behind Roberto Arce. A young kid stood behind her. After a few minutes, Schauer exited the chemical toilet making a big show of how bad it stank, waving his hand near his rear end. At the truck, he took out a wad of money from his front pocket, counted out sixty dollars, and handed it to Roberto.

Roberto looked at the three twenties for a moment. He rubbed each one to see if the bills were stuck together.

"*Something wrong?*" Schauer asked. "*¿Problemo?*"

Roberto considered it, shook his head, pocketed the money, and climbed in the back of the truck.

"That's bullshit," the young man behind Nadia said. "He said eighty."

"If you want to work tomorrow." Nadia turned to the young man. "Take the money and keep your mouth shut."

"It's not fair. He can't do that."

"He can," Nadia said.

The young man wasn't wrong about the money. Schauer had promised eighty dollars. Nadia didn't know what the kid was complaining about though. He was the laziest person she had ever met. He had only worked when Schauer was around and always took the easiest tasks. When Nadia had taken her afternoon break, she had caught sight of the kid going into the house with the bikini-clad owner. The kid was lucky to get paid at all.

Nadia didn't see the difference between sixty dollars and eighty. It made no sense to say anything, no more so than complaining to someone who slapped her in the face nine times after they had promised ten slaps. Life had not been fair in Mexico. Nadia had no expectation of finding fairness just because she crossed a border.

When Nadia reached Schauer, he counted out forty dollars. "*I should pay you less. Charity, letting a woman work for me.*"

Nadia smiled, acting like she didn't understand. She held out her hand waiting for the rest of her money.

"*Just kidding. I'm a fair man.*" He placed a third twenty on top of the other two.

She turned to the young man and shook her head. She knew that the kid would ignore her warning.

Schauer handed three twenties to the young man.

"Veinte *more*," he said in broken English. "*You say* ochenta."

"*You heard wrong, Paco*," Schauer said. "*Language barrier.*"

"Veinte *dollars.*"

Schauer looked at the money, chuckled to himself, and turned his back on the kid. He was still laughing when he climbed into his truck. The young man fumed, but did nothing else.

"Come on, kid," Nadia said, leaning out of the bed of the truck and offering a hand.

He walked away. The look of disgust and anger on his face was one Nadia recognized, even if she no longer had the passion for it herself.

THREE

Ostelinda's fingers frantically tried to rethread the sewing machine. An action she had performed a thousand times, yet her hands shook uncontrollably. She anticipated Sra. Moreland's reaction if she couldn't get her work done fast enough. The woman rarely raised her voice, but her insults hurt more than a slap. Her threats gave her nightmares. Ostelinda's heart raced in anticipation.

When she got the machine threaded, Ostelinda looked around the factory's third floor to see if she had been caught struggling. Sra. Moreland had been too busy berating one of the Guatemalans to notice. To make her daily quota, Ostelinda would have to work double-time sewing the linings into the knockoff suit jackets. If she skipped her bathroom break, she could get it done by the end of the day.

It didn't matter. Sra. Moreland would find a reason to call her worthless or stupid or pathetic. She always found a reason. On the worst days, the woman poked and prodded Ostelinda until she believed the insults. She would become convinced that everything was her fault. The abuse made her unsure of who she truly was.

Ostelinda had thought the United States would be different. If she had wanted a menial job with no future, she could have stayed in Coatepec and married one of the cuter campesinos. But she had wanted more, desired adventure, and found people that made many promises of a new life. None of them turned out to be true.

The man her cousin Pocho had put her in contact with had come into town with the evangélicos. They preached love and acceptance. They gave out Bibles. They fed the poor who lived by the river. The man had been friendly, always smiling. He had told Ostelinda and Maite that the journey north would take one week. He had told her that she didn't need to pay up-front. When they arrived in the U.S., a job would be waiting at a factory. She would work until the cost of her travel was repaid. The arrangement sounded fair.

The journey had not taken a week, but four months. Ostelinda had hated the small house outside of Mexicali where they stayed before crossing the border. Thirty people in two small rooms and one bathroom. Barely enough floor space for everyone to sleep. They had not been allowed to go outside or prepare their own food. Beans and tortillas—sometimes meat—were brought to them. It got so hot that she thought her insides would cook. The water from the faucet was brown and tasted like dirt. Every night, Ostelinda fought off men's hands.

Without Maite, she didn't know if she would have survived. A struggle never seemed as insurmountable when fought alongside a friend. They gave each other strength.

After weeks in Mexicali, the coyotes announced that it was time for the entire group to make the journey north. Ostelinda barely had time to grab her things before she had been corralled with the others into a truck.

The truck did not bring them to the United States. It brought them to a barren desert. They were each given a gallon of water and told to walk. The heat was like nothing Ostelinda had felt. She and Maite had drunk all their water by the end of the first day. She did not know how long they would walk. When her mouth became so dry she choked, Ostelinda let a man touch her breasts over her bra for a drink of water. Even on the brink of death, men couldn't resist such urges.

At one point, La Migra rode past on their three-wheeled motorcycles.

The group huddled in a small patch of scrub brush. Ostelinda and Maite held each other, waiting to be caught. They cried together, hurt and scared. The coyotes had warned them La Migra raped young women. When the motorcycles were dust in the distance, the journey continued. They walked six more hours, ending at a road that ran through the hardpack. Another truck waited. The coyote yelled them into the trailer. Fewer people ended the journey than had started.

The heat in the back of the truck was twenty degrees hotter than the desert. People got sick, vomiting and passing out. There was no room to move.

After ten or fifteen hours, Ostelinda and Maite were taken to another house. The house was larger. Only eight women stayed there. They still couldn't leave or look out the front windows, but they were allowed to cook their own meals. Once a day, they were allowed to go into the backyard.

She was told she was in Yuma.

One final trip in the back of a mobile home and she had reached her current destination. The mobile home was driven by two old white people. The coyote guaranteed old white people were never stopped by La Migra. It was the only thing the man hadn't lied about. They drove through the checkpoint without slowing down.

Ostelinda, Maite, and two Guatemalan women had been brought to the Los Angeles factory in the middle of the night. The Guatemalan women spoke K'iche' to each other, only knew fifty words in Spanish and no English. They communicated with nods and smiles and hand gestures. Even after a year, Ostelinda didn't know their names.

Sra. Moreland laid down the rules. She was a tall, thin white woman who reminded Ostelinda of the witch in El Mago de Oz. She spoke fluent Spanish to explain again that they would work off their debts in the factory. Sra. Moreland didn't tell Ostelinda what rate she would be paid or how long it would take to pay off her debt. She didn't even tell her how much she owed. She only told Ostelinda that she was to work and when the debt was paid, she could leave.

Ostelinda asked about going outside. Sra. Moreland warned her that United States Immigration was everywhere in Los Angeles. Agents regularly patrolled the streets. Checkpoints all over the city targeted anyone who looked Latin. Immigration agents were often violent and could get away with anything, because immigrants had no rights. Ostelinda knew that her presence in the country was illegal, but she'd had no idea it was so dangerous.

A row of three storerooms had been converted to living quarters for the permanent workers on the third floor of the factory. Three or four women to a room. Thin foam mats acted as beds. There were other workers on the second floor, but they went to their homes at the end of the day. The women on the third floor weren't allowed to speak to them. Sra. Moreland explained that it was a sure way to get deported. Substantial rewards had been offered to citizens for information that led to the apprehension of undocumented workers. Sra. Moreland was taking large risks on her behalf. The least Ostelinda could do was follow her rules.

After six months, Ostelinda asked when her debt would be paid. Sra. Moreland told her only: "You eat so much that we had to add the cost of food." "We thought you would be a better worker." "Even for illegals, there are taxes to pay." It was all a theater show. Ostelinda knew that Sra. Moreland didn't want to tell her the truth, to say, "You will never get paid. You will never leave. You are a slave and I own you."

Sra. Moreland stepped behind Ostelinda and picked up a completed suit jacket. Ostelinda's hands shook as she continued her work. Sra. Moreland flicked at a seam, made a sound of disgust, but didn't say anything. She set the jacket in the pile and walked to Maite's station.

Ostelinda exhaled, but her chest and stomach ached. She used to pray to God for him to rescue her. To send someone to save her. She never got a response and gave up on the idea. She tried to understand what she had done in her seventeen years on earth to make her deserve this life.

FOUR

Luz had two and a half hours between the end of her hotel housekeeping job and the start of her office janitorial job. She could have stayed in the neighborhood, but the twenty-five minute bus ride allowed her to come home and take a hot shower. The quiet luxury rejuvenated her for the rest of the long workday. Luz was thirty-three, but had been working full-time since she was thirteen. Those twenty years took a physical toll that made her feel older than her age would suggest.

"How long are you going to be in there?" Eliseo shouted through a crack in the door.

"A few more minutes," Luz said, her peace disrupted.

"What's for dinner?"

"I don't have time. There might be leftover tamales in the refrigerator."

"I have to do everything myself," Eliseo said. "I'll get dollar Chinese."

"Don't waste money," Luz said. "That orange stuff is too sweet."

"It's my money," Eliseo said.

"Did you work today?" Luz wrapped the curtain around her body and poked out her head. She was talking to a room full of steam. Eliseo had left, not bothering to close the door completely.

It had been seven years since she had said goodbye to Eliseo and headed north. Work had dried up and she had been desperate to find a way to keep her mother and her ten-year-old son fed. It had been hard, but the journey to the United States had been for him.

Within six months, Luz had found enough work to support herself and her family back in Mexico. She lived simply. After Luz paid for rent, food, minor living expenses, and calling cards, she sent the rest of the money home. She called it "home" but knew that she might never return. The longer she stayed away, the further it became.

Luz's mother took on the task of raising Eliseo. Life could not have been as good as her mother described in their phone calls, but Luz preferred the fantasy. Thousands of miles away, it was too painful to accept that her absence had negatively affected her son. She had always known that Eliseo had been more trouble than Luz's mother let on, especially once he reached his teens.

On the rare occasions Eliseo spoke to Luz, he sounded angry and full of complaints. Nothing was good. Everything was unfair. The older he got, the less they talked and the angrier he was when they did. By the time he was sixteen, all remnants of the boy she had left were gone. She didn't recognize him anymore.

Luz's mother had died suddenly six months earlier. Grief hit her hard, coupled with the shame and heartbreak that she could not attend the funeral. She had lost her connection to family. The loneliness of life in a foreign land. She needed her son.

Working extra shifts and borrowing money from friends, Luz found the necessary funds. Eliseo arrived in Los Angeles four months later with a single backpack. She cried all seven years out as she held him tightly, pinning his arms to his side.

It had been awkward from the start. Eliseo treated her with the cold distance of a stranger. Over time, the indifference became annoyance. Eliseo spent his days in the apartment complaining and evenings out with his "friends." Luz didn't know where he went, what he was doing, or who he was with. It worried her, but he always came home, no matter how late. She saw him less than an hour a day, and when they were together, he ignored her.

It didn't make things easier that there had already been three people living in the Boyle Heights one-bedroom when he arrived. A fourth person was the second person too many.

Fernando and Rosa Cardenas had lived with Luz for two years. Rosa had worked at the same hotel with Luz. She left when she got a better job, but still took a few shifts for extra money. Fernando repaired cars out of a garage in East LA. They both worked long hours and were in the house as rarely as Luz. Fernando and Rosa were saving to get their own place and eventually send for their children.

The apartment had no designated rooms. If a person needed to sleep and the bedroom was unoccupied, that was where they slept. If it was taken, they slept on the couch in the living room. With their schedules, it somehow worked out. Luz often slept next to Rosa, back to back. Luz liked to feel the warmth of another body. She missed it.

Eliseo usually ended up on the floor somewhere. He complained about most things, but never that. He seemed to prefer the floor.

Her son didn't get along with Fernando and Rosa either, which made the air in the apartment feel thick and musty. Fernando and Rosa had said nothing to Luz, but she caught them giving Eliseo dirty looks when he didn't clean or said stupid things.

Dressed in her janitorial uniform, Luz dried her hair. When she turned off the hairdryer, she listened for Eliseo, wondering if he was still in the apartment. Now that she thought of it, Chinese food sounded good. If Eliseo hadn't left yet, he could pick up some shrimp fried rice.

Luz's heart broke when she caught Eliseo rifling through Rosa's things in the living room. He picked up a coffee can, popped off the lid, and pulled out a wad of money and some jewelry. Luz didn't say anything, hoping that he was only being curious. He returned the jewelry to the can, counted out a few bills, and put the rest of the money back.

"What are you doing?" Luz said.

21

Eliseo jumped, dropping the can. Jewelry spilled across the carpet.

"Put Rosa's money back right now!" Luz yelled.

"It's…this…I…this money is…Rosa borrowed this from me."

"Do not lie to me," Luz said.

"She…" Eliseo started, but didn't bother to construct a new lie.

"Put the money back. Rosa worked for that money."

"I could have taken it all."

"None of it is yours," Luz said.

Eliseo shrugged, grabbed his jacket, and walked to the front door.

"If you leave with that money, do not come back."

Eliseo opened the door and walked outside.

"Eliseo! Wait!" Luz shouted. "Eliseo!"

Luz took a few steps to follow but stopped. She wanted to grab him. She wanted to shake him and yell at him more. Instead, she found her purse and counted out a few bills. She picked up Rosa's coffee can, scooped the jewelry back inside, added her money to Rosa's, and put it back where it had been hidden.

She heated up the tamales in the microwave before she went to work. It made strange electrical sounds and one loud pop as the food cooked. She ate her dinner in silence. The tamales were rubbery and flavorless in her mouth.

FIVE

The pigeons that lived under the eaves of the storage facility roof sounded like the purring of a large cat. Nadia listened to the haunting chorus as she stared at the ceiling of the Winnebago and admired the shapes of the water damage stains, a poor man's clouds.

Nadia shifted her body on the bench seat. Piles of magazines and newspapers covered the dinette table. A full-size American flag acted as a curtain above the functionless kitchen sink. Gillies had told her that the US government had given him two things when his father had died: a flag and a tombstone. "I kept the flag and pissed on the stone," he had said. The only words he had ever spoken about his family. The flag didn't keep out the light, but it was Gillies's RV. He made all the interior decorating decisions.

Nadia stood, kicked an empty can of Dinty Moore across the floor, and stretched until her fingers touched the ceiling. The digital clock on the table said five o'clock. Still dark outside, but if she was going to get work, she should be at the underpass in a half hour. Luckily, her commute was twenty yards across the street.

She walked down the short hall and knocked on the accordion partition.

"*Are you working today?*" Nadia asked in English. While they were both bilingual, Nadia and Gillies had developed a habit of speaking to each other in both English and Spanish, depending on mood and degree of intoxication.

The growl that came from the room wasn't any language, all a's and r's and strange sounds from the back of the throat. Like she had awakened and angered a Scottish pirate.

"I'll start the coffee," Nadia said.

She turned on the coffeemaker Gillies had jerry-rigged to run off a car battery. While she waited, she poured wine into her Donald Duck glass and took a drink.

The partition unfolded and Gillies lumbered out in his baggy white underwear. The scars on his shoulder and arm glinted in the light. He pulled some camouflage pants from the hall closet and put them on. His unkempt long white hair and beard made him look like a down-on-his-luck wizard.

Nadia held up the glass of wine in her hand.

"Why not?" Gillies said. He found his Goofy glass and blew into it, a thorough enough cleaning. "*Holy Christ. Those pigeons sound like a couple ghosts are getting violated at the bottom of a well.*"

Nadia had left Mexico in a hurry, desperate and with no direction. Upon arriving in Los Angeles, she had been so afraid of ICE picking her up, she lived on the street rather than sleeping in a bus station or shelter. A stark contrast from the sixteenth-floor apartment she had been living in a year earlier. A reminder that no matter what a person had, it could be taken away.

She didn't fully understand her drive to survive. A primal instinct, maybe. She couldn't think of one reason to continue living other than as punishment. Her stubbornness and spite revealed themselves to be greater than her apathy. Nadia might have lost everything, but that didn't mean she could let them win.

In those first months, Nadia spent her nights tucked into small spaces away from view or on the roofs of buildings with easy access.

Sometimes, she walked the streets, remaining in motion, sleeping off the day in a park or cemetery. She lost a tooth fighting off a man that had tried to assault her in an abandoned squat.

She drank every day to dull the pain. The alcohol addiction and rough living took its physical toll. She developed a cough she couldn't shake. Her skin was rough and scabbed.

Then she met Gillies.

Nadia had seen him at the underpass the few times she had felt strong enough to work. As the only white man who stood for work with the Mexicans, Guatemalans, and Salvadorans, he was hard to miss. Each nationality tended to stay with their own, but Gillies floated between them, standing a foot above everyone, making jokes in fluent Spanish, and laughing his booming laugh. On the days he didn't work, he sat across the street on a lawn chair in front of his RV.

The day they met, she had given up on work and found a shady spot on the sidewalk to take a nap. On a piece of discarded cardboard, Nadia leaned against the wall of the storage facility and dozed.

When Gillies's large frame cast a shadow over Nadia, it had woken her. He stood over her with a beer in one hand and a cigarette in the other, wearing camouflage pants, a stained US Army tank top, and a bandanna with an image of an eagle on the front. It was impossible to tell his age. Somewhere between forty and two hundred.

"You look comfortable," Gillies said.

"Good Spanish for a gabacho," Nadia said.

"I had a couple Mexican wives. Not at the same time. One after the other."

"Okay." Nadia closed her eyes.

"I got a joke for you," Gillies said, "but I got to tell it in English."

"*I speak English*," Nadia said, a little bite in her tone.

"*Without an accent, too. There's a story there, I bet.*"

"*One you'll never hear.*"

"*Fair enough*," Gillies said. "*How many Mexicans does it take to screw in a light bulb?*"

"*I don't know, but can I wager on whether or not the punchline is racist?*"

"*Nope.*" Gillies smiled. "*Just Juan.*"

Nadia laughed. A quick, unconscious nose snort. It was the first time she could remember laughing since she left Mexico. The moment should have felt profound, the first step toward coming to terms with her pain. It didn't. It felt wrong. Like she was grieving incorrectly. She reminded herself that when convicts laughed, it didn't mean they weren't being punished.

"I need a drink," Nadia said, switching back to Spanish. If she was going to talk to the mountain man, it would be on *her* terms.

"I got beer in my RV," Gillies said.

Nadia took a closer look at the Winnebago and its peeling paint and spider-webbed windshield. "Has a woman ever taken you up on that offer?"

"There's a first time for everything," Gillies said. He had the smile of a mischievous child. "If it's a selling point, the beer is warm."

"I don't think so."

"Suit yourself," Gillies said. "I was planning on drinking it all myself anyway. Nice meeting you, señora."

Nadia glanced at the ring on her finger. She closed her eyes and put her head back against the wall, but she remained awake. When she opened her eyes again, Gillies was sitting on his lawn chair. He wore a pair of granny glasses and was doing a crossword puzzle.

"I can sense you looking at me," Gillies said, without looking up. "Me and my delicious warm beer. The offer stands."

"Maybe *one*," she said.

Nadia moved into Gillies's RV that day. Four months later, she was still there.

Their relationship was platonic, if you set aside a couple of drunk evenings ending in desperate attempts at human contact. Half-naked fumbling and groping that resulted in the unsuccessful pressing together of groins. They had ground their bodies against each other until the realization of its pointlessness returned them to drinking.

They lived like an old couple and accepted the other's strangeness. She loved him and he loved her, but mostly they were good at drinking together and doing what they could to forget who they used to be.

SIX

At the end of the night, Sra. Moreland locked Ostelinda and the other women inside the storerooms. No bathroom, only a bucket in the corner. The women on the third floor were locked in at eight o'clock and released at six in the morning. Their dinner would be waiting for them, usually cold sandwiches or unheated canned meals.

For the first three months, Ostelinda had accepted that fate. Until she figured out that with a pair of scissors and some patience, she could open the storeroom door. The first night exploring the empty factory had been terrifying. It soon became a regular thing, although she never descended the stairs to the lower levels. The freedom of the third floor was as much freedom as she dared.

The Guatemalans refused to break the rules and venture outside their small cage. Maite had gone with her once but had gotten so scared that she returned to the storeroom after ten minutes. The risk of the unknown punishment wasn't worth it to her.

Ostelinda's days held no variation, all work and pressure and abuse. But outside of the storeroom, in the expanse of the empty factory, Ostelinda could be free. The other workers were gone. The building was quiet. Sra. Moreland was asleep in her lair. The white guard stayed on the first floor. Ostelinda had watched him from the third floor landing. He rarely left his small office.

The windows didn't open, but once the grime was removed, Ostelinda could see out to the dark and foreboding industrial neighborhood. Factories, warehouses, and salvage yards surrounded her, the lights of the massive city in the distance. A few billboards. The courtyard of her prison was surrounded by a tall fence with razor wire at the top, and filled with cars and abandoned machinery.

When Ostelinda accepted that she was a prisoner and would never work off her debt, her mind shifted to thoughts of escape. She didn't know where to start. Even if she could pry a window open, it was too high and would only land her in the sea of rusted metal. She was trusting liars that she was even in Los Angeles, a city that she only knew from American movies. Then there were the immigration patrols and checkpoints. She knew no one. She didn't even know the word for *help* in English.

She sat at the north-facing window and drew the scene outside. Sketching relaxed her, going inside the picture to get every detail right. Over the last six months, she had drawn the women from the factory, friends and family from memory, and the view from every window. Some nights, she drew until dawn. The lack of sleep hurt the next day, but the small amount of happiness was enough to take any abuse that Sra. Moreland dumped on her.

At three in the morning, Ostelinda returned to the storeroom, quietly closing the door behind her. Maite rolled over on her mat and gave Ostelinda a weak smile. "Let me see."

Ostelinda sat and handed Maite her new drawings. Mostly darkness with some power lines and the closest billboards. The drawing captured the view to the northeast.

"It is very good. Dark," Maite said. "You should sleep."

"Yes, mother."

Ostelinda tucked the new drawings under her mat. She would have to find a new hiding place soon. The lump was getting big enough to hurt her back.

"What are you doing awake?" Ostelinda asked.

"Waiting for you."

Ostelinda knew that was a lie. For the last few weeks, Maite had been sick and getting sicker. All the women on the third floor had persistent coughs from the chemicals they used on the fabric, but Maite's had grown worse, raspy and full of phlegm and blood. Ostelinda felt Maite's forehead. She had a fever and shook with chills.

"I'm going to talk to Sra. Moreland," Ostelinda said. "I'm going to get you help, a doctor."

"No," Maite said weakly. "Please don't."

"They will help. They have to."

"It will only bring trouble. I am getting better." Maite coughed into her hands until there were tears in her eyes.

Fifteen minutes before the morning shift, Ostelinda found Sra. Moreland. It was only the third time she had been in the second-floor office. Little more than a cluttered desk and some filing cabinets, the small room was adorned with religious imagery and small posters in English with pictures of angels. A crucifix with a cracked Jesus hung at an angle over the door.

"What do you want?" Sra. Moreland snapped.

"Maite will not say anything," Ostelinda said. "I am sorry to ask, but she needs a doctor. She has had a fever, a bad cough, for many days."

"Doctors cost money," Sra. Moreland said. She rose from her desk and walked to a cabinet against the wall. She found a white plastic container with a red cross on it. She handed Ostelinda a bottle of pills. "Have her take two of these every four hours. It will reduce the fever."

"Thank you," Ostelinda said.

"Is there anything else?" Sra. Moreland said, returning to her desk.

"She could very much use a doctor."

"No."

"She is too sick to work," Ostelinda said. "She needs rest."

"She will find the energy. The work needs to be done."

"I will do her work for her."

Sra. Moreland looked up. "You have your own work to do."

"I can do both. I will work into the night."

Sra. Moreland shrugged. "I won't give you special treatment tomorrow if you're tired."

"I understand."

"Okay. You can do the work. I can't wait to see Lou's face when I tell him he has to climb the stairs to lock you up."

"God bless you," Ostelinda said. "If the pills and rest do not heal Maite's fever? Then a doctor?"

"Haven't I done enough?" Sra. Moreland said. "You people want everything handed to you."

SEVEN

Luz had told Eliseo to never come back, and for the first time, her son did what he was told. She regretted the words the moment they had come out of her mouth, but it had happened and he was gone. She had to try harder. She had to quit failing him.

Luz had forgotten how to be a good mother, if she had ever been one. She had been so young when Eliseo was born. In the first year, the stress had made her hair fall out, a patch gone above her ear. It had been overwhelming to be responsible for a life. The opportunity for work had not been the only reason she left Mexico.

In abandoning her son, Luz's absence had made Eliseo the man he was. Seeing her son steal Rosa's money crushed her. The anger and frustration only added to the disappointment she felt in herself. She had finally reunited with her son—a day she had dreamed of—but she found no joy in it. She had worked so hard to make it a reality, but she couldn't get around the fact that she didn't like him. Eliseo wasn't a good person.

The Bible taught Luz that nobody was beyond hope. All sinners had a chance at redemption. Luz was Eliseo's mother. She could do her job. She could still get it right. She wouldn't let her son become a thief. He might be in the country illegally, but that didn't mean he was a criminal. Luz and five men got off the bus at the underpass. They walked as a group to the open lot across from the storage facility. None of the men said anything to Luz or even gave her a second glance. They didn't have the same casual air that the men in Mexico had. These men looked tired, determined, but mostly cautious. She was glad they weren't harassing her, but also disappointed that they had lost their spirit.

Back home, she had avoided certain roads when walking to school, a child of eleven or twelve. The roads where men gathered to get coffee before work. They would flirt and shout at her in her school uniform. Some would jokingly flip up her skirt or pinch her behind.

At the underpass, she waited. To anyone who grew up poor, waiting wasn't a challenge. When a person spent their whole lives waiting for something—anything—good to happen, patience came easy. Hope, on the other hand, faded.

Rosa had been happy to take her shift at the hotel. Luz didn't know anyone that couldn't use extra money, but it felt strange to be outside in the middle of the day, free to do what she wanted. Luz had not taken a day off work since Eliseo arrived. She had worked seventy-hour weeks to repay the loans she had taken out for his travel.

Luz bought a cup of coffee at the food truck and surveyed the men. She did not see Eliseo. She was surprised to see a white man and a woman among those standing for work.

A stake truck pulled up to the curb. The men stampeded toward it, shouting and waving their hands. A black man stepped out of the truck and climbed into the back. He shouted in rough-but-clear Spanish, "I need four. Roofing. All day. A hundred dollars. If you don't have roofing experience, don't say you do. I won't pay you."

Like choosing teams for a pickup soccer game, the black man assessed the crowd and pointed to a man. "You. You've worked for me. Joaquín, right?"

The man nodded and climbed into the back of the truck with the black man. They shook hands and talked. Joaquín nodded and pointed to three other men. They climbed into the back, the black man pulling up each one. In less than a minute after arriving, the truck drove away.

After an hour, Luz felt stupid for coming down to the underpass. She had been optimistic to believe that Eliseo would be there looking for work. On his best day, he had dragged himself around, as lazy as an old dog after an uphill walk.

A Chevrolet Caprice with a primered front quarter panel pulled to the curb. It had a metal Jesus fish on the back. The engine rattled. A few men stepped toward the car, holding up their arms and shouting for work.

Two young men got out of the car, one white and one Latino. They were both nineteen or twenty with heads shaved close, baggy jeans, crisp white T-shirts, and tattoos up and down their arms and necks. The thick gold rope hanging around the white boy's neck was the only difference in their attire. The white kid with big ears was smaller, but Luz got the impression he was in charge.

The presence of the two young men changed the energy on the lot. Luz felt it immediately, like when a wasp flew into a room. They looked like criminals to her. At the very least, trouble.

When Eliseo got out of the backseat of the Chevy, Luz felt an ache in her chest. She was relieved to see him, but couldn't understand what he was doing with these two young men.

Luz walked quickly along the jagged asphalt toward her son. Eliseo talked to the two men facing the other way, heads close to each other. When Luz was within a few yards, she shouted, "Eliseo!"

The three men flinched and turned.

"What are you doing, Eliseo?" Luz said. "Why are you with these people?"

"These people?" the white boy said, replying in Spanish.

"What do you want?" Eliseo said. His cheeks grew red. He glanced to his friends.

"I am sorry for getting angry," Luz said, "but you can't leave home and not call."

"You kicked me out," Eliseo said. "I'll get my things tonight."

"*Get the fuck out*," the white boy said, laughing. "Is this your mom?"

His friend joined in the laughter. It sounded like a balloon deflating.

Eliseo's face fell, but only for a moment. He thrust out his chest in a childlike display of toughness. "Go home."

"Not without you." Luz grabbed Eliseo's arm and pulled him toward her.

"*Your mom don't fuck around,*" the white boy said.

Off balance, Eliseo pushed Luz with his free hand. She lost her grip and stumbled back a few steps, but stayed on her feet.

"Go home!" Eliseo shouted.

Luz shook her head. "I am not leaving without you."

"Go!" Eliseo pushed her again, this time with both hands.

Luz fell, tripping over her feet and landing on her back. A sharp pain shot up the back of her leg.

Eliseo's face flashed momentary regret, as if he was about to ask if she was okay, his hand rising to help her stand.

"*What the hell do you think you're doing, punk?*" a voice shouted in English.

Luz looked up, squinting into the sun. The tall white man who had been standing for work walked forward and eclipsed the light. He stepped between Luz and the three young men, looking like Moses in camouflage pants.

"I don't care what country you're from," Moses said, switching to Spanish. "You don't touch a lady like that."

"*This ain't none of your business, old man,*" the white boy said. "*Back the fuck off.*"

"I suggest the three of you take a few steps back—give the lady some room—before I get mad."

"*What happens when you get mad?*" the white boy asked, a hand reaching into his pocket.

"*People bleed.*"

EIGHT

Nadia and Gillies had been discussing plans to get out of town and head to Slab City, when Gillies spotted something over Nadia's shoulder. He stopped talking mid-sentence, squinted his eyes, and walked past her. By the time Nadia turned, he was stepping between a woman on the ground and three men.

Helping Nadia must have gone to his head. Now he was saving every Mexican woman he saw.

Nadia had seen Gillies angry, watched him go to war with inanimate objects—but she hadn't seen him in any physical altercation with another person. He carried himself like it wasn't uncommon. Not showy, but confident and relaxed.

Gillies rarely talked about his time in the military, which meant that there was more to tell. When he did tell stories, they were consciously mundane, usually involving the challenges of defecating outdoors in a warzone while your buddies avoided eye contact.

When Nadia saw the young men, her instinct was to run. She recognized the hothead kid from the masonry job for Dan Schauer and knew he was mostly talk, but the other two reminded Nadia of men she came in contact with in Mexico. Young, dangerous men with a nihilistic view of existence. Men too reckless to see past the next minute. She wanted to run, but she froze.

The hothead pushed Gillies with one hand, but Gillies didn't budge. He laughed. Not a boom, but a dismissive chuckle. It angered the kid more. His open hands turned to fists.

"Careful," Gillies said, calm.

"This isn't your business!" the boy shouted.

"Knocking a lady to the ground is never right. No excuses. You did wrong."

"It's okay," the woman on the ground said, getting to a knee. "I am his mother. We had an argument."

Gillies held out a hand to the woman. "Your mother? That's worse."

"*How tough are you?*" the white boy said, lifting a revolver halfway from his pocket. He used two fingers, more display than threat.

Gillies stood upright, his eyes on the revolver. "*That's a pretty gun. Did you borrow it from your sister?*"

The white boy's crime partner laughed, until he got a hard look from the white boy.

Nadia could not watch anymore. Her breathing felt forced. Her hands shook. Panic overcame her. She walked quickly to Gillies's Winnebago. With every step, she expected to hear a gunshot ring out behind her and for Gillies to be shot dead.

Inside the RV, she sat down on the only chair and covered her ears with her hands. She rocked slightly and sucked in air, her breathing shallow. She felt lightheaded. Her heart raced so fast that it hurt her chest. The skin on the back of her neck tingled.

The yelling of the men outside burrowed through her hands into her ears, escalating violence in their voices.

She looked at the mess that was her home—the home that Gillies had given her. He had saved her. She couldn't imagine what her life would be like without him. He was all she had.

"Damn you," she said.

Nadia took a long pull from the open wine bottle on the table. Then one more. She threw boxes and cans and papers to the side, finally finding the small wooden box that Gillies had made her hide on a particularly bad night. She opened the box and grabbed the gun inside, a revolver that Gillies had named "Wyndorf," because, "A gunslinger's pistol is his best friend and your best friend needs a name."

Gun in hand, Nadia walked out of the RV and marched across the street.

Gillies and the young men stood where she had left them, chests out and ready to fight. The shouting match had ended, but the standoff hadn't. What remained was the deceptive quiet of a burning fuse. The other men at the underpass felt it. They had backed away. Some left the lot entirely.

"*Do you want to die, old man*?" the white boy said, on the balls of his feet, dancing from one to the other.

"*Some days*," Gillies said, "*but not by your hand, asshole*."

"Stop it!" Nadia shouted, stepping forward and pointing Wyndorf directly at the white boy. "Stop all of this."

The three young men looked at Nadia like they couldn't figure out what had happened. Like a woman with a gun was an impossibility.

"*Easy*," Gillies said, turning to Nadia and holding up both hands. "*Don't go shooting no one over this macho bullshit*."

"This your bitch?" the Mexican said.

"Are you stupid?" Gillies said, turning back to the men. "Can't you see she'll shoot you? That she wants to? Look at her eyes."

"Please, stop," the woman on the ground said, getting up and patting the dirt off her pants. Nobody looked at her, all eyes remained on Nadia and the gun. "He is my son. Families fight."

"You aren't my family," the hothead said.

The woman opened her mouth to answer, but ended up saying nothing. With tears in her eyes, she looked at the ground, defeated.

Nadia thought about pulling the trigger. How easy it would be to kill the white bully. How good it would feel. He had probably hurt people. He was young, but people don't change. How many lives would he ruin in his lifetime? She had the power to change the future with one small motion.

The men that remained on the lot stirred, moving even further away from the group. They whistled and shouted, "Policía!"

Gillies moved quickly to Nadia, reaching her in three quick steps. He took Wyndorf out of her hands and tucked the gun under his shirt. Nadia looked at him, confused, but didn't fight. The young men didn't move.

A police cruiser headed their way down Olympic Boulevard. Like school children about to get in trouble, everyone at the underpass dropped into character, smiling and laughing and acting like they were having normal conversations. Only the hothead and his mother didn't laugh, instead, staring at each other.

The patrol car slowed to a crawl, then stopped. Nobody looked directly at the car or the officers inside. They continued their pretend conversations, keeping their hands in sight.

Nadia looked up at Gillies, lost. He put an arm around her. "Breathe. Just breathe."

The white boy and the Mexican walked slowly to the Caprice. By the time the patrol car drove away and turned out of sight, the Chevy was gone.

"I would have shot him," Nadia said. "I would have."

"I know," Gillies said.

"Come home, Eliseo," the woman said. "We can work this out."

Her son walked away without a reply, joining the group of men at the underpass.

The woman stepped to follow, but Gillies put a soft hand on her shoulder. "Let him calm down. He can't hear you now."

The woman nodded. "Thank you."

"Are you all right?" Gillies asked.

She nodded again. "You could have been hurt."

"I was thirty—no, thirty-four percent—sure he wasn't going to shoot me."

"That's your son?" Nadia asked.

"If I had talked to my mother like that," Gillies said, "I would've needed a closed casket."

"Eliseo no longer respects me. I have lost him."

"Sons need mothers," Nadia said, almost to herself.

"I got to put Wyndorf to bed," Gillies said, patting the gun under his shirt. He gave a nod toward the woman and walked to the RV.

Nadia silently watched the woman stare at her son.

After a few minutes, a Volkswagen Jetta with a U-Haul trailer pulled up to the lot. The back windshield of the car was adorned with USC and sorority decals. The young blonde woman in the passenger seat looked overwhelmed by the crowd of Mexican men that pushed up against the door. She adorably butchered Spanish. "*Uh,* yo quiero dos hombres."

All the men laughed. A few made randy comments. Whistles. "Cállate. Cállate," Eliseo shouted at the men, edging his way between the crowd and the car. He pushed the men back. A few lobbed complaints, the rest quieted down. He turned to the woman and in the slowest most careful English, he said, "*I can help.*"

"*We need help moving. Mostly boxes. Some furniture. Like a mattress.* ¿Comprendo?"

"*Yes. I can help. And another one to work?*" Eliseo grabbed the shoulder of the man closest to him, a pudgy man with no hair.

"Si," the blonde woman said.

The woman's son and the ugly man climbed into the backseat of the Jetta. As it drove away, her son's arm stuck out the window. His middle finger held high in the air.

NINE

Ostelinda tried to stand, but her legs had fallen asleep. Every small motion sent tingling pain through the lower half of her body. She squeezed the muscles of her thighs and gave them light punches. An inch at a time over a full minute, she eventually rose to a standing position, one hand on the table, an ache deep in her back.

She had never worked so many hours in a single day—eighteen hours from when Ostelinda had sat down at the sewing machine, her workday finally ended. She had completed both her and Maite's work.

The third floor of the factory was empty. Maite had slept all day and the two Guatemalans had been locked inside the storeroom hours earlier. Ostelinda hoped Maite had gotten the rest that she needed and that her fever had finally broken. Her breathing had been weak that morning, her skin hot to the touch. The aspirin had done very little.

After an urgent trip to the bathroom, Ostelinda walked down the stairs to the second floor. She was supposed to summon the guard so that he could lock her in the storeroom, but she was in no hurry, even if she could just let herself out afterward. She would rather explore.

The second floor landing looked down on the loading dock. Her eyes locked on the only ways in and out of the factory: the garage door and the regular door next to it. Ostelinda sat down on the top step and ran her finger along a crack in the concrete floor. An ant crawled near her finger, looking lost. As she was about to crush it with her thumb, she stopped herself. The small insect had a better chance of finding its way home than she did. It should get that chance.

The corrugated garage door rattled and shook, someone knocking from outside. Ostelinda scooted along the railing to get a better look.

The guard walked out of his small office and buttoned the top of his pants. He rolled up the garage door a few feet. Three young men squeezed under and entered the warehouse. She didn't recognize the two Mexicans, but the white one was Corey, Sra. Moreland's son. Corey spoke to the guard in English. The guard nodded and guided the three of them toward the stairs.

Corey scared her. He had mean eyes and looked at her without blinking. He didn't show up at the factory that often, only to restock the storeroom and bring clothes to the women. When he did, Ostelinda avoided him and his stare.

As the men climbed the stairs, Ostelinda scrambled to her feet. She didn't want to be alone with them. She found a spot behind a supply cabinet, mostly out of view. Through a gap between boxes of steel fasteners, Ostelinda watched the guard guide the three young men up the stairs to the third floor.

Ostelinda stepped out from her hiding place. She moved quietly to the stairs and looked down. The garage door remained open.

She took off her shoes and walked down the stairs as quickly as she could. The grating cut into the bottom of her feet. She wanted to scream, but didn't slow down.

Before she reached the bottom, she heard women screaming and yelling, immediately followed by the men yelling back and the sound of a confrontation.

Ostelinda took one step back up the stairs and hesitated. Maite might be in danger. Ostelinda hesitated. She told herself that she would escape and then come back for Maite. The door was thirty yards away. She wouldn't get another opportunity. It was a chance to save them both.

The screaming stopped and the men's voices grew louder, closer. The sound of feet on the metal stairs.

"Quit complaining," one of the men said from above. "I got the heavy end."

Ostelinda looked up and saw movement on the stairs. The guard and Corey led the way. Behind them, the two Mexicans carried a person. Ostelinda recognized Maite's clothes immediately. She gasped and covered her mouth.

One last look at the door told her she wouldn't be able to cross the dock floor without being seen. She ducked behind the boxing machine in the corner.

When the men reached the first floor, they set Maite on the ground. Her body was limp. Her eyes closed. Her complexion was pale. Luz couldn't tell if she was breathing.

"What does she have?" the smaller Mexican boy asked, "Is it contagious?"

"How am I supposed to know?" the tattooed man said.

"She looks like she was hot before she got sick." Corey lifted up the front of her loose shirt to take a look underneath.

Ostelinda couldn't allow that. She stepped out from behind the boxing machine. "Don't touch her."

The men turned, surprised but not concerned.

"Where did you come from?" Corey asked.

"Where are you taking her?" Ostelinda asked.

"She's sick," Corey said. "We're the ambulance."

The guard said something to her in English that she didn't understand.

Ostelinda squinted toward Maite. She tried to see if she was breathing but was too far away.

"You're taking her to a doctor?" Ostelinda asked.

"Sure. That's what we're doing." Corey laughed. He turned to the other two. "Grab her feet."

"You are lying," Ostelinda said. She picked up a metal pipe that sat on the machine and held it high over her head with both hands.

43

The men spread out. Ostelinda took a big swing at the tattooed Mexican closest to her. It hit him in the elbow. He yelped in pain.

Corey stepped forward. She swung and missed. He hit her in the mouth with a straight jab. She dropped the pipe and landed hard on the ground. As she scrambled to get up, Corey and the tattooed Mexican stood over her. They kicked and stomped. She rolled into a ball, her arms around her head. Their feet connected with her stomach, her back, her legs, her arms.

When the kicking stopped, she remained still. The blood was warm on her face. The pain so intense that she couldn't quite feel it. She was surprised she was alive. She hadn't passed out. She had felt every blow.

The two young men gasped, out of breath from the exertion. Corey spit on her.

"I don't know about this," the smaller Mexican said, inching toward the door.

"Shut up," Corey yelled. "Move that one to the car."

The smaller man nodded. He and the tattooed man picked up Maite and carried her outside.

"No," Ostelinda said just above a whisper. Maite disappeared into the darkness.

Corey squatted down next to Ostelinda. He smiled. "I should take you with us, but we've already lost one worker. I'd warn you to keep this a secret, but it doesn't matter who you tell. You don't exist."

TEN

It had been six days since the confrontation at the underpass, and Eliseo still had not returned home. On that first night, it had been for the better. Luz hadn't been ready to talk to him. By the third night, Luz was concerned. After a week, she was nearing panic.

Luz bought a six-pack of beer on the walk after her night job. She had planned to drink all of them and get a little drunk, but after two she got so sleepy that she gave up on her plan. Heartburn from the beers on an empty stomach woke her at three in the morning. In the dark, she scrambled eggs and warmed tortillas over the steaming pan. She ate her snack over the sink while Fernando slept on the couch.

The next morning, Luz went to work as usual. While she cleaned and vacuumed, she couldn't help replaying her fight with Eliseo over and over again. Questioning her choices, imagining what else she could have done. She told herself that mothers and sons fought all the time. It was normal. Had she been too hard on him? After all, he was the product of her abandonment.

Returning home between jobs, she stopped expecting to find Eliseo on the couch. She had stopped rehearsing her apology in her head. She had dreaded his awkward presence in the apartment when he had been there, but now wished only to see him.

No matter how angry Eliseo had been, she had been sure he would come home to get his things. He hadn't called, even to yell at her more. The silent treatment was not her son's style. He was a yeller. He was an angry kid, but not a cruel one.

If Eliseo didn't want to see her, there was little she could do about it. The company he was keeping worried her, though. That white boy had a gun and if he wasn't a criminal, he was trying to be one. She regretted she hadn't written down the license plate of the Chevrolet, although it wouldn't have done much good. It wasn't like she could go to the police.

It bothered Luz when she noticed how much happier and relaxed Fernando and Rosa were with Eliseo not in the house. They said nothing outright. When talking to Luz, they expressed their concern for the boy and for Luz's well-being, but Luz knew what they were thinking. The house was quieter. There was less tension. She didn't care what they thought. She wanted her son to come home.

A week after Luz had last seen her son, she lay in bed staring at the cottage cheese ceiling. Rosa snored next to her, mumbled words in every exhalation. Luz usually liked the warmth of Rosa's body, but that night, it felt awful. Luz pushed away, trying to maintain a distance between them. Every time she moved away, the sleeping Rosa wiggled closer. When Luz reached the edge of the bed, she put one foot on the ground to avoid falling off. She remained in that awkward position, stuck between bed and ground.

Luz felt lost. There were too many possible scenarios that could have happened to her son. He might have left on his own, deciding that he didn't need his mother. But what if it was something else? The police could have picked him up. There might have been an accident. Immigration had showed a bigger presence in the last few years. And that white boy and his friend were troubling.

Rosa shifted again, moving closer to Luz and making a loud snort that seemed to surprise even her. Luz slid off the edge of the bed, just catching her feet underneath her. She ended up falling quietly on her rear end off the side of the bed. She sat there for a moment, chuckling to herself. Despite her fears and spinning dread, life went on and sometimes funny things happened.

Luz let Rosa have the bed. She would take the floor. It wouldn't be the first time she'd slept on the ground. It brought back memories of her youth. A time when family was at the center of everything. When they were all close.

When Luz rolled over, she spotted something under the bed. Besides the thin layer of dust and hair. Eliseo's backpack. Tattered and shiny with grime, it looked like it had been dragged through the desert. Which it literally had been.

Luz felt a sickness rise in her belly. Her heart beat loudly in her head.

She knew in that moment that something was very wrong.

That backpack represented everything Eliseo had brought with him from Mexico. All his current possessions. If she dug in the closet, she would find the bag that she had brought over. An important memento. A symbol of her journey. The backpack had meaning—even to a teenage hothead. It was not something Eliseo would leave behind.

Luz stared at her son's backpack. Her son wasn't just gone.

Eliseo was missing.

THE SOUTHLAND

PART TWO

THE SOUTHLAND

ELEVEN

Luz and Rosa stared at the unopened backpack on the kitchen table like it was a priceless artifact. And in a way, it was. When one's entire possessions were whittled down to the contents of a small bag, each item held meaning.

"What are you waiting for?" Rosa said. "Open it."

"Give me a moment," Luz said, wanting to treat the decision with the reverence it deserved. It was like reading someone else's diary. Going through another person's possessions was a violation in any context, but going through another person's only possessions was a breach of something sacred.

"What do you think is inside?" Rosa asked.

"Hopefully something that will lead me to Eliseo."

In the light, Eliseo's bag was more weathered than at first glance. Soiled and frayed at the edges. One shoulder strap was broken. Luz made a mental note to sew the small tear near the zipper. There was no reason to leave fixable things unfixed.

"Even if he is upset," Rosa said, "he will come back for his things."

"I just want to know he is okay," Luz said. "He is so angry."

"Taken by the devil. Men do not like to be told what to do."

"He's a boy."

"Who thinks he's a man," Rosa said. "Much worse."

Luz slowly unzipped the backpack. She glanced at the front door, half-expecting Eliseo to walk in and catch her in the act. She reached inside and pulled each item out one by one, setting them gently on the table and evaluating their importance.

A shirt. Socks. A hairbrush. Three disposable razors. A CD player with headphones and a CD by a band named Control Machete. A copy of *Presidio Magazine* with an illustration of a woman with a very large behind on the cover. Luz set the magazine facedown. She also found a pocket knife, some keys on a Tecate key ring, and loose pesos in a plastic bag.

Luz made a small sound—almost a whimper—when she pulled out the small compass that she had given him. She hadn't known he had brought it with him.

Before Eliseo's journey north, Luz had mailed him the compass, some money, and a note that read, "When in doubt, use this compass to find north. Head in that direction and you will find your new home." She worried that it had been sentimental, but had sent it anyway.

At the very bottom of the bag, Luz found a sock with something inside. She pulled out the contents, a roll of American bills. She stacked each denomination in its own pile. Six fives, eleven tens, twelve twenties, and one fifty. In total, four hundred and thirty dollars.

"I didn't know Eliseo had worked that much," Rosa said.

"He hasn't," Luz said.

"It's a lot of money to leave behind."

"Too much." Luz felt a catch in her voice.

"It's only been a week." Rosa put a hand on Luz's forearm.

"I am going to the police," Luz said. "They will help."

"They won't. He's illegal. They won't care. They'll ignore him and deport you. It will do no good."

"What do I do?" Luz felt hopeless asking Rosa, knowing that she didn't have the answer.

"You look for him."

"Me? How?"

"What does Señora Fletcher do on 'Reportera del Crimen'?" Rosa said. "She looks for clues. She talks to suspects. She finds leads."

"I am not a detective," Luz said.

"Neither is Señora Fletcher," Rosa said. "The only person who can find Eliseo is you."

Luz felt the conviction and dedication to find her son, but she did not know where to start. She had no experience. Most of Los Angeles was still foreign to her. She had no one to ask for help. And the people she knew were as powerless as she was. Luz had very little money or resources.

She felt like she was taking the first step on the road to hell.

Luz called Immigration and Customs Enforcement, but when she spoke to a real person after an hour on hold, she hung up immediately. The moment the person had asked for her information, Luz's instincts kicked in. ICE could never be trusted.

She had better luck calling the hospitals in the area, but each one took a half hour of being transferred from department to department before getting a vague answer. When she tried to get ready for work, Luz ended up sitting on the edge of the tub and staring into space. Rosa found her and agreed to take her shift.

"What do I do?" Luz asked.

"Get outside for a while," Rosa said. "Go to the park. This will be here when you return."

"Eliseo."

"Fernando will be home soon," Rosa said. "If Eliseo comes back, he will be here."

Luz took her advice. She walked through the neighborhood. But she was searching, not relaxing. If she remained out on the street, there was a chance of seeing him. Or something that would lead to him. She studied every face in every car that passed. She looked for the Chevy. She had to be active. Luz could no longer sit at home and wait for Eliseo to walk through the door.

Luz asked shop owners, waitresses, and bartenders if they had seen him. She showed them the only photograph she had of Eliseo. A blurry picture that she had taken when he first arrived, one of the last times she remembered him smiling, even if it was forced.

After three hours, Luz ended up at St. Mary's. The big columns in the front of the church made it look like a bank or some kind of fortress. It was one of the few buildings in the neighborhood with no graffiti, a sign of either respect or fear of God.

In the middle of the day, with no mass or confession, the church was almost empty. Two ancianas sat in the back pew softly gossiping.

Luz genuflected and walked down the center aisle to the front. She inserted a quarter to light one of the electric candles and got on her knees to pray. She didn't know where Eliseo was, but she knew that God watched over him. He gave her hope.

"Lord, like you, I have one son. He is nothing like Jesus. Not perfect. But young and impetuous. Please, I need to know that he is unhurt. That he is safe. I want nothing else. If he never speaks to me again, I will live with that. I pray not for myself or for my pain, but for Eliseo. I have failed him. I need to know that something bad didn't happen. That's all I ask. In your precious name. Amen."

She looked up at the crucifix, hoping for a sign, anything to signal that she had been heard. She knew that God didn't exist to grant favors, but she trusted him to help her on her path. The car alarm outside didn't feel divine nor did the thump of helicopter blades overhead. She would have to wait and listen for something subtler.

She whispered the Lord's prayer and crossed herself. Luz had faith in God, but she still felt alone.

TWELVE

Nadia hadn't slept more than an hour at a time since her confrontation with the young men a week earlier. The threat of violence had brought up the past in a fury. As hard as she pushed the images down in the day, they rose from the depth of night. She couldn't remember her dreams, only flashes: the steps of the church, the men on the motorcycle, the blood and the dead. Wrenched awake, flooded by her past failures. Nadia's stomach ached for hours afterward. She knew she had TEPT, survivor's guilt, and a half dozen other acronymic mental conditions, but that didn't make the pain go away. So Nadia drank, and Gillies was happy to join her to abate his own demons.

Over the course of the week, the two of them destroyed both mind and body. Dulling emotion into oblivion, they settled into a workmanlike consumption of alcohol. No activity. Sitting and drinking. Eating for constitutional balance. Not a wild night on the town, but a static high, sinking into a hole as deep as they could dig. Living life beneath the quicksand.

In case of retribution by the young men in the Chevrolet, Gillies decided it was time to pull up stakes as planned and head to Slab City. Nadia didn't care where they were. She wasn't ready to work. One place was as good as the next.

Slab City didn't work out. They made it thirty miles before the engine overheated. The dream of the desert died in West Covina. They limped back to LA, ending up a few miles from where they had started. In the heart of Bell Gardens, Gillies parked his RV on an industrial stretch that had since become a makeshift village. Mobile homes, buses, campers, and cars sat permanently parked on the street. Tents lined the sidewalk against high warehouse walls.

Their home in Bell wouldn't last. The police rousted the homeless in the tents. The authoritarian knock on the Winnebago's door came soon after. Gillies and Nadia stayed silent, pretending not to be home. The police left a written notice to remove the RV within twenty-four hours. Lacking any imagination or ambition, Nadia and Gillies returned to their old spot by the underpass. It wasn't safe, but it was familiar. It felt as close to home as their transient existence could manufacture.

They sunk their flag in the ground, got their supplies in order, and drank until they spent their last dollar. It did nothing to relieve Gillies's paranoia or Nadia's insomnia, but it felt good to be proactive.

Nadia swayed in the light of the rising sun. She hadn't had a drink in fifteen hours and felt like she had rolled down a mountain. Standing for work with a hangover and the shakes wouldn't have been her first choice at six in the morning, but she and Gillies needed money.

Nadia's alcohol sweat made the almost freezing temperature feel colder. Her stomach lurched, the taste of bile rose in the back of her throat. She wanted a coffee, but the thought of it made her queasier.

She had to get it together or no one would hire her. Nadia wasn't even sure if she was capable of work, but if Gillies was going to try in the same rough state, she would too. In an effort to center herself, she focused on the fuzzy letters of the "No U-Turn" sign. Her eyes wandered, the sign splitting in two.

If she didn't get hired by nine, she could panhandle down by the liquor store. There were usually only a few people begging and they were nasty men that people avoided. It shouldn't take more than a few hours to get enough for a bottle. Or, she could show some initiative and walk to a better neighborhood where people might be more generous.

She vetoed that idea quickly, a sure way to get ICE on her. One complaint in a white neighborhood and they would pick her up. They would process and deport her as quickly as the law allowed. And the moment Nadia returned to Mexico, she would be killed.

She hadn't made the effort to stay alive these last months to die for a bottle of wine. She would die in the United States. That would be her victory.

The lack of sleep was more debilitating than the hangover. If she took a half-hour siesta, Nadia was sure she would be rejuvenated. What had that white woman in the bikini at the work site called it? The one that kept asking her about her difficult life in Mexico? A *power nap*. Nadia needed a power nap.

She found a spot in the shade of the underpass, kicked some bottles and rocks to the side, and curled into a ball. Sleep did not come easily. She could smell her stink and the urine on the ground around her. She needed a shower and a change of clothes. Through half-open eyes, she watched the men on the lot, finding Gillies's tall frame among the squat Latinos.

Nadia didn't know if he was a good man, but he was good to her. His madness showed at times, but she didn't fear him. He would never hurt her. There was a monster inside him, but Gillies managed to hold it down with the power of his will. It kept him in pain. Something she understood.

Nadia must have fallen asleep. Because the next thing she knew, Gillies was shaking her awake. He wasn't alone. The woman with the hothead son stood next to him.

"Hello," the woman said. "Are you okay? You are on the ground. You look ill."

"We've both been fighting the flu," Gillies said. "Nadia, this is Luz. You remember her, right?"

Nadia nodded, shifting to a sitting position. "What's this about?"

"My son Eliseo," Luz said, "he hasn't come home. He hasn't called. I'm worried."

"That was a nasty fight," Nadia said.

"He has anger, yes, but it has been a week. That is a long time. He left money at home. He hasn't been in the country long enough to understand things."

"That's terrible," Nadia said. "I hope you find him."

"*Oh, she will,*" Gillies said. "*We're going to help her.*"

"*We're going to what?*" Nadia asked.

"*The good Samaritans that we are, we're going to help this concerned mother find her son.*"

"Thank you," Luz said. "You're the only people that have tried to help."

"It's nothing," Gillies said.

"*What are you doing?*" Nadia asked. "*What do you know about finding someone?*"

"*You know things,*" Gillies said. "*You were a journalist in Mexico.*"

"*When did I tell you that?*" Nadia practically screamed, her body tingling all over. "*What did I tell you?*"

"*Calm down,*" Gillies said. "*It's no big deal.*"

Nadia couldn't believe her carelessness. How much had she told Gillies about her past? She had to be more careful.

"If you are trying to talk privately," Luz said. "*I speak English. Just so you know.*"

Nadia stood up. "I can't help you. I'm sorry."

"You weren't afraid of those men," Luz said. "Neither of you. And Mr. Gillies can go places I cannot. Talk to people that I cannot."

"I'm white," Gillies said to Nadia, winking.

"Gillies might not have been afraid, but he's an idiot," Nadia said. "I was terrified."

"You're a mother," Luz said. "You have children."

"What?"

"You're a mother. I can tell."

"How can you—I'm not." Nadia walked away.

Gillies caught up to her. He turned back to where Luz stood, out of earshot.

"*She already paid us,*" Gillies said, lifting a small stack of bills a little way out of his pocket. "*Two hundred bucks.*"

"*She paid you. Not me.*"

"*We ain't in no shape to work,*" Gillies said. "*Nobody's going to hire us today.*"

"I'm not going to help."

"*It'll tide us over until I get my VA check. I'll pretend to ask around, a couple days later, I'll tell her I couldn't find nothing. The kid will probably show up by then.*"

"You're going to steal from a woman whose son is missing?"

"We need the money," Gillies said.

"Do what you want," Nadia said. "I'm going to sleep."

Nadia walked toward the RV. A few steps away, she heard Gillies say, "Don't worry, Luz. We'll find your son."

THIRTEEN

It took a week before Ostelinda could see out of her left eye. Her ribs hurt too much to sleep on her side. When she slept on her back, coagulated blood clogged her nostrils and woke her in desperate gasps. She slept in twenty-minute intervals. It hurt to cry.

Despite the pain, her thoughts were of Maite. Her best friend's fate had been Ostelinda's fault. She should never have spoken to Sra. Moreland. Maite could have gotten well on her own. They said they were taking her to the doctor, but Ostelinda knew that was a lie.

She would never see Maite again. Maite had been the only person that knew where Ostelinda was and Ostelinda had known where Maite was. Even if they were both trapped in the same factory together, that had meant something. None of the other people that she had known in her life knew where she was or even if she was alive. She was now lost and alone. There was no excuse for hope.

Ostelinda had been sure that she would die on the loading dock floor, but she managed to drag herself to the stairs, dripping blood from her mouth and nose. That was as far as she had gotten before fading out of consciousness.

The events that led to the beating played in a loop. Like a corner kick goal, in multiple angles, over and over again in slow motion, with commentary.

She could have stayed hidden. She could have run. Neither option would have changed the outcome. They would have caught her. Maite would have been taken away. Sometimes there were no good options. Her life had been spent choosing the worst of all the bad choices.

Ostelinda woke in the guard's arms being carried up the stairs. He breathed heavily with each step, but still managed to hold her gently. When he accidentally bumped her head on the railing, he softly cursed and apologized.

The guard brought her into the storeroom and placed her on her mat as quietly as he could. He didn't wake the two Guatemalan women, who could sleep through an explosion. He gave her one last look and said under his breath, "*I hate that kid.*"

Ostelinda tried to thank him, but couldn't speak. She was glad she hadn't, as the sound of the lock reminded her of his role. He didn't bandage her wounds. He didn't clean her cuts. He had shown the slightest mercy, nothing more.

Ostelinda closed her eyes. If she never woke, that would be her escape.

Ostelinda was awake when Sra. Moreland came into the storeroom in the late morning. She had tried to get up to work an hour earlier, but had been unable to move. Staring at the corner where the walls met the ceiling, Ostelinda laid frozen. Her muscles had stiffened. Her back spasmed. Her bruises stung, the color of beef liver and tender to the touch.

"What are you doing in bed?" Sra. Moreland said. "Work started an hour ago."

Ostelinda rolled over, yelping at the sting in her ribcage.

The anger on Sra. Moreland's face disappeared the moment she saw Ostelinda. She closed the door behind her, got to one knee, and took Ostelinda's chin in her hand. Inspecting the wounds on her face, she turned Ostelinda's head from left to right.

"Corey said you tried to leave," Sra. Moreland said. "That you fought him."

Ostelinda tried to speak, but nothing came out.

"You weigh a hundred pounds," Sra. Moreland said, shaking her head. "This wasn't necessary."

Sra. Moreland left the storeroom. Ostelinda closed her eyes. She didn't know for how long. When Sra. Moreland returned, she cradled medical supplies in her arms. She dabbed Ostelinda's cuts with a wet cloth that smelled like medicine. The liquid stung more than the cut hurt. Ostelinda bit down so hard she thought that her teeth would crack.

"It's okay," Sra. Moreland said, placing a hand on her forehead. "You can scream if you need to. The sewing machines will drown it out."

Sra. Moreland cleaned her cuts and bandaged the open wounds. She inspected under Ostelinda's shirt and poked at a few of the bruises around her ribcage. She never would have guessed that the woman could be capable of any kind of compassion or gentleness. The simple kindness made Ostelinda cry. The salt from her tears felt like acid in the cuts near her eyes.

"Thank you," Ostelinda said.

"You did not deserve this," Sra. Moreland said. "Did Corey—did any of them—violate you?"

"No," Ostelinda said. "What happened to Maite? Where is she?"

"My first husband hit me," Sra. Moreland said, ignoring her question. "By the end, so often, I thought it was normal. He hurt me bad enough to send me to the hospital three times. I always came back, though. Then I found God. I needed to know that I was not alone. I asked him to help me, to save me. The Lord listened. He sent me another man, one who loved me, who wanted to help me. And that man was willing to hurt for me."

"I ask God to help me," Ostelinda said, her voice a whisper. "He has abandoned me."

"He hasn't," Sra. Moreland said. "We all have our crosses. I would never go back to the abuse, but I am glad for it. God challenged me, and

I am stronger because of it. You will see. You will be stronger, too. You have to trust, to believe. Do you have Christ in your heart? Do you pray to him?"

"Prayer is all I have. Even if it goes unanswered."

"He hears you. Have faith."

"I fear my faith is gone," Ostelinda said. "I have not been to church in over a year. Without it, I feel less whole as a servant of Christ. I am incomplete without that fellowship."

Sra. Moreland held her gaze for a moment. She bowed her head and closed her eyes. "Pray with me."

Ostelinda had been raised in an Evangelical Church. Her parents and many of the other gitanos had embraced the faith and the message of the Protestant missionaries that had arrived decades earlier.

When she was a child, Ostelinda dreamed of being a Catholic like her friends at school. She loved the big stone churches with their stained glass. She wanted to walk among the images of saints and worship in the magnificence of a cathedral. Instead, her family attended services in a ranchero's refurbished barn.

By the time Ostelinda was fifteen, she no longer believed blindly in what men told her. God might have been powerful, but he had poor taste in the people that spread his message. The first time she refused to attend Sunday services, her mother slapped her but let her stay home. She received a slap the next Sunday and every one after, but Ostelinda proved to be as stubborn as her mother. She hadn't walked into a church since.

Sra. Moreland believed the same way the people back home believed. They selected the messages that made them feel better about themselves without making changes in their life. She had known thieves that would lecture people on the sin of drinking alcohol. The thought of her slaver believing she was on a righteous path should have made Ostelinda angry. It didn't. It restored her faith. It could end up being her way out.

When Ostelinda recovered enough to work again, she found small moments in the day to talk to Sra. Moreland. The woman no longer made her feel small. At times, she was even friendly. When Ostelinda asked for a Bible in Spanish, Sra. Moreland gave her the one she kept in her desk, a thick faux-leather bound book with a number of passages highlighted and underlined.

"Daniel's sermon yesterday spoke to me," Sra. Moreland said. "It was about sacrifice. About the seed we plant in our life. And the tree of faith that grows from that seed. Very powerful."

Ostelinda smiled and nodded.

Sra. Moreland leaned in close, her lips almost touching Ostelinda's ear. "Next Sunday. Be ready at eight. I'll try to find you a decent dress."

"God bless you," Ostelinda said, tempted to hug the woman. She didn't. She went back to work.

For the rest of the day, she tried not to smile. She tried to keep her expectations low, but it was difficult. She was going to leave the factory for the first time since her arrival.

FOURTEEN

Luz felt stupid. She shouldn't have given that man Gillies any money. A bad idea driven by desperation.

Two hundred dollars had been excessive. While she didn't think he was trying to steal from her, she doubted his ability to find Eliseo. He had been confident and had helped her before, but Luz wasn't blind to Gillies's situation. He lived in a mobile home under an overpass. The woman he was with had been sleeping in trash. He reeked of alcohol sweat. He didn't own a cell phone. Although, to be fair, neither did Luz.

She had felt so lost and alone that she had paid the first willing person that she came across to be on her side. It wasn't that she was too proud to ask for help. It was that so few of the people she knew could help in any way. Zeroes added up to zero. Ten people with no power had as little as one.

It wasn't like Luz had options. She only knew poor people, many of them struggling and in the country illegally. Gillies was white and a US citizen. He didn't live in fear of being picked up by the police or immigration. He didn't risk everything by talking to a person of authority. Luz had heard too many stories about ICE waiting outside of courtrooms and police stations, about immigration agents in schools and hospitals.

Her friend Isabela Hernández had told her a few weeks earlier about her cousin Arturo who had been in the U.S. for fourteen years. He was robbed and assaulted on his way home from his restaurant job. When the nurse at the hospital heard his story, she contacted the police. She was trying to help. It's what a person did to assist a victim of crime. While filing the report, the police learned Arturo had no papers. By the time they wrapped the last bandage, ICE was waiting to take him into custody. According to Isabela, he was still in detention awaiting a hearing to determine his status.

Luz stood on the sidewalk looking up at her apartment complex. It needed a coat of paint. The palm tree in the front drooped a little more each season, its fronds touching the roof. The stucco on the entire first floor had multiple layers of graffiti. Luz's American Dream.

She walked in the front door of her apartment. Fernando slept on the couch. She closed the door quietly behind her. Rosa read a romance novel at the kitchen table. Luz gave her a half-smile. Rosa stood, shook her head at her sleeping husband, and pointed to the back. Luz followed her into the bedroom.

"Anything?" Rosa asked. "Has anyone seen him?"

Luz shook her head. "I have work in a few hours. I'm going to take a shower."

"I need to tell you." Rosa put a hand on Luz's forearm. "Fernando and I found a place. A house in Montebello."

"That's great, Rosa." Luz gave her a hug. "I'm happy for the two of you. It's great to hear good news for a change."

"The problem is—and I know it couldn't be a worse time—we have to move in right away. Beginning of the month. We can't pay next month's rent here, too."

"That's ten days from now."

"I'm sorry, Luz."

"What am I supposed to do?" Luz asked. "You know what I'm dealing with. I'm supposed to find new housemates on top of everything else?"

"It was too good an opportunity. I'll help you find someone. I'm so sorry."

"I have to get ready for work." Luz walked out of the bedroom, slamming the door behind her. She hoped that she woke up Fernando.

Luz replaced the toilet paper roll in room 1285, then went to work cleaning the sink. It looked like a large dog had shaved but didn't understand how faucets worked. Every surface was wet. Small hairs stuck to the sink and mirror. When she thought she had cleaned the marble, she would spot another scattered hair she had missed. They were endless. Frustrated, she fired up the hairdryer and blew the hairs onto the floor trying to corral them into a corner.

Luz caught sight of herself in the mirror. She looked older than she thought of herself, her face drawn and tired. She had aged a decade in the last year. Or maybe it was the last week. Luz looked like her mother.

She smashed the hairdryer against the end of the sink. Turquoise-colored plastic shards flew like shrapnel into the air. Luz smelled smoke. She pulled the plug from the wall and dropped the hairdryer on the bathroom floor.

When Dolores came in the room, she found Luz sitting on the corner of the bed staring at the small red light at the bottom corner of the wall-mounted television. Dolores glanced at the scene in the bathroom, walked to Luz, and put a hand on her shoulder. Luz jumped, noticing for the first time that Dolores had entered the room.

"Are you okay?" Dolores asked.

"Yes." It took a moment for Luz to figure out where she was. "I got dizzy. I had to sit."

"What happened in there?"

Luz shook her head and shrugged.

"I radioed you," Dolores said. "Everyone has to go home."

"I started two hours ago. I have twelve more rooms to clean."

"Immigration raid. Supposed to be in an hour."

"The last two were false alarms."

"You should be glad they warn us."

"I need money for my son. Will I get paid for today?"

Dolores shook her head and walked out the door. "You get paid to work, not to sit at home."

Luz missed her stop, getting off the bus several blocks past her apartment. Whether lack of sleep or simple avoidance of going home, she had been lucky to snap out of her daze before the bus made it all the way to East L.A..

Across the street, a serious young man on a bus stop bench advertisement stared back at her. He was handsome, wore glasses, and had good hair. Mateo Fitzsimmons. *Reasonable rates. Immigration Expert. You Do Not Need To Fight Alone. Free Consultation.* Hablo Español. Luz wrote the phone number down on a piece of scrap paper. He looked smart.

Two blocks down the street, she passed the New Life Apostolic Church. She remembered when the building had been a jewelry store. Now it had a big cross on the roof. "Jesus Lives" and slightly smaller underneath "Jesús Vive" were handwritten on a board just above the door. While she was Catholic, the church was an appreciated addition. The neighborhood could use more religion of any kind. There wasn't enough community. Too much isolation. A city composed of strangers.

The congregation inside the church sang an upbeat song, clapping along. Luz considered going inside, but it felt like cheating. To go to a different church for a wedding or funeral was acceptable, but to sit through a Protestant sermon wasn't right.

Some things needed to remain sacred.

FIFTEEN

Nadia jumped when the RV door flew open. Gillies walked in with a full grocery bag under each arm. From the items that poked out of the tops, it looked like a child had filled the shopping cart for him. Funyuns, Lucky Charms, and a bouquet of Slim Jims rested on top of what was almost certainly a massive volume of alcohol.

"*Come and get it*," he hollered in a bad actor's version of a Southern accent.

He cleared off the table and laid out his bounty as if displaying treasure. A ridiculous amount of junk food and booze. He tossed Nadia a small package of Sponch.

"Your favorite, right?" Gillies said.

"You know it is," Nadia said. "You make fun of the name every time I eat them."

"*It's circus food*," Gillies said, biting into a Slim Jim. "*The guy at the store told me a joke.*"

"How much did all this cost?"

"*What do you call a barefoot Mexican that stepped in dogshit?*"

Nadia stared at him. She wasn't going to let him funny his way out of the situation.

"*A poo-toe.*"

Nadia shook her head.

"*Not even an eyeroll*," Gillies said. "What are you mad about? We made money. It's a good day."

Nadia went back to the book she was reading, a mystery novel by Paco Ignacio Taibo II. She stared at the next sentence, but didn't see the words.

"Here," Gilles said, holding out the money. "This is what's left. You take it. Hide it. Spend it. Do what you want. I tried to do a good thing. Now it feels dirty."

Nadia took the money and put it inside the book.

"You're acting like I stole a puppy," Gillies said.

"I thought I knew you, that's all."

"I never said I was a good guy."

"I never thought you were one, but I thought I knew what kind of bad you were."

"*This ain't no big deal*," Gillies said. "In a way, I'm helping her."

"You're giving a worried mother false hope."

"All hope is false hope."

"What happens when her son never shows? When you don't find him?"

"I might find him."

"You aren't looking for him," Nadia yelled.

"*Fuck. What do you want from me?*" Gillies yelled back.

Nadia flinched at Gillies's volume and his switch back to English. He was geared up to fight now.

"*I don't want anything from you.*" Nadia snatched the book off the table and stormed out of the RV. She walked down the street, listening to Gillies call after her.

When Nadia was a child, the small library in her town had been her sanctuary. The building was also one of the only buildings with air-conditioning. It didn't work well, but on a hot day eighty-five degrees was better than one hundred. While other kids settled for shade or swam in the river during the summer, Nadia tucked herself at the end of one of the short rows and spent hours inside a book.

It was in that same library where she later decided that stories could change the world. When she moved to the city and started working for the newspaper, the library remained an essential part of her life. It acted not only as a resource, but an oasis from the chaos of the city.

She expected an American library to have the same churchlike atmosphere. College students studying and a librarian reading from a picture book to a small group of children. The reality of Robert L. Stevenson Public Library was different, more grounded in reality and the necessities of the people that it assisted.

Banks of computers lined the walls. The center of the first floor was filled with long tables, each chair filled by a man or woman that spent more time outside than inside. The familiar must of old books was replaced by the pungent smell of sweat and mildew.

A few men slept with their heads on the table. One man had a small box that held three-by-five cards. He made small chicken scratches on a card and then carefully filed it in the box. Next to him was a stack of eight thick books including a Bible and Eight Days to Slimmer Thighs. He looked like Rasputin.

Nadia found an empty chair at the end of one of the long tables. She opened her book to read. After ten minutes, she had barely made headway into the chapter. She was too distracted, thinking about Gillies, Luz, and Luz's estúpido son.

"Damn it," she said.

In the corner, she found a free computer and Googled, "How Find Relative ICE Detention" which led her to ICE's Detainee Locator search engine. It made no effort to be user-friendly, asking a number of questions without providing context or explanation. She didn't know what an A-number was, so she skipped that part. Below the search area in red, it stated, "Online Detainee Locator System cannot search for records of persons under the age of 18." It gave no indication on how to locate a detainee under the age of 18.

Frequently Asked Questions wasn't much help either. Under the heading, "I can't find the person in ODLS. What should I do?" it offered the sentence fragment, "If you are unable to find the detainee using ODLS, please contact the—" followed by nothing. "Please contact the—" No punctuation.

It had been ridiculous to think the government would be clear about how the government operated. ICE blatantly wanted to make it as difficult as possible to navigate the system, even for people trying to follow the rules. It's why Nadia hadn't applied for asylum. It hadn't mattered that she was a legitimate candidate. If she had gone by the book, she would have been dead before asylum was granted.

She returned to Google. The internet consensus was that if you were looking for a juvenile in ICE custody, you needed to hire an immigration attorney.

Nadia didn't think that the kid had been detained. If he had been, he would have phone access. Regardless of how angry he had been at his mother, a seventeen-year old in custody would be scared enough to pick up the phone. He would look for help anywhere he could find it.

When Nadia looked up from the computer, she caught sight of a security guard strolling the rows in the center of the room. He carried a police baton, an item that did not seem like standard issue for library security. As he passed sleeping men, the security guard pressed the end of the baton into their ribs until they woke.

When he reached Nadia, his thigh brushed against her back. It could have been an accident, the product of his wide body and the narrow space. But having no reason to walk in her direction, she took it as a threat.

It was one of those moments that immigrants had to deal with daily. An insult that had to be swallowed. A coward with a tiny amount of power could quickly ruin the day of someone powerless. Nadia hated and pitied people like the security guard. Weak men who thought their power was earned, that it was meant to be abused.

Nadia had spent her career as a journalist exposing people that casually uttered the phrase, "What are you going to do about it?" People that believed they were untouchable. The problem was that in Mexico some people were untouchable. She hadn't been one of them.

Nadia thought of Luz, a mother who had lost her son. Her gut told her that Luz's story would not have a happy ending. Exploiting her pain by giving her hope didn't sit well either. It would raise her up in the present, but the plummet would be from a greater height.

She opened her book and looked at the money inside. Giving what was left back to Luz would have been the thing to do. Give it back and call it done. The only other choice was to earn it, for Luz to get the work she had paid for.

Nadia shut down the computer. As she walked to the exit, she scanned the room one last time. The security guard gave her a cruel smile. Nadia gave him nothing. She didn't exhale until she reached the sidewalk outside of the library.

SIXTEEN

Ostelinda had never been on a rollercoaster. She had seen pictures. Large wooden structures built by a bridgemaker gone mad. Thoughts of the heights and speed both frightened and excited her. The look of fear and glee on each rider's face.

The drive from the factory to the church was as close to a rollercoaster as Ostelinda would ever experience. She did not like it. It made her sick and disoriented.

Sra. Moreland drove the twenty-year old car like a bank robber in a film. One foot on the brake and one on the accelerator. She darted from lane to lane and ignored the colors of the streetlights, the lines on the road, and pedestrians. Sra. Moreland explained that her aggressive driving helped her to evade the many immigration patrols in the area.

Ostelinda pressed a hand against the roof and another against the dashboard, preparing herself for the inevitable impact. Miraculously, it never came. Maybe God was looking down on her, after all.

The chaos of the wild ride had derailed Ostelinda's plans. She tried to remember the path of their journey, counting distances and turns, but the streets and directions made no sense to her. She memorized signs and street names, but could only retain the Spanish names. English words were unfamiliar to her, impossible to memorize. By the time they merged onto the freeway, she was completely lost.

Many of the people that she saw out the window looked Mexican, but it didn't look like Mexico. Too many nice cars. Too many Black and Asian people. The buildings looked different. She was sure for the first time that she was in the United States, even if it was not how she had pictured California. No movie stars or swimming pools. The only blonde people were Latina women with dyed hair or wigs.

Sra. Moreland turned onto a street with small houses and dying trees. Peeling paint, graffiti, and cracked sidewalks. Metal bars on the windows and doors. She parked in an open lot next to a group of older cars. A handwritten sign in Spanish read, "Church Parking Only. Violators Will Be Towed."

Ostelinda walked with Sra. Moreland down the sidewalk. The tall woman walked as fast as she drove. They passed an elderly man mowing his lawn. He looked up at them. Ostelinda smiled. The man looked straight through her.

"It's about three blocks this way," Sra. Moreland said. "The church needs a real parking lot."

"Thank you for the dress," Ostelinda said.

"It's two sizes too big, but it's what I could find."

"It is very pretty."

They walked by a house where two young men sat on the steps in the shade. One of the men stood and walked to the chain link gate that separated the sidewalk from the yard. Ostelinda recognized him. It was Corey's friend, the older of the two Mexican men who beat her and took Maite.

"Hey, girl," the man said to Ostelinda.

Ostelinda stepped slightly behind Sra. Moreland.

"Quit scaring her, Juanito." Sra. Moreland said.

"Everyone calls me Lobo."

"No, they don't." Sra. Moreland turned to Ostelinda. "Wait for me at the corner. I have to talk to Juanito—I mean Lobito."

Ostelinda wanted to be far away from the man. She gave Lobo one last look. He made a growling sound. Behind her, Sra. Moreland said, "Where is Corey? He's avoiding me. We have to talk about the other night."

Sra. Moreland turned to Ostelinda. When she turned back to Lobo, she spoke in English.

Ostelinda leaned against the stop sign thirty yards from Sra. Moreland. She could have run. She was in the open, nothing restraining her, but she didn't know where she was or where she would go. She doubted a stranger would help her. If she was only going to get one chance for escape, she wasn't going to waste it.

The church looked like every other building on the busy street. A one-story stucco structure with barred windows and graffiti. The cross on the roof with the sign below that read, "Jesus Lives" was the only indication of what was inside.

Before entering, Sra. Moreland gripped Ostelinda's bicep, squeezing hard. "We are here because I care about your soul. But these visits will only continue if you follow my rules. Today, we are attending the English sermon, which I know you don't understand. If you behave, we will try the Spanish sermon another time. If someone talks to you and I am not around, smile, be friendly, but say nothing. You are here to worship, nothing more. Understood?"

"Yes," Ostelinda said.

"You could have run when I was talking to Juanito. Thank you for not being difficult."

"I would have missed church," Ostelinda said. "God bless you and thank you for this gift."

"It's the Christian thing to do."

The lobby looked more like a store than a church. Stacks of books, CDs, crosses, and other religious items covered two tables on either side of a large door into the auditorium. A few people milled around, talking to each other or looking at the merchandise.

Sra. Moreland didn't socialize. She guided Ostelinda through the door. The auditorium was large. The seats were a quarter full. They sat down in the back row and waited in silence for the sermon to begin.

Despite her inability to understand what the man said, he reminded Ostelinda of the preachers that she had heard as a child. The white man had a thick beard and shoulder-length brown hair, like American portrayals of Jesus. He talked with enthusiasm, pacing the small stage. He often held a Bible in the air or pointed at it.

At the end of the service, the congregation broke into small prayer groups. Ostelinda and Sra. Moreland joined four other people in a circle. One man talked and then they prayed together. A woman spoke. They prayed. Another woman talked. They prayed. She didn't know what they had said, so she prayed for God to listen to them.

Then it was Ostelinda's turn. She didn't know what to do.

Sra. Moreland said something in English to the rest of the group. When she was done talking, she gave Ostelinda a nod.

Ostelinda spoke softly. Sra. Moreland translated for her.

"I would like to pray for my sister, Maite. She was sick. I pray that she gets well. That her pain is gone. That I can see her again soon. I am afraid that I will not. I put it in God's hands. I have to. Thank you all. Being here, I no longer feel alone."

Everyone bowed their heads to pray, except Sra. Moreland. She held Ostelinda's eyes until Ostelinda bowed her head.

After the prayer group said their last amen, Sra. Moreland and Ostelinda stood and headed straight for the exit. They walked to the car in silence. Ostelinda worried that she had made a mistake, that she had done something wrong. She shouldn't have mentioned Maite. She didn't know why she had. Ostelinda was sure that they were bound for the factory and she would never leave that building again. At least not alive.

"I didn't know what to say," Ostelinda said.

Sra. Moreland didn't say anything, staring straight ahead.

"I'm sorry," Ostelinda said.

Sra. Moreland put a hand on Ostelinda's arm. "Let's get you a new dress. You should have something that fits if you're going to church next week."

Ostelinda smiled. With so little compassion in her world, even a sadist's kindness was welcome.

SEVENTEEN

The lawyer's office was on the same block as the bus stop advertisement. Sandwiched between a taquería and a nail salon, the single door held a plaque with the name Mateo Fitzsimmons in small letters. Nothing else was small. On either side of the door, a Mexican flag and an American flag projected from wall mounts. The same slogans from the advertisement covered the reflective silver window's peeling laminate. *Reasonable rates. Immigration Expert. You Do Not Need To Fight Alone. Free Consultation.* Hablo Español.

An electric bell buzzed when Luz opened the door and walked into the empty waiting room. Five chairs sat in an L with a small table in front of them. In front of the only other door, there was an empty reception desk with a telephone and a small row of flags representing the US, Mexico, and all of Central America. The wilting plant in the corner needed water, a circle of dead leaves on the ground beneath it.

Luz waited, expecting something to happen. She couldn't decide whether to knock on the door or not. She could hear a man's voice talking in rapid-fire English, but it was too muffled for her to understand.

She was fifteen minutes early for her nine o'clock appointment. The lawyer was probably in a meeting or on an important call. Lawyers on television were always very busy. She sat down and picked up a magazine.

Luz was in the middle of an article about Queen Elizabeth of England in the new issue of *Vanidades*, when the office door opened and a young white man in glasses walked out. He was considerably paler than the photograph on the bus stop bench, unfinished wood to the deep stain of the advertisement. His hair was wonderful though. His suit looked new but unpressed. He turned and looked at the clock.

"*I'm so sorry for making you wait.*" Fitzsimmons held out his hand. "*You must be my nine o'clock. I'm Mateo Fitzsimmons.*"

Luz introduced herself and they shook hands.

"*I'm sorry. Would you prefer Spanish or English?*" Fitzsimmons asked. "*¿Español o Inglés?*"

"Spanish, please," Luz said. She wanted to make sure that she understood everything.

"Again, my apologies for the wait," Fitzsimmons said in formal, book-learned Spanish. "My mother called and once she gets going, she's impossible to shut up. I try to be a good son."

"My son is missing."

Fitzsimmons coughed and nodded seriously. "Of course. Please, come in."

Luz followed him into the small office. She sat on one of the two chairs on the other side of his desk. In the tight space, his aftershave made her eyes water. The desk had a laptop computer, a legal pad, and a cup of coffee on it. She had imagined stacks of files and books and papers, but it was surprisingly tidy. She would have preferred a lawyer with a messy desk.

"Can I get you anything? Coffee, tea, water?"

Luz shook her head.

"I really do apologize. My receptionist's daughter came down with a fever. There was no time to get a temp."

"I hope the child is okay. It is best for a sick child to be with her mother."

"You are more understanding than me," Fitzsimmons said. "Now tell me about your son. Whatever you say to me is in confidence. You are safe here regardless of your own legal status."

Luz laid out everything she could remember. Fitzsimmons took notes as she spoke. He asked a few questions, mostly for clarity. He let Luz talk, never looking at the clock or making her feel rushed. When she finished, he reviewed his notes. She didn't know if he was a good lawyer, but he was a good listener.

"You hired an investigator," Fitzsimmons said. "Can I ask what firm?"

"He is not a detective like that. His name is Gillies. He is a friend. Someone that knows the people that my son worked with."

"I hope you didn't give him any money."

Luz felt her face get hot. She didn't want to tell him that she had. "Can you help me find my son?"

"Before I lay out your options, you need to know who I am."

Luz didn't, but could see that he was going to talk regardless.

Fitzsimmons set his pen down and tented his fingers to his chin. "You're looking at me, saying to yourself, 'Who is this gringo?' I might look white, but I identify as Latinx. My abuelito on my mother's side was half-Mexican. Your culture is my culture. I eat tamales on Christmas."

"I am only interested in finding my son."

"That's why I can help. I understand the plight of the immigrant. La Raza. Hard-working people like yourself are treated like criminals. It is indecent and unfair that people who want a better life are seen as less. You are called illegals, when you are refugees."

Luz didn't interrupt but hoped that he would finish soon.

"Even so-called 'good people' don't care about the circumstances that brought a person here. They don't care about your living conditions. About crime in immigrant ghettos. They don't care about the poverty, families forced apart, or the emotional toll of living in constant fear. These people only want you gone. And that makes me angry."

"My son?" Luz said.

But the lawyer had only stopped to take a breath. "I used to think that the United States represented freedom, but it stands for the worst kind of hypocrisy, a form of selective empathy. I became a lawyer to fight that injustice. To be a voice for the voiceless. That's who I am and why you'll never have to fight alone."

Luz waited, counting to five in her head. When she was sure he was done, she said, "My son Eliseo has been gone for more than a week."

"Right." Fitzsimmons glanced at his notes. "I see a few things that I can do immediately. I can contact ICE and find out if he's been detained. I can also call the police and inquire about recent arrests without you risking any repercussions. Let's hold off on filing a missing persons. I doubt its effectiveness. I'd rather keep his name off any reports for now."

"How much will it cost?" Luz said. "I have very little money."

"Since I made you wait this morning, I will give you twice that for free on your first bill. Twenty minutes for free. That's enough to get started. A few emails and calls shouldn't take much longer than that. My work would really begin when we find him. A two hundred dollar retainer should cover it."

Luz nodded. She had what was left of Eliseo's money. "What should I do?"

"Not much you can do. Wait by the phone and hope he calls or comes home. Or your friend finds something. I'm not a detective. I can only do so much. I'm not going to sell you a fantasy. I grew up in LA. It's an easy place to get lost. And when I say lost, I mean that in a lot of ways."

EIGHTEEN

Nadia entered the RV slamming the door behind her. Gillies's head shot up from the table where it had been resting. His eyes darted around wide-open and bloodshot. Gillies kicked the chair out behind him, stood up, and raised his fists to fight. Eventually, he focused on Nadia.

She threw a wirebound notebook onto the table in front of him. "If you're going to take a worried mother's money, you're going to do the job."

"Where were you last night?" Gillies's voice was equal parts spit and sound. His body dipped forward. "I was worried. I looked for you."

"You don't look like you left the RV."

"I looked all over the trailer," Gillies said. "Even in the drawers. You weren't in any of them."

"I needed space."

"The streets are dangerous."

"I survived before I met you," Nadia said.

"Where did you go?"

"I sat in King Taco for a few hours, then grabbed some sleep in one of my old spots."

"I didn't think you were coming back."

"I wasn't sure I was," Nadia said. "You have to do the right thing with this woman, Luz."

"You want wine?"

Nadia looked at the bottle in Gillies's hand for a moment. She was tempted, but shook her head. She would wait until the afternoon before she had her first drink of the day.

Gillies poured himself more wine. He took a big swig, letting some drip out of the side of his mouth, staining his beard. "Don't leave like that again. I'm used to you here."

"How much have you had to drink?"

"No more than usual."

"That much."

Gillies picked up the notebook and thumbed through the first few pages. "What's all this? What are all these names and lines? Who is Ugly Man? The Greek?"

"I'll explain everything," Nadia said. "I wrote you a plan. For your investigation. Different threads to unravel in your search."

"My search for what?"

"It's infuriating," Nadia said. "To find Luz's son."

"Right, right. Sorry. I'm tired from looking for you last night."

"You didn't look for me."

"Exactly. You can't find someone who doesn't want to be found."

"I'm going to make coffee," Nadia said, pushing him to the side to get to the coffeemaker.

"This looks a lot like work." Gillies tossed the notebook back on the table.

"I'm sorry." Nadia waved the empty coffeepot in her hand. "I forgot that your schedule was packed with activities."

"There's only a few things that could have happened to the kid. One being the most obvious. He got mixed up with those two assholes in the Chevy, something bad happened—like it does with assholes—and that's the end of it. The only mystery is where the body ended up."

"That's not the only thing that could have happened."

"You're right. He could have been abducted by a UFO. Or maybe a C.H.U.D. dragged him into the sewers. Except C.H.U.D.s live in New York."

"You're unbelievable. Making jokes? You took money from a mother looking for her missing kid."

"*Because I needed money,*" Gillies shouted, but immediately dropped his voice. "I can't help her. No matter what I do, this ends the same. Her son is gone. There's no point in making the effort if we end up where we start."

"You don't know that. It's not always the obvious thing. You sound like..." Nadia trailed off.

"Who? Who do I sound like?"

"Someone. No one. It doesn't matter," Nadia said. "You once said you would do anything for me."

"I would. I will," Gillies said, "but this isn't for you. It's for a stranger."

"If you don't help Luz, I will leave and never come back."

Gillies shook his head violently. "Why is this so important to you?"

Nadia set the empty coffeepot on the table and picked up the bottle of wine. She took a pull directly from the bottle. And then another one.

"What is it, Nadia?"

"That's not my real name," Nadia said. She didn't know how much she could tell him, but it was time Gillies knew some of it. He was the only person she trusted. "When I told you I was a journalist, did I tell you anything else? Anything about my past?"

Gillies shook his head. "It wasn't like you were telling your story. We were arguing about...I don't remember what. You were telling me that I didn't know what I was talking about. Which was probably true. You kind of said it as a claim of your expert knowledge or whatever. Like 'I know what I'm talking about, stupid, I was a journalist.' That kind of thing. Nothing more than that."

Nadia nodded. "I was a journalist for a decade. Up until a few months ago. The last three years, I wrote stories exposing the corruption of certain government officials and their ties to the cartels."

"I see where this is going," Gillies said. "Even I know that journos that cross the cartels don't last long down south."

"With the aid of worse men, somebody in the government put a contract out on my life. I had no choice. I ran north. With the reach of the cartel, I will never be safe. Those contracts and the money attached to them won't ever expire. If my name goes into any system in México, here, or anywhere, they will find me. They'll kill me."

"What's your real name?"

"It doesn't matter. Nadia is my name now."

"Okay," Gillies said. He took a drink from the bottle and handed the wine back to Nadia. She set it on the table without taking a drink.

"You can't tell anyone any of this," Nadia said. "The reason I didn't tell you until now is because it could put you in as much danger as me. The cartel does not discriminate. They destroy like God or nature. They kill the guilty and the innocent."

"Who am I going to tell?" Gillies said. "Wouldn't that make you less likely to want to find Luz's kid? You need to stay hidden, not run around asking questions."

"That's why you're going to run around and ask the questions. I'll tell you what to do, who to talk to, where to go, and what to ask. We can do this right."

"And this is important to you?"

"Luz deserves our effort. She paid for it."

Gillies picked up the notebook and opened it to the first page. *"Then let's crack this sucker open, put on our deerstalkers, and find out what I'm supposed to do next. The game is afoot."*

NINETEEN

Ostelinda admired herself in the cracked mirror. The dress that Sra. Moreland had bought for her was the nicest piece of clothing that she had ever owned. Against the dirty green of the storeroom, the reds and yellows of the flower print glowed like the first day of spring. Even her Sunday dress back home had been a hand-me-down from a cousin, out of style and threadbare under the arms.

She picked up a safety pin, opened it, and pushed the tip into her index finger. A trickle of blood ran down the back of her hand. She pushed in the pin. The sharp pain made her body jolt. She gritted her teeth and focused on herself in the mirror.

Ostelinda concentrated on the flowers of the dress. The roses were beautiful, but they had thorns, even if she couldn't see them. The prick of the safety pin affirmed where she was, and who Sra. Moreland was. Ostelinda couldn't let seemingly kind gestures like the visit to church and the new dress make her forget that Sra. Moreland was the woman in charge of her imprisonment, the woman who treated her as a piece of machinery. Sra. Moreland didn't care about Ostelinda beyond the work that she did.

A new dress changed nothing.

Ostelinda pushed the pin deeper. As far as it would go. Until it hit bone. Punishment for her failure, for letting them take Maite. Even if she could not have stopped the men, she was the one who had brought her friend with her from Mexico. Ostelinda may not have killed Maite, but she was to blame.

She removed the safety pin and put her finger in her mouth. The pain receded to a dull throb. The familiar taste of her blood kept everything in perspective.

The two Guatemalan women walked into the storeroom, drying their wet hair. The moment they spotted the new dress, they whispered to each other and gave Ostelinda nasty looks.

Since Ostelinda's visit to the church with Sra. Moreland, the Guatemalans had become increasingly belligerent toward her. Even if they never spoke, it had hurt. They knew nothing about each other, but they were in the same situation. Ostelinda had considered them to be extended family by circumstance, but as she knew too well, family doesn't always get along.

"You don't have to whisper," Ostelinda said. "I can't understand you."

One of the women made her voice high-pitched and walked like a fancy lady across the storeroom. The other woman laughed and followed, doing the same exaggerated strut.

Ostelinda tried to ignore them, looking up at the ceiling. All three of them had to get ready for work. They couldn't keep it up for long.

Not giving the women her attention made it worse. The Guatemalans walked in a tight circle around Ostelinda, screaming into her ears. Their voices were shrill enough to hurt her head. One of them bumped her, knocking her to the side.

"Stop it," Ostelinda said, covering her ears.

They screamed. She got bumped again.

"Please. Stop," Ostelinda said. She felt tears in her eyes, her frustration and anger rising to the surface. When she tried to move to the other side of the room, they stayed with her.

One of the women pushed Ostelinda in the back. She fell forward a few steps. At the same time, the storeroom door opened. Everyone turned.

"What's going on in here?" Sra. Moreland asked.

The two Guatemalans went silent. Like children in trouble, they looked at the ground. Their anger turned instantly to fear.

"Nothing," Ostelinda said. "They were helping me with my dress. I lost my balance."

Sra. Moreland looked back and forth to the two women. "Be at your station in ten minutes. You don't want to know what happens if you're late."

She said something in K'iche'. The Guatemalans nodded, eyes still to the floor.

"The dress looks nice on you," Sra. Moreland said and left.

When the door closed, the Guatemalans walked to their spaces and got dressed in silence. They gave Ostelinda a few nasty stares, but mostly concentrated on getting ready for work.

Ostelinda took off the dress, carefully folded it, and put it with her small inventory of possessions. She got into her work clothes.

Her ribs remained tender, but the rest of her wounds had healed. Cuts and bruises, however, were nothing compared to the feeling of helplessness and humiliation that came with a beating. Loud sounds made her flinch. Memories made her heart miss a beat. She broke into sweat at random moments.

Ostelinda had left Mexico to get away from violence. She had not expected to find more in America. She had escaped her stepfather and the slow increase in his violence toward her. It had started slow. He had shaken her, thrown her against a wall, but it took months to build to a hard slap. The real bruises came later.

She had prayed for a savior back them. She had prayed for someone to see her pain, to remove her from the situation. Her mother saw it, but did nothing. Everybody in her family and neighborhood must have known, but she was still alone.

Ostelinda had needed God then, as she did now, but she knew that He would never come. He either didn't care or didn't exist. Ostelinda was done with God. Her survival had been up to her in Mexico and would be in America. That didn't mean that she couldn't use some assistance.

If she could find a person she could trust at church, someone who spoke Spanish, she would have someone on the outside that could help. With an ally, there would be a way to escape that place.

Ostelinda had to be careful. She couldn't trust just anyone. She had to be sure of the person. She would get only one opportunity, so she needed to be patient. Even if patience seemed impossible after a year of imprisonment.

Sra. Moreland walked by her station. She stopped behind Ostelinda and put a soft hand on her shoulder. Sra. Moreland didn't say a word. She watched Ostelinda work. When she silently moved down the row, a chill ran through Ostelinda's body. Sra. Moreland had been treating her nicely, but Ostelinda knew the monster that lived under the surface. Sra. Moreland hadn't changed. She was the same person, the same abuser. One mistake and the punishment of the past would return.

TWENTY

Luz had discovered Hollenbeck Park on accident. A few months after moving to Boyle Heights, she had gotten lost looking for the house of an acquaintance. The woman owned a car and was going to drive Luz to Santa Monica to talk to an optometrist's wife about a job. A half hour late and no closer to finding the house, Luz knew that she had missed the opportunity, but she had found this oasis. Even with a freeway running straight through it, the park felt removed from the chaos of the city. Well-maintained, clean, and safe enough during the day, the park was her favorite place when she needed to relax.

Things had started to become overwhelming. Luz worried about her son, about money, about her job, about the future. She was always aware that her feet weren't firmly planted in the place she currently called home. The danger of getting stopped every time she left the house hung over her head. All it took was one medical emergency, traffic stop, or a random interaction with an authority figure, and she could be sent back. The seven years meant nothing to those in charge. She didn't understand what harm they thought she was doing.

Luz waited by the pond and watched the ducks. She liked it when the ducks stuck their heads under the water with their behinds in the air. A brief break from the weight of the worries in her life.

Gillies and Nadia approached from the distance. Gillies gave her a big wave. Luz watched the tall white man walk with his slight limp, the educated Mexican woman next to him. She wondered what their story was. They spoke to each other like a couple, but it didn't seem that simple. The woman wore a ring. The white man did not.

Luz steeled herself to be strong, confident, and insistent. If they didn't have information about Eliseo—show her that they were serious about finding her son—she would demand her money back. Her desperation had made her act impulsively. She wouldn't let it happen again.

When Gillies and Nadia reached Luz, she didn't offer a handshake or any niceties. "Do you have any news? Have you found out anything?"

Gillies sat on the picnic table and opened a school notebook. Luz could see writing in three different colors ink, each page full. She was surprised that he was that well organized.

"I'm making progress," Gillies said. "I hope to have some hard leads in the next few days. I know patience isn't easy, but it's going to take some time to track down and talk to the other workers."

"It's been almost two weeks."

"That's the thing," Gillies said. "If I had started right away, the trail would have been fresh. Time is a factor. People have bad memories. I'm talking to everyone, and we're focusing our attention on finding the man that Eliseo left with that day. The moving job with the college girls."

Nadia stood behind Gillies. She nodded, but said nothing.

Gillies read in his notebook. "I'm creating a timeline and establishing Eliseo's movements from the point he was last seen. I'll talk to the college students, everyone he had contact with."

"What about those two criminals? One of them had a gun. I am certain they have something to do with this."

Gillies turned to Nadia. She gave him a look that confirmed to Luz that she was the one in charge. Nadia nodded toward the notebook.

"We...I haven't been able to locate them," Gillies said, turning the page in the notebook. "They are our best lead, but also a dead end. It's not like I have a series of contacts in the underworld or in law enforcement.

Even if I did, I don't have a license plate. The best I can do is rule out the other leads until we get lucky."

"I went to see a lawyer," Luz said.

"I hope you didn't give him any money," Gillies said.

"That's what he said about you."

"Lawyers want it all for themselves."

"He's contacting Immigration, hospitals, maybe the police," Luz said. "He suggested I get my money back from you. At least half until you show results."

Gillies turned and looked at Nadia.

"Fifty, at least," Luz said. "I need a phone. We need to be able to contact each other."

Nadia shoved Gillies's shoulder and held out a few bills. He took the money and handed it to Luz.

"Thanks for understanding," she said. "I need every penny right now."

"Of course," Gillies grunted.

"Is that Eliseo's backpack?" Nadia spoke for the first time, pointing to the bag at Luz's feet. "May I?"

Luz picked up the backpack and handed it to Nadia. Meticulously, she took each item out, inspected it, and then set it on the table. She read the labels of shirts and smelled them. She thumbed through each page of the magazine, held it by the spine, and shook it for anything loose. She took out the compass.

"I gave him that compass," Luz said. "For the trip north."

Nadia nodded, not interested. When the backpack was empty, Nadia turned it upside-down and fished around inside. She ironed the fabric with her hand, feeling for bulges. She inspected the outside and smelled it, as well. She returned everything to the backpack and handed it back to Luz.

"I didn't tell you," Nadia said. "I worked a bricklaying job with your son. A day or two before he—that day when you fought."

"Was he a hard worker?"

"Yes," Nadia said, but she had paused long enough for Luz to know she was lying. It was a nice gesture, but poorly executed. "He fought with the boss. Seemed angry."

"He is." Luz felt tears coming. "He fights with everyone. Do you think he got mad at the wrong person?"

"No, maybe, I don't know," Nadia said. "I didn't mean it that way. I meant it as a good thing."

"How is his temper good?"

"When you're looking for a person, the best you can hope for is someone remembering them. Quiet isn't memorable. An angry person, someone who yells or makes a scene, isn't as forgettable. If he showed that temper, someone might remember seeing him. It could help us find him."

"You sound more like a detective than a journalist."

Nadia flinched at the word *journalist*.

"I was wrong about that," Gillies said. "Nadia was never a journalist. I misunderstood her. My Spanish isn't very good."

"Your Spanish sounds fluent to me," Luz said.

"I watch a lot of mystery television shows," Nadia said.

"¿Reportera del Crimen?" Luz asked.

"Señora Jessica Fletcher." Nadia smiled. "The television detectives do it the same way every time. And they always solve the case. Gillies is using those methods. Deduction, logic, and observation."

"Señora Fletcher solved murders," Luz said.

Nadia didn't reply. She looked down at the ground.

Gillies looked away.

Luz realized what she had said. That she had said aloud for the first time what she had been thinking for the last week. Speaking the words, she had opened the door to the possibility of Eliseo being more than just missing. It made her feel sick.

TWENTY-ONE

Nadia walked five blocks from the bus stop into University Park. The neighborhood near the USC campus remained a stark contrast to the working class areas that surrounded it. The students and residents treated the outside like a contaminated zone, rarely going beyond their given boundaries.

She said good morning to the Mexican man who trimmed the low hedge that spelled out the Greek letters of the sorority house. The same Greek letters that had been on the car that Eliseo Delgado had gotten into on the day he disappeared.

Despite their recent efforts, the investigation wasn't going anywhere. Gillies had spent the better part of the week asking around for the man that did the moving job with Eliseo. They nicknamed him Feo. Nadia thought Eliseo might have known the man, but Gillies contended that Eliseo had chosen Feo because he was the shortest and ugliest in the bunch. In Gillies's most elegant words, *"If Eliseo was going to try to bang some coed poontang, he didn't want competition."*

Gillies had no luck with the men at the underpass, the lumberyard, or the Home Depot. Without a name and only a vague description, most of the people couldn't commit to knowing or not knowing the man. Nadia and Gillies needed a name.

Nadia felt good in the suit from Goodwill. She looked like a lawyer or a detective, which gave her confidence. It made her feel like the times when she had been tracking a story. She thought about all the clothes that she had left in her closet in Mexico—the life that she had once had. A life that was gone forever.

She stood in front of the big wooden door, looking for a ringer. Finding none, she knocked. A bright-eyed redhead opened the door. She looked twelve years old, but Nadia knew that she was probably nineteen. The young woman started talking before Nadia had a chance to introduce herself.

"Awesome. You're here. That's perfect. You're a lifesaver. It's been a fucking shit show. Come in. Come in."

Nadia stepped into the large foyer. Red and gold streamers ran down from the staircase, landing, and ceiling. There were an inordinate number of red and gold balloons in the room, as well. She couldn't tell if they were for a party or a political rally.

"The other girl was supposed to have the dining room cleaned by now. I hope you're a harder worker. Let me show you where we keep the cleaning supplies, mops, all that stuff. Do you think you can get it done in an hour and a half? The charter president is coming at one. It's super important. Like life and death."

Nadia stared at her.

"Oh, for fuck's sake. Do you even speak English? Hablo *whatever?"*

"I speak English," Nadia said. *"Does it look like I'm dressed to clean your dining room?"*

"I don't know. You're a—you're not with the party planner?"

"I am with no one. I am here on serious business. I am looking for someone."

"Oh, shit. Are you Lety's mother? I'm so sorry. I thought you were a Mexican, I mean, like, a Mexican Mexican. I mean—you know what I mean."

Nadia blinked. It took her about five seconds. She exhaled. *"A young man has gone missing. He was last seen with two of your sorority sisters."*

"Are you with the police? I can't have the police here. The charter president is going to be here at one."

"Did two young ladies, both blonde, move into or out of the house eleven days ago, on the twenty-eighth of last month?"

"Probably Hannah and Bey. That's what happens when you accept pledges from Orange County. So you know, we're totally diverse here. Lety isn't the only Latina Chicana. And we have like tons of African-Americans and Asians, too. Tons."

"I don't care. Hannah and Bey? Are they here?"

"A total fucking shit show." The young woman made a groaning sound that teenagers had both invented and perfected, her hands straight at her side. *"I'll be right back."*

Nadia had been to the USC campus once before. Three years earlier when she was still working for the newspaper. She had been invited to speak as part of an international lecture series. The event had one of those academic names, "Borders, Barriers, and Barbed Wire: A Roundtable Forum Reimagining the Contemporary Landscape of International Journalism from Its Global Impact to Its Real Dangers." She had been joined on the stage with her colleague Pepe Guerrero and journalists and photographers from Kazakhstan, Egypt, Kenya, and Bolivia. Of the six people on that forum, only Nadia and the Bolivian were still alive. Pepe had tried to gain asylum in the U.S. two years earlier when he got word that there were legitimate threats on his life. His request was pending, but they didn't bother waiting for him to return to Mexico. He had been gunned down in his cousin's driveway in Denver.

Nadia had chosen not to make the same mistake. The system didn't work. It shouldn't have taken them that long. He should have had protection. Nobody had cared about his well-being. Bureaucracy and incompetence had killed him as much as the assassin that pulled the trigger.

Mexico would always be Nadia's home. She loved the people—the kindest and friendliest in the world—but the country had rotted long ago, corruption and unfairness imbedded in the political culture. Not drastically different than the United States, but further out of the shadows. She had fought for Mexico and she had lost. The war still waged, but she could no longer step on the battlefield. There had already been too many casualties.

The swimming pool in the backyard of the sorority house was full of balloons. A big banner spanned its width, reading *"Welcome."*

Hannah and Bey sat at a small table across from Nadia. They were the two blonde girls from that day at the underpass. The last people to see Eliseo.

"Thank you for talking to me," Nadia said.

Hannah gave her a weak smile. *"I can't believe that I was in the same car with someone that is missing. I'm totally traumatized. It could have been me. Like, if he can go missing or that girl in Aruba or whatever, then how safe am I? You know?"*

"Is it okay if I share this?" Bey asked.

"Share with whom?"

Hannah turned to Bey and mouthed the word *whom* and made a face.

"Share with whom?" Nadia repeated.

"I don't know," Bey said. *"Twitter. Instagram. Maybe it could, like, help. I mean, not just with traffic and retweets, but like a social media blast. Bring awareness."*

"It would be better if you didn't," Nadia said. *"Tell me what happened the day you moved. Any detail. Do you remember the name of the man Eliseo was with?"*

"César," Hannah said. *"His name was César. I remember because he kept correcting me on how to pronounce it."*

"Excellent." Nadia said. *"Anything else?"*

Bey cleared her throat and looked over her shoulder. *"You can't tell anyone, but we kind of made out. Nothing big. Clothes on stuff."*

"With César?" Nadia asked.

"No," Bey screamed. *"Gross. With Eliseo. He was cute and did a lot of the work with his shirt off. His body was like bam! He wanted more, but I wasn't going to fuck a Mexican worker. No offense."*

Nadia wanted her to keep talking, so she didn't say what she was thinking.

"He was pissed when I dropped him off. You know how guys get, like, fighty when they're horny and frustrated. Like that."

"*You're such a cocktease,*" Hannah said.

"*You know it, slut,*" Bey said.

They both laughed and high-fived each other.

"*Do you remember the address where he got out?*" Nadia asked.

"*I don't remember the street. It was a few miles from here, somewhere off Vernon. Not like the 'hood though. Houses, mostly. I dropped him and César. They went in opposite directions.*"

Nadia caught sight of the redhead standing at the French doors giving her the stink-eye, one foot tapping nervously. She decided that she'd gotten all she would get. "*That's all for now. I have your numbers if I have any more questions. Thank you for your help.*"

"*Of course. And you'll tell me when I can post this?*"

TWENTY-TWO

Ostelinda folded the pieces of paper and slid them into the Bible. There were too many drawings to include them all. She carefully selected the ones that would be the most effective.

She had spent hours writing the note, drafting three different versions. The other two copies, she had torn into small bits and eaten. She had to be very careful. She would only get one opportunity.

Her final draft read, "I need help. I am a prisoner in a factory. It is one and a half miles from the church. There are nine of us here. I'm afraid my friend Maite might be dead. The woman named Morlen who brings me to the church, she is dangerous. I have been her slave for over one year. Please contact the police. Thank you and God bless you."

She had never been a good writer and knew that the letter was filled with mistakes and poor spelling. Taking her time, she made sure that her penmanship was legible and the ink unsmeared. She would try to include a few of her drawings of the area and Maite. They might help her rescuers find her location or her friend.

Ostelinda's plan was to attempt to pass the notes to the preacher at the Spanish sermon. He was a man of God. He would help her. The police would believe him. He would know what to do. She could only hope that she would be giving him enough information to be found. If the plan worked, Ostelinda could be free by the end of the week.

Or she could never be found. Or she could get caught. She had to risk it. The prospect of another year living in the factory was unthinkable. She wouldn't survive. Ostelinda knew with certainty that her captivity would end soon. Freedom or failure. If the plan failed, it would end by their hands or her own. She wouldn't wait until they dragged her out like Maite.

Ostelinda and Sra. Moreland arrived at the church late. Boisterous singing echoed out of the auditorium. The sermon had already started. Sra. Moreland guided Ostelinda to their spot in the back, but it was taken. The Spanish sermon drew a bigger crowd. They remained standing. Ostelinda set her Bible on the chair and clapped and sang to the music. She had hoped to pass the note to Father Daniel before the service, but would have to wait until the break. Cold sweat dripped down her back.

Even though she understood this sermon, the preacher's words were little more than sound to Ostelinda. Her mind was elsewhere. She focused her attention on the pocket of Father Daniel's suit jacket. That's where she would place the note. As they said goodbye, she would give him a hug and slip the note into his pocket. She had practiced on one of the milliner's models at the factory.

At the close of the sermon, Father Daniel announced the ten-minute break before the start of the prayer circles. Everyone rose. A group of women rearranged the chairs. Others found friends and talked in small groups.

With the Bible tucked under her arm, Ostelinda helped move some chairs against the wall. A woman greeted her, but Ostelinda didn't respond. She had seen the woman talk to Sra. Moreland the week before. She couldn't be trusted. Father Daniel was the only person who she would give the note to.

Walking to the farthest corner with her back to the crowd, she found the note in her Bible and folded it into a thick square. She had practiced palming the square of paper every night during the week. She could move it from hand to hand, keeping it concealed. She wanted to include a drawing or two, but the thickness worried her.

The note would have to be enough.

She walked through the crowd looking for Father Daniel. She spotted him across the room, at the center of a small circle of people. He broke loose from the group. Ostelinda followed. It was like trying to catch a butterfly. Every time she tried to anticipate his movement, he zagged in the other direction. When Ostelinda finally got him cornered, Sra. Moreland stepped in front of her, and she lost her chance. The thick piece of paper had become damp in her sweaty palm.

"Church has given you energy," Sra. Moreland said. "You've been on your feet since the sermon ended. It must be nice to walk around. Not cooped up."

"It feels like I have woken from a long sleep."

"Praise Jesus. I can see the change in your face. In your eyes. A positive change in your attitude. It's been wonderful to see this rebirth."

"I needed to rediscover the Lord more wholly. Thank you for your kindness."

Ostelinda found Father Daniel with her eyes as they spoke. She watched him hang his jacket on a coat rack. It would be easier to get the note in the pocket now that it wasn't a moving target. She needed to get away from Sra. Moreland.

Ostelinda squeezed her left thigh with one hand and stretched. "I spend so much time sitting."

"I know what you mean." Sra. Moreland put a hand to the small of her back. "Let's walk some more."

After a lap around the room, Ostelinda managed to guide them to the coat rack. She stopped next to it. Father Daniel's coat pocket was a foot from her hand.

"How long have you been going to this church?" Ostelinda asked.

"Two years. From the day it opened."

"You must know everyone here."

Sra. Moreland looked out to the people. "I used to live in this neighborhood. I probably know more people here than not. It's been exciting to see the church grow."

While Sra. Moreland's attention was on the crowd, Ostelinda reached slowly for the jacket. She lifted the flap and felt for the pocket. It wasn't there. There was a flap, but no pocket. No place to get her finger inside. She scratched at the material. When she gave up, Sra. Moreland was staring at her.

"What are you doing?" Sra. Moreland said. "Are you stealing? Whose jacket is that?"

"No. No," Ostelinda said. "I wanted to see if this was a real pocket or a decorative one. I sew so many, I wanted to look at the stitching. It's silly."

"Don't lie to me."

Ostelinda stood with her mouth open, not knowing what to say.

Like the savior that she hoped he would become, Father Daniel stepped in with perfect timing. His welcoming smile and positive energy immediately softened Sra. Moreland. "How are you two doing on this beautiful Sunday morning that God has been so gracious to grant us?"

Sra. Moreland gave Ostelinda a glance, but didn't pursue her line of inquiry.

Ostelinda smiled. "I enjoyed the service this morning. A beautiful message. And the music was lovely."

She reached out to shake Father Daniel's hand. He took it. Ostelinda passed the note to him, pleading with her eyes to not give her away.

Nothing happened for a moment. Everything seemed to stop.

"She's one of yours?" Father Daniel asked Sra. Moreland, opening his hand and showing her the note. "I told you it was a bad idea to bring one of them here. We'll talk about this at home."

TWENTY-THREE

When Mateo Fitzsimmons had asked Luz to come down on a Sunday, she had expected him to have new information for her. On the walk to the lawyer's office, she tried not to convince herself that it was good news, but a dangerous amount of optimism shaded her thoughts.

"Thanks for making time on a Sunday," Fitzsimmons said, answering the door himself. "I'm heading out of town for a few days. Arrowhead. Ever been?"

Luz shook her head. "Is there news?"

"Only in the sense that I've crossed out a few things. I wanted to give you an update. The LAPD, Sheriff's Department, and ICE don't have anyone in custody with your son's name."

"He could have given them a different one."

"There isn't really an upside to that. Is your son dumb?"

Luz felt her face get hot, somewhere between anger and embarrassment.

"I'm sorry," Fitzsimmons said. "That was inappropriate. Dealing with these agencies is infuriating. What I meant to say was that it would do him no good. If he gives them trouble, they could 'accidentally' lose him in the system, detain him indefinitely."

"They can do that?" Luz asked.

"They do a lot of things they can't do. Not legally, but most detained immigrants don't have help. No advocate. No knowledge of the law. No power. They're pretty much on their own."

"But he's not in custody in any of those places," Luz said. She had known that sliver of optimism would hurt later. She didn't want him in a cage, but at least she would know where he was.

"Is there new information? Something else I should know?" Fitzsimmons asked.

"No. I am his mother. My son is lost to me. I just know."

"Don't give up." Fitzsimmons handed her a Kleenex.

Luz took it, even though she wasn't crying and didn't feel like crying.

"We're at the point when you should file a police report. I'll walk you through the process and make sure it does not impact your status here."

"I do not see the point of telling the police if they will do nothing."

"You don't have a lot of other options. We can talk more when I get back from Arrowhead."

Like many cities in Mexico, Los Angeles was dedicated to not providing shade for its pedestrian population. Luz felt the heat of the sidewalk through her soles as she walked down the street. The bright sun made her squint, forcing her to keep her eyes to the ground.

Luz cut through a residential neighborhood toward her apartment building. She thought she might find some shade, but there were only a few palm trees mocking the concept.

A block in the distance, Luz caught sight of a struggle between a white mother and a Latina girl she assumed was her daughter. The girl held a book to her chest. The mother pulled the daughter along the street. She gripped her upper arm tightly and threw the young girl forward. The daughter stopped and mumbled. The woman grabbed her arm again and threw her a few more steps. They repeated the process down the street.

Even though she was the punisher, it was the mother who cried. Makeup smeared the older woman's face, black streaks and raccoon eyes.

Luz understood. She had wept the first time she had spanked Eliseo. She couldn't make out what either of the women were saying, but the mother looked terribly disappointed in her daughter.

Intrigued by the conflict, a tattooed young man in a tank top left the porch of one of the houses and walked to the edge of his yard. He whooped and hollered at the show on the sidewalk. "You need help, señora?"

The mother ignored him.

"I can give her a good spanking."

The mother stopped, wiped the tears from her eyes, and turned to the man. His expression changed. He looked down. "I'm sorry."

The mother grabbed both of her daughter's arms. She pulled her closer until their foreheads touched. The mother said something through her teeth. The daughter nodded. The mother let go.

Luz was impressed. You had to be firm with young people. She should have been stricter with Eliseo. Maybe things would have been different.

The two women walked into an empty lot being used for parking. The moment the daughter's foot hit the gravel, she dropped the book in her hands and ran straight in Luz's direction. The mother swore and chased after her. The young man watching in the yard opened the gate, and fast-walked toward them.

Luz froze. She didn't know what to do. She didn't think the girl was attacking her, but she didn't know if she should stop the girl either. Luz had her own problems. She didn't want to get involved in a family dispute.

When the girl was ten yards away, Luz saw the daughter's face clearly. She had never seen anyone as frightened as that young woman, wild-eyed and desperate.

The daughter wrapped her arms around Luz. The force almost knocked Luz off her feet. The heat of the girl's breath burned her ear. Through gulping breaths, the girl said, "My name is Ostelinda. I am their slave. In a factory that is a prison. One and a half miles from here. They make me work all day. Help me. Please."

The older woman pulled the girl away from Luz. The girl spun and slid in the gravel.

"Stop," Luz said. "You're hurting her."

"What did she say to you?"

"I'm going to get the police," Luz said.

"You don't want to do that," the young man said. He stood behind the older woman, who was definitely not this girl's mother.

The woman grabbed the young girl by her hair and the shoulder of her dress. The girl tried to stand, but kept falling as she was dragged away.

Luz took a step forward. "Let her go."

The young man stepped in her path and put a hand on her chest. "This is not your business, lady." He said it casually, but the threat was there.

The girl kicked, trying to get to her feet. She grabbed the older woman's wrists in an attempt to pry them from her hair. Most of her chest was exposed, as the flower-print dress was pulled from her body.

"Get out of my way," Luz said, trying to push past the big man. He gave her a gentle shove.

The older woman dragged the screaming girl to her car and pushed her inside.

Luz stopped fighting. She stepped back, almost falling. Not from the force of his blow, but what she saw. She started to hyperventilate. The woman and the girl had gotten into a Chevrolet Caprice with a primered front quarter panel and a Jesus fish on the back.

It was the car Eliseo had gotten out of that day at the underpass. The car driven by two young men similar to the young man blocking her path.

The Chevy drove out of the empty lot. The young man watched it leave, took a look at Luz, and then walked back to his house. "Go home, lady," he said over his shoulder.

Luz ran the two blocks back to Whittier Boulevard. She looked for a policeman or a taxi. She ran up and down the street, expending effort but achieving nothing. By the time she finally spotted one, too much time had passed. The Chevy was long gone. It didn't matter.

When the taxi driver saw her, he kept driving.

TWENTY-FOUR

Nadia was glad to return to the underpass. University Park had made her nervous. She preferred to be invisible.

The sorority girls hadn't given her much, but they now had César's name to go with his description. Armed with the new information, Nadia and Gillies canvassed all the men at the underpass about César. It got them nowhere, until Nadia realized that they had only been asking the men. Not the only woman who spent every day down there.

Lupe García parked her food truck near the underpass from five o'clock until ten o'clock every morning. For the rest of the day and into the night, she moved to a pod downtown near Olvera Street. Her menu switched to English and her prices rose by fifty percent for the foodies and tourists. She joked about how white people loved when she added arbitrary ingredients to the tacos. As long as she could charge an extra two dollars by adding kimchi or haggis, she didn't care.

Nadia didn't want to wait until the next morning to talk to her, so she and Gillies hopped on a bus downtown. They found her truck in its usual spot and waited for a lull in the crowd. Approaching the window, Lupe recognized them immediately. The only female and the only gringo at her morning stop, they were hard to miss.

"What are you two bichos raros doing down here?" She said it with a smile.

"We're looking for someone," Nadia said. "You see everyone. Thought you could help."

Lupe drank a beer slowly, enjoying her break. She knew who Nadia was talking about the moment she had said César's name.

"I only saw him that one day. It was strange to see him down there. César's a cook. We worked the line at an Italian restaurant together. Four years ago. Before I had the truck. He must have been desperate if he was willing to work labor. No offense. Work is work, but he's got burnt hands, not callused ones."

"Do you know how to contact him?" Nadia said.

"We didn't keep in touch." Lupe shook her head. "He was a good cook, but a pinche pendejo. Always grabbing the waitresses. He tried it with me once. I burned him with a pan and he backed off."

"I sure as hell wouldn't mess with you," Gillies said.

"Do you know how we could find him?" Nadia asked.

"I haven't seen him since then. Probably found a job. I'll ask a few people. Kitchen workers move around, but we all know each other. Even in a city as big as LA. He's a cabrón, so easy to remember. Give me a couple days. You know where to find me."

"Thanks," Nadia said. "And his last name? Do you know his last name?"

"Castillo, I think? Kitchens aren't formal."

Nadia and Gillies walked back from the bus stop. Some kids rode by on bicycles, but other than them, the streets were empty. Creepy to some, peaceful to others. For Nadia, it was home.

Old feelings rose for Nadia. Feelings that she had thought were long ago in her past. She had missed the chase.

"Do you want to pick up a bottle of wine?" Gillies asked. "Or two? To celebrate closing in on César?"

"Let's celebrate when we find Luz's son," Nadia said, "but of course we need wine. We're off the clock."

They stopped at the liquor store down the street and bought two bottles and assorted Bimbo products. Nadia laughed when Gillies did his imagined version of the Bimbo bear's voice. High-pitched and foul-mouthed, Gillies played out a scenario where the mascot spoke about destroying his competition. Oh, the things he would do to Little Debbie. The more violent and profane his descriptions, the harder she laughed.

Around the corner from the RV, acrid, thick smoke stung Nadia's eyes and made her cough. Gillies picked up the pace, walking ahead of her.

"What is it?" she asked.

"No!" Gillies shouted the moment he turned the corner.

Nadia caught up and saw the RV down the street. Fire billowed out the small windows, the entire vehicle engulfed in flames. The American flag curtain flapped ablaze. Black smoke rose and swirled, darker than the night sky. The glow of the streetlights receded down the road in a brown haze. It looked like a war photograph.

"No, no, no!" Gillies yelled, running toward the RV. He dropped the bag of groceries. One of the bottles broke on the asphalt, wine filling the plastic bag and pouring into the street.

"Gillies!" Nadia yelled.

Nadia watched two figures step from the shadows across the street. The fire lit one side of their faces and bodies, the other side still in darkness. If Nadia hadn't seen them both before, she might have mistaken them for demons. She didn't know their names, but hadn't forgotten the faces of the two men who she had threatened with Gillies's pistol. The white boy with the big ears and his Mexican friend haunted her thoughts.

The two young men drank beer from forty-ounce bottles in paper sacks and watched the Winnebago burn. They laughed, toasted, and took big pulls.

Gillies stopped in the middle of the street thirty yards from his RV. Nadia could feel the heat from where she stood. She couldn't imagine what it felt like that close. He said something under his breath, turned, and marched toward the young men, fists at his side.

"Gillies!" Nadia shouted. "Don't!"

Nadia was aware that she hadn't moved. She couldn't. She was frozen in place, a witness but not a participant.

When Gillies reached the two men, he threw a big overhand right at the bigger Mexican. The kid easily feinted to the side and Gillies missed badly. The white boy didn't miss.

He might have been small, but a thick-glassed bottle was a powerful equalizer. He hit Gillies on the side of the head. The bottle didn't break, but Gillies crumpled to a knee. The bigger man hit him on the top of the head with his bottle. It shattered and Gillies collapsed facedown onto the pavement. He didn't move, aside from a twitch in one leg.

The two men turned to Nadia. She took a step to run. Not this time, she told herself. Nadia willed herself to face them, to confront her attackers. She ran straight at them, screaming wildly, her hands windmilling in front of her.

She scratched and punched at the two men, feeling skin dig under her nails. Until the white boy hit Nadia in the jaw. It knocked her off her feet. The taste of blood filled her mouth.

"*You thought you could pull a gun on me and I would forget?*" the white boy said. "*That I would let that shit go? You're lucky you're old and skanky, or you'd have gotten more than a punch in your mouth.*"

He kicked Gillies's unconscious body.

Nadia scrambled to her feet, but the big Mexican stepped forward and easily picked her up. He slammed her down on top of Gillies. The wind knocked out of her, Nadia gasped for breath.

The two young men walked away, laughing.

Nadia rolled off Gillies. She pulled at his body until she turned him over. She held his bleeding head in her lap, rocking slightly, frantic and anxious. Pushing panic down, Nadia did her best to keep it together. She had to stop the bleeding. Nadia removed her shirt and pressed it against the cut on his head. The cloth quickly became saturated with blood.

"Gillies," Nadia whispered, the air still trapped inside her. She wanted to throw up.

"*I'm okay,*" he said, his eyes fluttering open. "*Just resting.*"

The words came out slurred. His eyes had lost focus, floating from place to place, never able to lock in on any single thing.

"Those chingados," Nadia said. "This cut looks bad."

"*Probably a concussion, too. Don't worry. This ain't my first demolition derby.*" Gillies smiled, his teeth stained bloody. "*The advantage to having a head full of rocks.*"

"*There's a lot of blood.*"

Gillies stared at her for a moment without answering. His head dipped, fading.

"*Gillies, stay awake.*"

Gillies popped his head back up. "*I'm fine. It's nothing. You need to go.*"

"*I'm not leaving you,*" Nadia said.

"*The fire department and the cops and whoever else are going to show up. There's a camper burning.*" Gillies took her hand. He opened his eyes wide in an attempt to concentrate. "*You can't be here. You can't risk it.*"

"I won't leave you."

"Yes, you will. You have to. You know I'm right."

"I can't."

"Let me win one damn argument." He squeezed her hand. "Please."

"Damn it. Once I hear the sirens." She turned to the RV. "You gave me a good home."

"*Fuck that piece of shit. We'll get something better. Bigger. One with extra rooms for the help. What do they call them? Servants' quarters. And a wet-dry sauna.*"

"How do I find you?" Nadia asked.

"Here. We'll meet here." Gillies watched his home burn and then focused back on Nadia. "Tell me your real name."

"It was Anabel," Nadia said.

"You look more like a Nadia to me."

Nadia grabbed his face and kissed him on the mouth. "Don't die, Gillies."

"Don't tell me what to do."

TWENTY-FIVE

Ostelinda couldn't tell if she was standing under her own weight. Her feet touched the bottom, but her body felt lifted. She was wedged so tight in the narrow space that she could barely move. It had been hours since Sra. Moreland had forced her into the tall locker. Her calves cramped. She tried to point her toes for relief, but her feet were at an awkward angle.

She moved her left arm upward in an effort to shift her position. When she got it past her shoulder, her legs gave out and her body slipped downward. The strain on her knees ached worse than the cramping. She clutched at a small shelf above her head and pulled, bringing herself back upright. She shifted until she found a position that wedged her back where she had been. The pain was bad, but pain was just pain.

Ostelinda had gotten most of the screaming out in the first few minutes of the drive back from the church. Sra. Moreland had tied her wrists to a bar under the passenger seat, forcing her head down below the dashboard. In that position, Ostelinda couldn't get any lung power. She eventually gave up and stayed quiet. Sra. Moreland gripped the wheel tightly and mumbled to herself.

While stopped at a light, Sra. Moreland shouted a rare profanity, reached out her arm, and pressed Ostelinda's head against the interior of the car door. The bindings at Ostelinda's wrist stretched. It felt like her arms would get pulled from their sockets and her head would crack like an egg. When Sra. Moreland let go, the release of pressure was as jarring as the pain itself.

By the time they got to the factory, her throat burned and her tongue felt like a bloated sponge. Between the tears and the screaming, Ostelinda desperately needed water. She tried to produce spit, but there was no moisture left in her mouth. She coughed uncontrollably.

Sra. Moreland pulled her car directly onto the loading dock of the factory. With the help of the guard, she put Ostelinda inside the tall locker.

Ostelinda had been there for hours. It smelled of mildewed clothes and body odor. Through the small slits in the metal door, she watched Sra. Moreland talk to the guard and then drive out of the factory. After the guard closed the rolling door, he walked to his small office. Ostelinda couldn't make out his expression when he glanced in her direction, but it wasn't a smile.

Ostelinda didn't know she had passed out until she woke to the sound of a voice and banging.

"*Hey*," the voice said, followed by something in English that Ostelinda couldn't understand.

She tried to answer back, but nothing came out.

"Agua," the voice said.

A straw emerged from the slit in front of her face. She dipped her head and got her lips around it. She drank until she heard the straw rattle at the bottom of the bottle. The water burned her throat. She was still thirsty.

"Thank you," she said, her voice barely above a whisper and not her own.

The guard said something in English.

"Please help me," Ostelinda said.

He said something else and walked away.

Ostelinda was glad to know that she wasn't alone. That there was someone who knew she was there. And no matter the pain, he wouldn't have given her water if they planned to get rid of her. This was punishment. She would survive.

Ostelinda was half-asleep when the locker opened. Sra. Moreland and one of the Guatemalans pulled her out. Her legs couldn't carry her full weight. The two women held her like a child jumping puddles, taking each step slowly and cautiously.

"I lost my temper," Sra. Moreland said. "For that I am sorry. I have prayed to God for his forgiveness and now I ask for yours. I felt betrayed. You violated the trust between us."

Ostelinda pictured Sra. Moreland slipping on one of the steps and breaking her neck on the impact with the concrete floor.

"I've had time to think," Sra. Moreland said. "I was wrong. I can't blame you for running. It's what I would have done. What anyone would do. But I also can't allow it."

The two women set Ostelinda on the floor in the storeroom. Sra. Moreland found a blanket and draped it over her. The Guatemalan left the room.

"You don't have to work tomorrow," Sra. Moreland said. "You couldn't if you wanted to. Get your rest. Work will be waiting. Everything will go back to normal."

Ostelinda's voice cracked, just above a whisper. "I can't work for you anymore. I won't. You do not own me."

"You're tired."

"You can't make me do anything."

"If you're not working," Sra. Moreland said, "what use are you? How are you going to pay your debt?"

"There is no debt. It isn't real. You don't have to play act."

"Outside of this factory, you're worthless. The world doesn't need you."

"I am not worthless."

"If you're not behind a sewing machine the day after tomorrow, I'll have to find another way for you to repay what you owe. You're a very pretty girl. There are men who would find you attractive. Your life could be much worse."

"You call yourself a Christian," Ostelinda said.

"Get your rest. No matter what you choose, you're going to need it. It's your decision, not mine."

When Ostelinda was fourteen, one of the girls at her school hanged herself. She hadn't seen it happen or the aftermath, but several of her classmates reported that they had seen Marta Angulo's body hanging from the train trellis before she had been cut down.

Rumors spread through the school and town about what events could have led to Marta's fate. Ostelinda had never thought of it as a mystery. She was an unhappy girl. Her mother had died when she was six. Her father was a violent drunk. Everyone knew it. The poor girl simply couldn't take it anymore.

While Ostelinda understood the why of Marta's decision, suicide hadn't made sense to her back then. No matter how bad things got for her, she had the hope that change was possible even if she couldn't see the path to it. She had survived her childhood knowing that it would eventually end.

On the floor of a storeroom in a clothing factory in Los Angeles, Ostelinda was forced to rethink those views. She began to understand the kind of hopelessness that led a person to take their own life.

Ostelinda had little hope left. Without it, she felt herself slipping. It was like being so tired that she could fall asleep at any moment against her will. She wanted to resist, to push forward, but at some point her body would take over and there would be no more fighting and no more pain and she would slip into the peace of oblivion.

It sounded wonderful.

TWENTY-SIX

Luz couldn't get the frightened girl out of her head. Ostelinda. An uncommon name, easy to remember. The desperation and fear on the girl's face wasn't the look of a daughter afraid of punishment waiting at home. It was the terror of a wounded animal. The girl was desperate for help.

Luz replayed the confrontation, convinced she could have done more. She had protested and fought, but with hesitation. She might have been Ostelinda's only hope and all she had done was yell at the girl's kidnappers.

The moment that the car pulled away, Luz had lost her ability to think. She had tried to follow the car, but adrenaline made her body shake and her heart pound in her ears. It didn't occur to her to get the license plate number until it was too late. She wanted to call the police, but wouldn't.

When Luz finally stopped and took a breath, she wrote down what the girl had said to her. Every word. Everything that she could remember. Ostelinda had said her name and that she was being held in a factory. Luz had heard stories of men and women that had been brought over by coyotes only to be forced into work with no freedom or pay. Ostelinda had said that she was one and a half miles away, but she didn't say in which direction. Luz didn't know what she could do with the information, but she needed to record it.

There was also the car. The Chevrolet Caprice with the Jesus fish. The white woman drove the same car that Eliseo had gotten out of the day he disappeared. The car that those two criminals had been driving. The white woman and those young men were connected. Luz needed to find the girl to find the car. Or the car to find the girl. One of them would lead to her son.

Luz didn't know where to start. She needed help, someone to tell her what to do. Someone to give her guidance. She called the lawyer, but got no answer and didn't know what to say on the voicemail. She wanted to call Gillies, but he didn't have a phone number. Rosa and Fernando had already moved out and were living their lives.

The person who she really needed to talk to was Nadia. While Luz had hired Gillies, she knew that Nadia was the brains of their operation. The woman had alcohol problems, she was shaky and thin, but Luz could tell that she was smart and capable. Her accent and vocabulary gave her away. She had the confidence of someone with an education, someone that had once been respected.

Luz knew that Nadia had lied about not being a journalist. Gillies had gotten it right the first time. Luz didn't care about the lie. Nadia certainly had her reasons. Luz had lied so often to so many people to protect her status in the United States that it had become second nature.

Nadia had claimed that she learned everything about investigating from Reportera del Crimen. Another lie, of course, but for Luz, that had been true. Everything she knew about criminal investigations had come from watching detective television shows. That had gotten her nowhere.

Luz accepted that it had been blind luck that she had stumbled onto the car and the girl and a potential link to her son, but there were times when accidents were not accidental. She had asked for a sign from God a week earlier. The car was as close to a sign as she would receive. Sometimes what we called luck was rewrapped providence.

Luz had been told that detectives were American men with square jaws or old British ladies with gardens, but this was real life. She might have been a housekeeper and not a detective. She might not have known the first thing about finding lost people. She had real life things to do that weren't about saving damsels in distress. But she wasn't about to turn around and go home. She couldn't. Work and money and rent and all those things were just that. They were things, not people.

Luz wouldn't be able to live with herself if she didn't make every effort to find that girl. And Eliseo. Her son.

There were a lot of choices in front of her, but the path was clear. She had to do the wrong thing because it was the right thing to do.

With all the confidence that she could manufacture, Luz descended the stairs of her apartment complex and walked onto the sidewalk. The street hadn't changed. The same tired palm tree drooped in front of the building. The same faded graffiti sat on the stucco wall. But Luz felt different, changed. One of those moments when life no longer moved at its usual, slow pace, and everything changed in a flash. One of those sharp turns that sent a person's life in a new direction.

Luz rounded the corner and headed back toward the church parking lot and the neighborhood where a mysterious white woman had taken a girl named Ostelinda.

PART THREE

THE SOUTHLAND

TWENTY-SEVEN

Luz took out her notepad. Not knowing what information was important, she wrote down all the numbers and names she saw: names of streets, addresses, license plates. Luz made a note in the margin to buy a map of the city. She would gather the information and process it later. With enough data, maybe she would see a connection, something that would bring everything together. Something that would lead her to her son or Ostelinda

As she neared the lot where the confrontation took place, she kept one eye on the house where the threatening young man had lived. She didn't see him or anyone else, but Luz's proximity to the building made her antsy. She wrote down the address and underlined it. At some point, Luz knew she would return there.

A handwritten sign at the lot entrance read, "New Life Apostolic Church Parking Only," in both Spanish and English. Near the entrance, tucked against the tire of a Kia was a Bible. Luz remembered Ostelinda carrying a book when she had seen her from a distance, but when the girl had pled to her, she held Luz with both hands. She must have dropped it.

The Bible was faux-leather bound, well worn, and heavily highlighted inside. The binding was cracked at the spine. The gold gilt edge was faded from wear. Dispersed throughout the pages of the Bible were folded pieces of paper. Luz opened the first one she found. It was a drawing of a girl's face. Not Ostelinda, but someone her same age. The remaining drawings were urban landscapes, drawings of rooftops and billboards, somewhere industrial, mostly drawn at night. She refolded each paper carefully and returned them to the exact pages where she had found them.

Taking a deep breath, Luz pushed open the door and walked into the New Life Apostolic Church. Growing up Catholic, she had expectations for what constituted a proper church. This space did not meet those qualifications. It wasn't that she felt a church required the opulence of a cathedral. She had been to and appreciated many humble churches. The difference was that this was a place of business more than it was a place of worship. The only thing it was glorifying was money. She walked to a woman selling books and crosses at a folding table.

"*Excuse me,*" Luz said in English.

"*Hello,*" the woman said. "*You're very early. Monday services aren't for another two hours.*"

"*Yes. Thank you. I am not here for the church. I am looking for two women. They were here yesterday. A white woman in her forties, taller than me. She was with a young Mexican girl, a teenager, pretty.*"

"*A lot of women attend on Sunday,*" the woman said. "*What are their names?*"

"*The older woman, I do not know. The girl's name is Ostelinda.*"

"*That's a pretty name. I don't remember hearing it. I'm sorry.*"

"*Thank you for your help.*" Luz turned toward the door.

"*Wait,*" the woman said. "*Father Daniel might know them.*"

Luz stopped and turned.

"*He's the boss around here. I mean, other than Jesus.*" The woman smiled and pointed to a door across the lobby. "*It's his flock. If anyone knows them, it would be him. He should be in his office.*"

"*Thank you.*" Luz walked to the door and lifted her hand to knock.

She hesitated, listening to the voice on the other side.

"*The people down there are becoming downright hostile. We don't have the base we did in Puebla. It's been working, but why take those risks? Mexico is a big country. We can send the missionaries farther south. Or put more efforts into Guatemala. We've saved some souls down that way.*" The man laughed.

Luz could feel the woman at the table looking at her. She knocked on the door.

"*Can you hold on for a second?*" the voice said.

The man that opened the door had shoulder-length hair and a trim beard. He looked like the white Jesus that is in all the images in the United States, down to the blue eyes. Father Daniel smiled. "*Can I help you?*"

"*I'm sorry to bother you. I'm looking for a young Mexican girl in her teens. She was here yesterday with an older white woman. The girl's name is Ostelinda. I saw her in the parking lot. She dropped her Bible.*" Luz held the book out for the man to see.

"*I don't know anyone named—what did you say?*"

"*Ostelinda.*"

"*It's not a name I recognize. If you want, you can leave the Bible here.*"

"*I will keep it to give to her myself.*"

"*Do you know the girl?*"

"*No.*"

"*How do you know the girl's name if you don't know her? If you only saw her drop her Bible?*"

"*It is written inside,*" Luz said. "*Thank you for your help.*"

"*You should leave the Bible with me. I'll make sure it's returned to her.*"

"*That's okay. I'll find the girl.*"

"*It's not your Bible,*" Father Daniel said.

"*It's not yours, either.*"

Luz might have gotten Father Daniel on the wrong day, but she did not like the look or the tone of his voice. There was nothing overt about the threat, but Luz felt it in the air.

"Why didn't the girl pick up the Bible?" Father Daniel said. *"It's a difficult thing to drop and not notice."*

"It was because she was scared. She was running, and then she got dragged by the hair into a car and taken away."

"That's terrible. Did you witness this? I mean, it sounds like a vicious crime."

"Yes. I saw it happen."

"Did you write down the license plate number of the car?"

"No."

"Did you call the police?"

"No."

Father Daniel rose from his desk. *"I hope the girl is okay. Usually when something like that happens, an American citizen would immediately call the police."*

Luz said nothing. She took a few steps away from the preacher.

"Is there a phone number where I can reach you?" Father Daniel asked, walking step for step with Luz.

Luz backed up, turned, and ran out of the church. She ran halfway down the block, convinced that Father Daniel would chase her. He didn't. When Luz turned the corner, she slowed to a walk, out of breath.

She had gathered clues, but didn't know how they fit together. Luz was even more confused than before she had stepped into the church. The Bible, the car, the house, the church, she couldn't see how they would lead her to Ostelinda or Eliseo.

Questions were supposed to have answers, but for Luz, they just seemed to lead to more questions.

TWENTY-EIGHT

Nadia had remained in some level of intoxication for two days, but still only managed to get halfway to oblivion. A built-up tolerance over the last year, or the sheer weight of her pain—there wasn't enough alcohol in the world to obscure her dark, inescapable thoughts.

She could hear Gillies's laughter in her head. She could hear his voice. She could see his face. His smile. And then she saw the white boy hit him with the bottle. She saw his blood. The heartbreak of seeing someone she loved hurt. The anger and helplessness of it. And the guilt.

It was her fault, after all. When Nadia had taken Wyndorf from its box and pointed the pistol at those two punk kids, she had set events in motion that led to Gillies's assault. Stories involving guns did not have happy endings. Guns led only to pain and grief, regret and death.

Nadia hated leaving Gillies bleeding on the street. She had waited in the shadows until a fire truck arrived and then she had walked away. She kept walking. Three hours later, her feet hurt. Her whole body hurt. She hadn't stopped walking the entire time.

As it got deeper into early morning, the traffic died down. When a bus approached, Nadia felt a pull. Nothing big, but a momentary temptation to jump in front of it. To end it all. It wouldn't be the first time that she had thoughts of suicide, but her self-preservation or cowardice always kicked in before she committed fully to the act.

Nadia walked through the neighborhood until she found the construction site off Olympic. Nadia had worked on the site two months earlier, doing brickwork on some walkways, short walls, and chimneys. In the middle of the job, everyone had been abruptly told to go home. The contractor said something about one of the investors embezzling from his partners. No money for anyone. Something about a dry well and blood and a stone. They weren't even paid for that last day.

While the remaining investors worked everything out with the authorities and the bank and whoever else rich people complained to, no more work could be done on the property. The condominium complex remained half-built. Equipment and building materials sat idle. Everything looked the same as the day Nadia had walked off the site.

She pulled at the corner of the chain link fence enough to crabwalk underneath. The metal scratched her back and tore her shirt. It didn't matter. It was already ruined by Gillies's blood, now stiffened dry and dark brown.

Once inside, Nadia walked the perimeter of the half-completed structure. She recognized her work at the base of one of the chimneys. A single brick jutted out at the corner, her signature on the unfinished painting. The only unique element of her work was its imperfection.

Using the bare concrete foundation for a bed and a bag of cement as a pillow, Nadia lay on her side, her eyes tightly closed. She felt her body tilt gradually to the side, but never quite tilting at all. She knew she wasn't moving, but that didn't make her any less nauseated.

"It's all your fault," Ignacio said.

Nadia didn't open her eyes at the sound of the voice. She didn't have to. She knew Ignacio wasn't there. Her husband was dead.

"It's all your fault," Ignacio repeated.

"Yes. It's all my fault," Nadia said.

There was no point in arguing with someone who wasn't there, someone who had been dead for a long while. Any sane person will tell you that. It wasn't an argument you could win.

She should have bought more wine, but the way the liquor store clerk had looked at her and her bloodstained clothes, Nadia was pretty sure two bottles were her limit. The effects of the wine were wearing off. More alcohol was about the only thing that might shut out Ignacio's voice, but it was too late to buy more. Maybe if there was a Safeway close, she could get some cough syrup.

He wasn't real. He was only in her head.

She knew that, but that didn't mean that she didn't hear it.

"You get people hurt," Ignacio said.

"I hurt people," Nadia agreed.

"It should have been you."

"It should have been me."

"I warned you."

"Yes, you warned me."

"You killed me."

Nadia opened her eyes. Of course, there was no one there. She was alone. She would always be alone. She would live that way and die that way.

"I killed you," she said, "and I could have gotten Gillies killed."

Ignacio was right. She put other people's lives at risk through her actions, through her existence. Every investigation that Nadia had been a part of had put innocent people in danger. She had gotten people killed.

The attack on Gillies was her fault. Those two pendejos could have killed him. They certainly wouldn't have burned his RV if Nadia hadn't pointed a gun at them. A yelling match—a non-fight—on the lot would have been forgotten, common to violent men. She had escalated things. A criminal cannot swallow the insult of a gun pointed at him without some kind of retribution.

Nadia had arrived in the United States less than a year earlier. It felt like decades. Her old life, a million miles away. Her life in Mexico was someone else's story. It was Anabel's story.

Anabel had done a lot of things wrong. She had ignored subtle threats and then overt ones. She had persisted when she knew it did no good. She had mistakenly believed that being right mattered. Most importantly, she had pretended that her actions only impacted her and not the people in her life.

Ignacio had begged her to quit her investigation and ditch the story. Even after seeing fellow journalists killed for far less scandalous work, Nadia didn't waver. The police had put a detail on her for the two weeks after the main article came out, a 9,000-word exposé on broad corruption within the local government. Nadia had tried to turn them down, but they had insisted. She hadn't refused because she didn't believe the threat was real. She had refused because she thought one of her guards might try to kill her.

The article was praised by the international journalist community and even translated and reprinted in English on a few prestigious websites. But for all that work, the impact was minimal. One government aide resigned. No investigations or convictions. The people that she had directly insulted—and that's all it was to them, an insult—were too powerful for a financial scandal to impact them.

There had been a public uproar, government committees were formed, accusations were made, but nothing changed. The powerful don't stop being powerful because the powerless learned how they got there.

In a practical sense, there had been no reason to kill her. The story hadn't hurt them. No matter how well she had done her job, she had been ineffective in doing any damage to their operations. But it hadn't been about damage. It was the insult. A housefly doesn't bite, but eventually the incessant buzzing gets it killed. Which is why she was sure that they were still looking for her, that the contract on her life was real. She would never be out of danger. There was no statute of limitation on this kind of crime. These were people that had a godlike opinion of themselves, infinite patience, a very long reach, and an army of soldiers willing to kill on command.

If she returned to Mexico or if her name appeared in any system— even in the United States—she had no doubt that they would find her.

132

Her death would soon follow. A kid with a razor would walk up to her on a job site or in a public bathroom or in a holding cell. A car would pull up next to her on the street. They would not stop until she was dead.

And if anyone was standing next to her, that person would be dead as well.

TWENTY-NINE

"I will not work for you anymore," Ostelinda said. "You cannot make me. I have nothing. You cannot take anything else away."

Sra. Moreland stood in the doorway to the storeroom, rhythmically tapping her foot. Ostelinda sat against the wall on her mat. Her back ached, but she refused to budge from the position. She tried to look as defiant as she could despite her fear.

"Very dramatic," Sra. Moreland said. "It's your decision and you're free to make that choice. Of course, there will be consequences."

"What are you going to do?"

"I'm going to show you that you still have much to lose."

Sra. Moreland left, locking the door behind her. Ostelinda's body shook. She closed her eyes and took a deep breath. As the minutes passed, Ostelinda wondered if this was Sra. Moreland's punishment. Making her wait. Letting her contemplate what was to come.

A half hour later, the door opened and Corey entered. He smiled without joy, his eyes lifeless. Without saying a word, he took off his shirt and dropped it on the ground.

Ostelinda scrambled to her feet. She looked around the room for a weapon and picked up her hairbrush. It was neither intimidating or an effective defense, but she felt better with something in her hand.

"I remember what you looked like when you first got here," Corey said, moving from side to side, but keeping his distance.

Ostelinda moved a step to the side to get a better angle at the door.

"You were worn from the trip, but still hot. Young and fresh. Even now, dirty and tired, beat to shit, you look good enough to eat. You ever had a boyfriend?"

"Stay away from me!"

"I haven't moved." Corey laughed. "How old are you? Forget it, I don't need to know. You ever been with a real man?" He flexed his muscles.

Ostelinda was scared. She had prepared herself for a beating, but hadn't considered this kind of threat. She had managed to protect her virginity to that point. At home, boys had been insistent, but she had resisted their advances and more forceful attempts. She had heard stories about the possibilities on the journey north. She had taken a birth control shot but had been able to fight off the men who wanted more than a feel.

With Corey standing in front of her with his dumb face and his big ears, Ostelinda thought of Maite. She had accepted her friend's death, but now wondered what her final minutes had been like. If she had been afraid. If she had been in pain. If she had been violated in some way by this clown. The weak of heart should never be given power.

"Tell me what happened to Maite," Ostelinda said.

"Who?"

"The girl you took away. My friend."

"I'm not going to tell you anything about that."

Corey moved quickly. He grabbed Ostelinda's wrist and twisted her arm. She dropped the brush, yelping in pain. He got her in a bear hug and walked her backward. Corey leaned forward with his full weight until she fell back onto the mat. He landed on top of her, their foreheads bumping. Ostelinda fought, trying to bite his face. Corey laughed and brought her hands over her head, holding both wrists in one hand.

"Let me go!" Ostelinda screamed. He was small, but strong.

With his free hand, Corey tore open her shirt from the collar, ripping the fabric and exposing her chest. The seams cut into her shoulders and armpits. Corey leaned down and licked her neck. His chest felt slimy against hers, both of them sticky with sweat. His breath burned her ear.

"My mom told me to be respectful, but you disrespected me first. She's not here. Why shouldn't I do whatever I want?"

Ostelinda's face was wet with tears. "Please."

"You going to work today?"

"Yes. I will work."

"And tomorrow?"

"Yes."

"Is my mom going to have any more problems with you?"

"No."

"Okay."

Corey released her wrists and leaned back into an upright position on top of her. He breathed hard, staring at her for a moment. With a hand on the top of her chest, he pushed off and rose to his feet. He adjusted his crotch with one hand. "Nice tits," he said and left the room.

Ostelinda clutched her torn shirt to her body, trying to cover herself. Her eyes watered enough to blind her, the world a blur. She let herself cry until she felt exhausted and sick and there was nothing left.

Fifteen minutes later, the storeroom door opened. Ostelinda had put on a clean shirt and was ready to return to her workstation. She couldn't fight anymore.

Sra. Moreland entered with a bottle of water and a paper bag with a grease stain at the bottom. She handed the bottle to Ostelinda.

Ostelinda drank, the water running down the corners of her mouth. Her throat still hurt from the day before, wounds on scars. All the crying had dehydrated her. She drank it despite the nausea.

"Did Corey clear things up? He can be persuasive. You ready to go back to work?" Sra. Moreland held up the paper bag to Ostelinda.

Ostelinda could smell egg, meat, cilantro, onions, jalapeños. Whatever was wrapped in tin foil inside the bag smelled like her abuela's kitchen. She rolled the top of the bag back up and set it on the ground.

"That's my breakfast. I want you to have it. Enjoy it. I respect your strength. The fight in you."

"Are you going to kill me like you did Maite?"

"What kind of monster do you think I am?" Sra. Moreland looked appalled at the possibility. "That girl's death was a tragedy. God took her too soon, but I certainly had nothing to do with it."

"You could have helped her. You killed her."

Sra. Moreland turned and waved for Ostelinda to follow. "Can I show you something?"

Looking down at the loading dock, Ostelinda watched Corey and his tattooed companion laugh with the guard. It made her ill that she lived in a world where they were allowed to be happy.

Sitting on the stairs were two girls, both younger than her. The older one was around sixteen, maybe even younger. The two of them looked around wide-eyed. Scared and excited and far from home. Ostelinda remembered that feeling. Arriving in Los Angeles had felt like the beginning of a grand adventure. The first week felt like freedom.

"They're sisters," Sra. Moreland said. "From Chiapas. I'm going to put them in your room."

"You could help them. Actually help them, if you wanted to."

"I am helping them," Sra. Moreland said. "I'm giving them an opportunity. Just like I've helped you and hundreds of other women achieve the American Dream. You have no idea the risks I take for you."

"You force us to work."

"If you aren't working, what use are you?"

"What about these girls?" Ostelinda asked.

"Corey heard about an opportunity from some business partners out in Riverside. That's a city inland from here. Some men are looking to employee girls about their age. About your age, now that I think of it.

The girls could pay their debt quicker, but the work is—let's say—more challenging."

"You would do that? You would destroy their lives?"

"I don't want to," Sra. Moreland said, "but it's not up to me. If you don't behave, I'll take Corey's friends' offer. I will cut my losses and send you and those two innocent angels down there to Riverside. And let me tell you a simple truth, nothing good ever happens in Riverside."

THIRTY

Luz wished she could devote all her time to the search for her son and Ostelinda. But if she wanted Eliseo to have an apartment to come home to, she needed new housemates in the next few days. Rent was due in one week and she couldn't cover it herself.

After an hour of calling friends, she had a few leads, but was running out of time. Her friend Yolanda had a cousin who might be moving to the city from Fresno. Israel, who lived a few doors down, worked with a woman that needed a place, but she had a green card and was worried about risking her status by living with someone without papers.

Word had travelled about Eliseo, and Luz received a lot of sympathy from those people who had heard. She had to correct two people who assumed he was dead. Each time, it sent shivers through her body. Luz had thought she had accepted the possibility, but she hadn't—she had to believe her son was alive.

Taking a break from her calls, Luz went to the refrigerator. She needed a beer. Opening the refrigerator door, Luz could have sworn that she heard a light scratching behind her. She froze, listened, then opened the door some more. She heard the sound again. Like the riffling of pages. Through the front door mail slot, the corner of an envelope poked inside, getting stuck halfway.

When Luz opened the front door, she found Nadia on her knees holding the thick envelope in both hands. There was no question that Nadia was drunk, but that wasn't the worst of it. Her matted hair and the dark circles under her eyes made her look like a mad bruja. Blood stained her torn shirt. Her hands shook and she smelled heavily of sweat and urine.

"It wouldn't fit," Nadia said, looking like her inability to put the envelope in the slot was about to make her cry. She tried to stand, but lost her balance and fell backward. She dropped the envelope, revealing a stack of loose bills inside.

"Why don't you come inside?" Luz said, reaching her hand out to help Nadia.

Nadia shook her head. "This is your money. Not all of it. I came to return it. I'm sorry. It's what's left."

"Let me get you something to eat. Some coffee."

"I have to go. I have to go away." She picked up the envelope and forced it into Luz's hands.

"Where is Mr. Gillies?" Luz asked.

"I don't know. Men beat him. I left."

"What are you talking about? What men?"

"The white boy with the gun. His friend."

"Come inside and tell me," Luz said. "Please."

"We weren't ever going to find your son. I have to go."

Luz reached down and got her hands in Nadia's armpits. Nadia stood with Luz's assistance. She didn't resist as Luz walked her into the house.

"Let me help," Luz said, navigating the coffee table, walking her to the bedroom, and setting her onto the bed. "Let me help you, Nadia."

"Not even my name." Nadia said, dropping her head back and closing her eyes.

It only took a few minutes before Nadia was talking in her sleep. Luz took off Nadia's clothes. Her body was bruised and scarred, thin to the ribs. Luz pulled the blankets over her. She dug in the closet and found something for her to wear. Nadia was six inches taller and considerably thinner, but Rosa had left a few things that might fit. Luz left the clothes on the corner of the bed and let Nadia sleep.

In the living room, Luz tripped over Nadia's backpack. She tossed it on the couch and a revolver spilled out along with packages of Bimbos. Nadia picked up the gun by the barrel. It was heavy, the weight oddly distributed. She put it in a kitchen drawer.

Nadia had more color in her face when she walked into the kitchen two hours later. Rosa's blouse and jeans hung on her like a scarecrow, but she no longer looked or smelled like she had been buried in a laguna de estiércol for a week.

"Do you have anything to drink?" Nadia asked, holding her forehead in one hand. "A beer? Some wine?"

"Is that a good idea?" Luz asked.

"Just one. To ease me back…maybe two."

Luz grabbed a beer from the refrigerator and handed it to Nadia. "I'm going to put on some coffee."

"Thank you, Luz." Nadia drank half the bottle in one pull. "You've been very kind."

"I need your help."

"I can't help you."

"We'll see," Luz said and jumped into a recap of the events of the last few days. She tried to be as detailed as possible from the scene in the church parking lot with Ostelinda and the woman, to the sinister energy she got from the preacher. The Mexican at the house, the drawings, but most importantly, the car.

"You're sure it was the same car?" Nadia asked.

"Yes. A Chevy with a gray front fender and a fish on the trunk."

"And this Ostelinda? A sweatshop worker?"

"Something like that. We have to help her. The police won't do anything. Nobody will listen to me. If we don't do something, nobody will."

"I'm sorry, Luz. I can't help you. I'm leaving."

"Please. You're smarter than me. You know about finding people.

Together, we can find the car or the girl or Eliseo. One will lead to the other. I can't do it without you."

"Thank you for your kindness. I've seen very little." Nadia stood up, using the back of the chair for support. She took a few shaky steps and walked to the front door.

"A few days. That's all."

Nadia stared down at the doorknob in her hand. "I want to help, but I only get people hurt. My intentions don't matter. I put people in danger. I get people killed. It's how I am."

"Maybe this time the person that gets hurt will be someone who deserves it."

"It doesn't work like that." Nadia opened the door.

"Where will you go?"

"I'll find something. I know places to sleep."

"These are the same people that hurt Mr. Gillies," Luz said.

Nadia let go of the knob, but didn't turn around.

"Stay with me for one week," Luz said. "That's how long I have this place. I'm six hundred dollars away from paying rent. When I get evicted, maybe you can show me some of those places where you sleep."

Nadia turned from the door and looked at the apartment. "You would let me stay here with you?"

"Of course."

"What if I don't help you?"

"That doesn't matter. You're welcome to stay as long as you need."

Nadia closed the door and came back inside.

Luz could feel Nadia's foot bouncing under the table. Nadia's hands shook and her eyes darted all over the apartment. Luz had watched the woman drink four cups of coffee with three big scoops of sugar in each.

"The church is involved," Nadia said, reading over Luz's notes. "From the parking lot to the preacher, there's a connection. You should go on Sunday."

"He's suspicious of me."

"It's a public place. You could blend in," Nadia said. "And the girl? What did she say? One and a half miles? From the church or the lot?"

"I don't know."

"We need a map," Nadia said.

"I bought one." Luz dug the map out of her purse.

"And a pen?" Nadia asked. "Where was the parking lot?"

Luz handed a pen to Nadia. She pointed out the lot and church on the map. Nadia put small Xs on the locations.

"Do you have a pushpin and some string?" Nadia asked.

After Luz found them, she watched Nadia stick a pushpin into the table where the church lot was. She looked at the table at the bottom of the map, tied a piece of string to a pencil, and twisted the end around the pushpin until it was the length she wanted. Nadia drew a big circle around the spot.

"That's one and a half miles," Nadia said. "If you walked the entire circle, that's eight or ten miles. It will take a couple days. Let me see those drawings."

Luz slid the drawings across the table to Nadia. She flipped through them, separating the urban landscapes from the portraits.

"Keep an eye out for these billboards. They might be the key to finding the right neighborhood. To help us narrow it down."

"What happens if I find her?" Luz asked.

"I have no idea."

THIRTY-ONE

After fourteen hours of sleep, Nadia was surprised to find herself alone in Luz's apartment. The space in the small one-bedroom felt decadent compared to her previous circumstances. She drank three glasses of water and wandered around the apartment. The clothes that Luz had given her were too large, but they smelled like detergent and felt soft against her body.

Luz had left a set of keys, ten dollars in cash, and a note on the kitchen table. It read, "Nadia, hope you got enough sleep. I'm going to walk the circle on the map. Make yourself at home. There's not much in the refrigerator, but places to eat down the block. Lock the door when you leave. If the top lock sticks, wiggle the key. Luz."

Nadia put the money and keys in her pocket. She opened the refrigerator and looked at the beer. The beer looked back at her. She grabbed an orange from the bottom drawer.

Without Gillies's RV parked across the street, Nadia expected the lot and the underpass to look different. It didn't. The same men stood around the same dirt waiting for the same bad pay. The burnt-out husk of the Winnebago was gone, towed and junked. A dark black mark scarred the curbside and bled into the street. Shards of glass and red plastic reflected the light off the dark ground. She didn't see Gillies.

Nadia walked to Lupe's food cart. If Gillies had returned to the underpass, she would have seen him. Gillies had an obvious crush on Lupe.

"Where have you been?" Lupe said.

"Long story. I'm looking for Gillies."

"Yeah, I heard about his camper. Tough break."

"Have you seen him?"

"No," Lupe said, "but I found César."

"Who?"

"You have a short memory," Lupe said. "The chingado cook you asked me to find."

"Of course. I'm sorry. I've been distracted."

Lupe wrote something on a napkin. "He's working at this restaurant on Fifth, downtown."

"Thanks, Lupe." Nadia took the note. "If Gillies comes by, tell him that I am staying with Luz. That's where I'll be. He has her number."

Before Nadia headed downtown to talk to César, she walked the six blocks to Ace Pawn and Loans. Gillies had told her this if she got into trouble, that Bambi at Ace would give cash for almost anything, but especially guns. Gillies insisted that if Nadia was ever in a real bind, that she was to sell Wyndorf.

Nadia pressed the intercom button next to the gated door.

"*Step back,*" a gruff voice said.

Nadia backed up and lifted her chin to the camera. The door buzzed and she entered the pawn shop. Guitars and bicycles on one side, power tools and stereo equipment on the other. Glass cases filled with jewelry. The only person in the space other than Nadia was a fat man behind the counter. Nadia approached him and set the backpack down at her feet.

"*Gillies told me to come to see Bambi.*"

"*I'm Bambi,*" the man said. "*How do you know Batshit Gillies?*"

"*We live together.*"

Bambi looked her up and down. "*Good for Batshit.*"

"*He said you would give me a fair price.*"

"*I give everyone a fair price,*" Bambi said. "*How is the son of a bitch?*"

"*He got assaulted the other night. He's in the hospital. They didn't kill him though.*"

"*He's hard to kill,*" Bambi said. "*I'll let him tell you the stories. We served together.*"

"*He never talks about that time.*"

"*They're not exactly humorous anecdotes. With the killing and the moral ambiguity. What have you got for me?*"

Nadia reached into the bag for the gun, but it wasn't there. She clawed at the inside of the bag. Nothing. In her drunken state, she must have lost it.

"*I'm sorry. I can't seem to find—*" Nadia stopped herself. The gun wasn't the only thing of value that she owned. She pulled at the ring on her finger, but couldn't get it off.

Ignacio had given her the ring on a trip to Belize. She remembered the dinner, the proposal, and the walk back to their cabaña down a rutted dirt road in Placencia. She also remembered taking notes to investigate corruption in Belize City after reading an article in the local paper. The two memories had defined her life at that time.

Ignacio and the hunt for a story.

Her two loves.

"*I got something for that.*" Bambi found a can of WD-40 under the counter. "*It happens a lot with wedding rings.*"

Nadia held out her finger. Bambi sprayed the lubricant onto it while she turned her hand.

She twisted the ring on her finger. It turned easily. Getting the ring over the knuckle took some effort, but she managed. She held the ring in her palm for a moment, silently apologized to her husband, and then handed it to Bambi.

The fat man pulled out a loupe, a small scale, and a measuring tool. He studied the ring with the magnifier, weighed it, and measured the size of the diamond.

"*It was insured for eighty thousand,*" Nadia said.

"*I'm guessing that's pesos.*"

She nodded. That was about four thousand dollars, if she remembered correctly.

"*It's a nice ring, good stone, but I got to be honest, jewelry depreciates. You take a diamond out of the Zales and it loses ninety percent of its value by the time you're at the Cinnabon. The platinum—my mistake, white gold—might be worth more than the diamond.*"

"*What is your best offer?*"

Bambi gave the ring another long look. Nadia watched the man study the last remnant of her relationship to her dead husband.

"*Five hundred. No bullshit. That's the best I can do. That price is based on what I know Gillies would do if he heard I lowballed you. We're friends, but that fucker scares me.*"

Nadia didn't argue. She watched Bambi count out the money from a stack of bills the size of a toilet paper roll. He wrote out a receipt and tagged the ring.

"*Anything else you want to sell?*" Bambi asked.

"*No. I have nothing left.*"

"I got five minutes," César said. "The lesbian manager hates when I take a cigarette break."

César sat on a milk crate in the alley behind the restaurant. He smoked a cigarette and scarfed down a torta. He ate quickly, bean paste painting his chin. Nadia felt sick watching him eat. She hadn't had a drink in a while and was sweating in the mild weather.

"Tell me about that night," Nadia said. "Where did the girl drop you off?"

"Somewhere off Vernon."

"Did you see Eliseo walk into any buildings or meet any people?"

"We went in different directions. The kid was mad that the bitch at the college hadn't put out. He said he knew a lady that was always horny and that's where he was going. He was probably bullshitting. Trying to impress a pussy magnet like me." César gave Nadia a smile that displayed his half-chewed torta.

"Did he say the woman's name?"

"No, just that she was a rich lady he met on some job. And that she looked great in a bikini. And out of one." César used a finger to dig out some food from his back teeth. "So, what's your situation? Put on a few pounds and I could be into it."

THIRTY-TWO

Ostelinda hemmed the sleeve of a suit jacket for what felt like the millionth time. She had lost. All she could hope for was that her defeat wasn't meaningless. She looked over at the new girls fumbling with their sewing machines. They were confused and scared, but not yet terrified. They knew the familiarity of hard work and it calmed them, the only moments in the day that made sense.

The Guatemalans were gone. Ostelinda did not know where they went. They had been working one day and gone the next. No tear-filled goodbye or even a neutral head nod. She had lived with them for over a year. She hoped that they had been put to work somewhere else or sent back south. Ostelinda didn't want to think about the worst possibilities. It only brought back dark thoughts of Maite's fate.

Ostelinda considered telling the two girls the whole truth. Or she could let them live with some optimism for a while. It wouldn't last. It wouldn't change their fate. But it would delay their disappointment and protect their hope a little longer. The pin was pressed against the balloon. She didn't know if she had the heart to push it in all the way.

It had crushed Ostelinda when the older of the two girls, Marisol, asked her, "How long have you been here?"

"A year."

"You must have owed a lot of money. I don't want to make you feel bad, but Sra. Moreland said it would take us only three months before we can go."

"I came from very far away."

"That must mean that you will leave soon. All the work that you've done."

"Yes," Ostelinda said. "I hope to leave very soon."

"America!" the girl said, smiling. "It is so exciting to be here."

Sra. Moreland inspected each worker's progress, walking the aisle between the workstations. She stopped behind Ostelinda, putting a hand on her shoulder. Ostelinda had grown to hate when she did that. It appeared to be a friendly gesture, but she knew it was about control and power. The woman's touch felt like the sensation of sticking a hand in river mud. Cold and thick and slippery, filled with crawling sickness.

"This isn't so bad, is it?" Sra. Moreland said. "Everything back to normal. Working gives us all purpose. The new girls look happy."

"It's going to break their hearts when they learn they're never leaving."

"The most important lessons in life are often the most difficult ones."

"What happened to the Guatemalans?"

"They moved on," Sra. Moreland said. "I heard they found a place in Fontana with some other Guats they knew."

"They're not with Maite?"

"I don't know why you insist on bringing up such a sensitive subject. A tragic event. It hurts me to relive those memories, as I take some of the responsibility for her death. I ask myself every day if I could have done more."

Ostelinda remained completely still.

"I pray on it every night," Sra. Moreland said. "I know Jesus forgives whatever small mistakes I may have made."

"May I take a bathroom break?" Ostelinda asked.

Sra. Moreland lifted her hand from Ostelinda's shoulder, probably checking her watch.

"A bit early. But to show you there's no hard feelings. Make it fast."

"Thank you," Ostelinda said, standing and getting away from Sra. Moreland as quickly as she could.

There were two restrooms on the third floor. Because they got so little time away from their workstations, the other third-floor workers used the closer bathroom. Ostelinda preferred the farther one that the others rarely used. The only rebellion that remained for Ostelinda was to walk slower than her usual pace.

She caught her reflection in the bathroom mirror. Her face looked gray, the color of a fish belly. Her hair was stringy. She saw three large pimples on her chin. Back home, she wouldn't have left the house looking that bad. Vanity died in chains. Ostelinda washed her face with cold water.

On the walk back to her workstation, she stopped to look out the window. It was one of her favorite spots in the evening. Through the clear spot that she had cleared of grime, she would look at the lights of the city. She came to this location as often as she could, but rarely in the day. Without the lights in the distance, everything looked smaller and dirtier and lacked magic.

The neighborhood below wasn't much to look at, but it was the world beyond the walls. She imagined herself standing in the street and looking up at herself in the window. One part of her soul free, the other captive.

She turned to return to work, but stopped when something registered out of the corner of her eye. She had caught some movement on the street.

Ostelinda rarely saw people on foot in the industrial area. Cars and trucks drove past. A stray dog she called "Perrito" strolled through the streets like he was on a mission, dutifully making his rounds to pee or sniff. He looked hungry and unloved, but did his job like a good soldier.

The movement Ostelinda saw wasn't Perrito. It was a woman Ostelinda recognized. It was the woman that she had pled to at the church parking lot. It could not be a coincidence.

151

The woman carried a folding map and traced the surface with her finger. She stood in the middle of the street, looking up at the two billboards. She made a few notes on the map.

Ostelinda tried to open the window, but it wouldn't budge. She wanted to shout down to the woman.

"What are you doing?" Sra. Moreland asked, making Ostelinda jump.

Ostelinda's heart skipped. She tried to appear calm. "Looking out the window. I got distracted. Not enough sleep. I'm sorry."

Sra. Moreland looked out the window. She stared out for some time, then turned to Ostelinda.

"There's a dog I see every once in a while," Ostelinda said. "I call him Perrito."

"I didn't see a dog."

"Me neither, but I always look."

Sra. Moreland glanced out the window again. "You have work to do. Best to get back to it. I'd hate to have to make you work late."

Ostelinda nodded. Had Sra. Moreland seen the woman on the street? Ostelinda didn't care. Sra. Moreland had no power over someone outside the factory.

She returned to her workstation and got back to work. She couldn't believe it. Someone was looking for her. All her thoughts had been about giving up and resigning herself to this life. After seeing the woman on the street, everything had changed. She had something that she had never had before. There was someone on her side. She wasn't alone.

Ostelinda smiled. It made her face feel strange.

THIRTY-THREE

Luz marked the spot on the map. They weren't Tecate and La Tricolor 103.1 FM billboards like in the drawing, but the layout of the buildings looked similar. It was hard to tell. The point of view of the drawing was higher up. From Luz's perspective, this area was the closest to the images that she had found so far. She looked at the buildings around her. Ostelinda could be in one of them right now.

There were dozens of potential sweatshop locations in the area. Many of the businesses had high fences or walls with razor wire at the top. Empty lots and junkyards abounded. Warehouses and factories. Code violations and a disregard for order. Like a border town down to the scattered stray dogs and cats for atmosphere.

Luz's feet hurt from the four miles she had covered, almost half of the circle complete. She should have brought water. She should have worn a hat or a scarf. Her face was hot to the touch and covered in sweat. Luz needed to be inside somewhere with air conditioning. She felt lightheaded. Trying to keep in the shade, she walked back to the main road fanning her face with the folded map.

She almost shouted when the Chevrolet with the primered front quarter panel turned the corner three blocks ahead and drove toward her. She squeezed her eyes shut, not convinced that it wasn't an illusion from her baked brain. When she opened her eyes, it was still there. She couldn't see the driver.

By the time she reacted, the car had turned the corner. She chased after it on foot. Rounding the corner, she caught sight of it again. She watched it reach the main road and turn into traffic. Luz was a block away. She kept running.

The siren of a police car startled her. She looked to her side to see a police cruiser pulling up next to her. She acted casual, although she felt her insides tighten. She couldn't catch her breath, gasping for air. She bent over, hands on knees.

The police car parked sideways across the road. A police officer got out and walked to Luz, one hand resting on his holster. He stopped about four feet from Luz.

"*Is everything okay?*" the officer asked.

"*Yes. I am good.*" Luz did her best to speak without an accent, her eyes still toward the ground.

"*You were running. You aren't dressed for exercise. Something is usually wrong when people run in street clothes.*"

Luz wanted to tell the police officer about the girl and Eliseo and the car that was getting away, but he wouldn't believe her. It would only extend the interaction. The longer they talked, the more dangerous it was for her.

"*Late. I'm very late,*" she said.

"*Can I ask you what you are doing in this neighborhood?*" the officer asked. "*I spotted you two hours ago walking down the road a ways back.*"

"*I have a job interview,*" Luz said. "*Well, I had one. I made a mistake with the address. I've been wandering around for hours. I am lost.*"

"*What address are you looking for?*"

"*It doesn't matter. They will not hire someone two hours late.*"

"*They might. It's confusing around here. The address?*"

Luz looked at the map, pretending to look for the address. "*Six hundred fifteen Euclid Avenue.*"

"*That's not far,*" the police officer said. "*Do you have ID on you?*"

The man had been toying with her. He didn't care about anything she had said. He knew it was all lies. It was illegal for him to ask for her identification. That didn't mean that he didn't. The police were never afraid about doing illegal things. They weren't going to arrest themselves. He could shoot her and nothing would happen. He was the police.

"*Did I do something wrong?*" Luz asked.

The radio in the police car squawked and a harsh voice blared on the other end of the radio saying numbers and words that meant nothing to Luz. The police officer glanced at the car and back at Luz.

"*If you keep walking down this street, you'll reach Euclid in about a half mile,*" the police officer said, and then in an awful American accent. "Tienes mucha suerte, señora."

Luz nodded. He was right. She had been very lucky. Interactions with police could end up many ways. Arrest, detainment, and physical harm were all on the table. She would have to be more careful.

The only positive thing to come out of the interaction was that the chill of fear had cooled her down.

When Luz walked through the door, she found Nadia at the dining room table. A half-empty bottle of wine sat among scattered notes and papers. Nadia looked like she was cramming for a college final.

"I saw the car," Luz said. "I was looking for the building and I saw the car."

"Where?" Nadia said, excitement in her eyes.

Luz pulled out the map and spread it on the table. She pointed to the location and ran her finger along the path that the car had taken.

"The factory must be in that area," Nadia said.

"I think so," Luz said. "I saw two billboards that matched the placement, but not the ads, in the drawing. A lot of those buildings have high fences. It's going to be hard to see the car if it is parked inside one of those areas. We'll have to catch sight of it when it's on the street."

Nadia poured herself another glass of wine.

"Are you sure that's a good idea?" Luz said. "The wine?"

"I'm tapering."

Luz nodded. It wasn't her business.

"I'm going to go to the church on Sunday," Nadia said.

"I can go."

"No, you were right. Both the preacher and the woman have seen you. It's safe. It's a church. I'm just going to take a look."

"What about the house by the parking lot? I didn't see the white boy or the other one, but I know that building is connected."

"You might be right, but I don't know what we do about it. These people are dangerous. We're not exactly the police or a couple machos. I don't see a plan for us to confront them."

"I'm not afraid of them."

"You should be." Nadia gulped down the glass of wine. "I found César. Eliseo saw a woman after working for the sorority girls. I'm going to talk to her tomorrow. Probably a dead end, but it will give us another piece of the timeline. If Eliseo was fucking—"

"You're talking about my son."

"I'm sorry. If Eliseo was with a married woman, it could be that the white boy and the car and all that is the wrong direction. It could be as simple as a jealous husband or a scared wife. The construction in the backyard is unfinished. It would be a good place to conceal a body."

"I feel sick."

"What am I thinking?" Nadia said. "I'm sorry, again. In the newsroom, there is so much dark humor. We would talk about this stuff freely, jokingly."

"And probably a little more sober," Luz said. "This is about my son."

Nadia nodded, her eyes down at the table.

"I'm going to bed. Good night" Luz walked to the bedroom without waiting for a reply. She closed the door and sat on the edge of the bed.

She knew that there was a strong possibility that Eliseo might be dead. That didn't mean she wanted to picture her only son as a corpse. Especially since she still saw him as the nine-year-old boy that she remembered.

THIRTY-FOUR

Nadia didn't see one white face among the manicured lawns and clean sidewalks. It looked like a Latinx army was renovating a recently vacated suburban ghost town. In the upper middle class neighborhood, immigrants mowed lawns, clipped hedges, and walked strollers down the sidewalk. Mexicans, Guatemalans, Hondurans, Salvadorans. Landscapers, gardeners, nannies, and maids.

The house hadn't changed from when she had worked there, where she had first come in contact with Eliseo. She hadn't known his name at the time, but she remembered his youthful rage.

A Cadillac Escalade sat in the narrow driveway. The ridiculously wide tires had dug a trench in the grass, missing the concrete.

Nadia walked to the front door and rang the bell. More nervous since the attack on her and Gillies, every interaction felt rife with danger. She told herself it was a simple interview. Nadia checked her breath. She only detected a hint of the wine she had drank that morning. She regretted not drinking a little more. Her hands felt shaky.

She glanced at the mail sticking out of the mailbox. Bills and advertising addressed to David and Brandy Maxwell. Nothing interesting, but now she had their names. A regular Jessica Fletcher.

Brandy Maxwell answered the door. She wore skintight exercise clothes. It was the first time Nadia had seen the woman in anything but a bikini. The tights had the same effect, little left to the imagination. Brandy must not have started her workout, as she looked fresh and wore thick makeup.

"*Yes?*" Brandy asked.

"*Mrs. Maxwell? I have a few questions about Eliseo Delgado. Would you mind if I came in?*"

"*Who is that? I don't know who that is. Who are you? What is this? I'm busy.*"

She talked quickly, one sentence starting before the last ended. Nadia had worked with enough journalists to recognize the effects of a chemical stimulant. She guessed cocaine, but it could be any number of drugs.

"*I won't be long,*" Nadia said. "*Eliseo Delgado was a laborer that worked for you a few weeks ago. He is missing. I have reason to believe that you saw him on the night he disappeared.*"

"*A laborer? You would have to talk to the contractor. You haven't said who you are. What this is.*"

"*I'm inquiring for the family. Can we talk inside?*"

"*No. We can't.*" Brandy looked Nadia up and down. "*You're not coming in my house.*"

The woman tried to close the door, but Nadia jammed her foot in the gap. It hurt. She tried not to show it. "*It's important.*"

Brandy looked down at Nadia's foot. "*Some Mexican looking for some other Mexican has nothing to do with me. Goodbye.*"

"*I don't care that you had sex with him,*" Nadia said loud enough to hear across the street. "*I won't tell David.*"

"*Shut your fucking mouth.*" Brandy said through gritted teeth. "*I will call the police or immigration or whatever.*"

Nadia shrugged and removed her foot. The door slammed in her face. The sound of the lock followed.

"*That's okay,*" Nadia shouted at the closed door. "*David should be able to answer my questions. Was he out of town that night or working late? Doesn't matter. I'll head down to his office.*"

The door unlocked and swung open. It was the first time being called a *fucking wetback* made her smile.

The house was furnished in mostly gold and white, glass and plaster. There was no art on the walls, only mirrors in gaudy frames. Brandy Maxwell sat on the couch opposite Nadia with her arms crossed over her chest. Her look of disgust was usually only reserved for people at fish markets on hot days. Nadia didn't care.

"*You and Eliseo were sleeping together,*" Nadia said. A statement, not a question.

Brandy said nothing, her stare retaining its hatred. She fidgeted in her seat, not nervous, chemically induced.

"*He was here that night,*" Nadia said.

Same reaction. As close to a confirmation as she would get.

"*Did anything strange or memorable happen?*"

"*We fucked.*"

"*You were the last person to see Eliseo. Is there anything you can remember that will give me insight into what happened to him?*"

Brandy let out a giant exhale. "*He came here around ten. He left after midnight.*"

"*Did someone pick him up?*"

"*Yes.*" Brandy nodded. "*About eleven thirty, he got a call. We were done. A half hour or so later he left.*"

"*Did you see the car? Did the driver come to the door?*"

"*They honked. Fucking savages. At midnight. Old people live across the street.*"

"*Did he say any names on the phone?*"

"*He answered, listened, that was it.*"

"*How did they know he was here if he didn't give them an address?*"

"*I don't know.*"

"*Had he been here before? Other than the work he did in the back?*"

"*He did plenty more work in the back.*" She smiled and winked.

Nadia stared blankly.

Brandy shrugged. *"Once before. What can I say? He was young and enthusiastic."*

"You don't seem to be too worried about him. A missing kid. Did you know he was seventeen?"

"It's not like there's a shortage of Mexicans."

Before she knew she did it, Nadia leaned over the small coffee table and slapped Brandy across the face. Hard. The sound of the strike sat in the room.

"Pendeja," Nadia said.

Brandy screamed and dove, her long fingernails reaching for Nadia's neck.

Nadia backed away, still assessing the severity of her actions. She had made a huge mistake.

Brandy fumbled for her cell phone. *"You're going to jail, bitch."*

She might have said something else, but Nadia didn't wait to find out. She was through the kitchen and out the back door in ten seconds.

Nadia remembered the landscape of the backyard. She rushed past the still-unfinished brickwork and through the gate into an alley. She ran toward the closest outlet, reached the sidewalk, and slowed to a walk. A Mexican woman pushed a stroller in her direction. The woman didn't make eye contact.

Ten blocks away, Nadia sat down on a bus stop bench, surrounded by enough men and women to blend in. No police car came. For all she knew, Brandy Maxwell never made the call.

As soon as she got on the bus, her stomach lurched. She couldn't remember the last time she had run any distance. Her morning wine hadn't settled. She vomited in the back of the bus and got out at the next stop.

THIRTY-FIVE

Ostelinda admired the resilience of Marisol and Anita, the two girls who had replaced the Guatemalans as her roommates. Their ability to accept the factory as their new home so readily made Ostelinda wonder what their lives had been like in Mexico.

"We have two brothers in Modesto," Marisol said. "Maybe Modesto. They have not written or called in over a year. After we pay our debt here, we hope to find them."

Ostelinda saw Marisol as a child. The girl was only two years younger than her, but the year in the factory had taken the last of her childhood. The girl's sister, Anita, was a year younger than Marisol. Children in a situation that no person of any age should endure.

"It was difficult for our parents. Tía Francisca and four primos stay at our home because Tío Jorge drinks. Too many in the house. We were the only ones old enough to work. Not enough work. We wanted to help."

"That was very brave." Ostelinda said. She looked toward Anita, sleeping on her mat in the corner. She looked so tiny curled up in a ball. Ostelinda had never heard the younger girl speak, her scared eyes like a cornered mouse.

"There was a man at the cantina," Marisol continued. "He worked two years in Arizona. He returned with money to not work. The man spent the whole day drunk on beer. He told us to talk to the evangélicos. They could help us get north in exchange for work. We had no money, but we are hard workers."

Ostelinda nodded. She wondered how many people Sra. Moreland and the preacher had brought into the country and enslaved. She had met dozens herself.

"And the journey here?" Ostelinda said. "Was it difficult?"

"The people who we spoke to said they were people of God, but the men that drove the trucks and fed us and took us through the desert mountains, they did not know God. They were devils. They were terrible. They left people to die."

The girl looked away. In that moment, she looked even younger. She shouldn't be locked in the storeroom of a factory in Los Angeles. She should be chasing boys and laughing with her friends in the plaza of her town. A child should never be forced to grow up that fast.

"What did they tell you about this place?" Ostelinda asked. "About the work that you would do?"

"They asked if I could sew. If I could work with my hands. We would owe six thousand U.S. dollars each for the journey. It would take twelve weeks to work it off. After that, Sra. Moreland said we could choose to stay or look for work elsewhere. We would be kept safe from crime and from La Migra. The agreement sounded fair."

Ostelinda held her tongue.

"It is nice to be here with someone closer to our age," Marisol said. "On the journey, all the women ridiculed us for wearing lipstick and makeup. They looked down on us and called us spoiled. Others called us farm girls. We are not from a farm."

"You two took care of each other."

"I tried to." She looked down at the ground. "Sometimes men are stronger, more vicious, more insistent. We can fight, but that doesn't mean we always win."

Ostelinda thought of Maite. She had wanted to take care of her, tried to fight for her, but all the will and hope in the world didn't win a fixed fight.

The best she could do was to make sure that Marisol didn't fail her sister like she had Maite. A reason for her to keep going. Another sign telling her to persist. The fight wasn't over until she no longer rose back to her feet.

Ostelinda knew nothing about the woman from the church parking lot, but she thought of her as her saint. While the Catholics got to pray to all their saints, the religion of her parents never allowed for it. Now she had a saint of her own. Santa Sin Nombre. La mujer con el mapa.

If her saint returned to the neighborhood, Ostelinda needed to help the woman find her. She needed to create some kind of signal to indicate that she was inside the building.

While the two girls huddled together listening to music on their small radio, Ostelinda walked to the third floor in search of inspiration. The supply cabinets were locked, but plenty of workers left tools and materials at their workstations overnight. Nothing useful, but she did find half a pack of cigarettes and a lighter.

Ostelinda had only smoked a cigarette twice before. Once in Mexico when she was fourteen and her cousin had stolen a pack from the old man bar. It made her cough, sick to her stomach, and lightheaded. She smoked for the second time on the journey north. A man had offered her one. He had looked like a man who insulted easily, so she pretended to enjoy it. She hadn't.

She assumed that she had smoked those wrong. Women in movies looked like they enjoyed smoking. They made it look sexy and cosmopolitan. Perhaps it was like eating a hot pepper or what she had heard about sex. Painful and unpleasant the first few times, but more enjoyable as time went on. Or maybe it was always awful and that was another lie that people told.

She went to the window, looking out at the familiar view of the two billboards. She lit the cigarette and took a very light inhale. She didn't cough, which made her feel sophisticated. She smiled and posed like a movie star actress.

"*How did you get out?*" a voice said from the staircase. "What are you doing?"

Ostelinda jumped, dropping the cigarette. She crushed it underfoot. "Nothing. Looking out the window."

"There's no smoking in here."

Walking from the shadows, she saw that it was Corey. She could still feel his hands on her body. The way he had looked at her. She wanted to attack him. She wanted to run.

"I am not allowed outside," Ostelinda said, trying to sound calm. "It's the only place I can smoke."

Corey laughed, stepping closer. "I'm messing with you. I don't care. Can I have one?"

Ostelinda nodded and held out the pack, inching toward him. It felt like petting a growling dog. She was scared, but hoped being nice would help. Corey took a cigarette.

"What's your name?" he asked. "I don't think I know it."

"Ostelinda."

"Maybe I did know it. I don't remember." He eyed her body up and down. "I remember you though—not your name maybe—but I remember the rest of you."

Ostelinda backed up a step, her eyes moving to the storeroom.

"Don't worry," Corey said. "I'm not going to tell my mom you were out here. You're tough. I like tough chicks."

"Are you here to take another girl?"

"It isn't like that." He shook his head. "Lou got shingles. I'm watching things at night for the next week. My mom doesn't trust a Mexican to do it."

Ostelinda realized that she was hearing the white guard's name for the first time. The man had watched her for over a year.

"The other man, Lou, never came upstairs," Ostelinda said.

"He's a fat, lazy bastard."

"You can have the rest," Ostelinda said, setting the pack of cigarettes on the table. She took small steps in the direction of the storeroom.

"Are you scared of me?" Corey asked.

"You hurt me twice."

"*Yeah, I have.*" Corey took a few quick steps toward her and grabbed her arm. He pulled her close, staring into her eyes and then moving his attention to her body.

"Your mother..." Ostelinda started to say.

"...doesn't matter. She can't stop me."

Ostelinda held his stare.

Corey let go of her arm. He walked to the stairs, turning after he took the first step down. "One night I'm going to come back up here. I don't know when. Whenever I want. I'm going to come back and I'm going to rape you. It's going to hurt. Buenas noches, Ostelinda."

Back in the storeroom, she jammed a chair under the doorknob. It wouldn't keep the monster away, but at least she would hear him coming.

THIRTY-SIX

Luz's thoughts darted between Ostelinda and Eliseo. Whenever she thought she was closer to solving a thing, it moved frustratingly further away. She had a rough idea where Ostelinda was—the neighborhood, at least—but finding the exact building in the maze of a Los Angeles industrial area was unlikely. Which made her just as far from finding Eliseo. Luz was failing two people. And herself, if she couldn't figure out how to pay the rent.

She turned off the hot water and stood in the shower. The heat had felt good, but she needed to feel the cold. One soothed, the other woke. She needed to be alert, not rested. After ten seconds, she turned off the cold water, shivering.

"Luz," Nadia shouted through a crack in the door. "Your lawyer's on the phone."

"Tell him I'll call back."

"You're going to want to talk to him," Nadia said. "A hospital responded to one of his calls. He might have found Eliseo, but—"

Luz grabbed a towel and wrapped it around her body. She slid on the bathmat hurrying out of the shower.

"Careful. It might be—" Nadia started to say, but Luz was already down the hall. In the kitchen, still dripping, she picked up the receiver.

"Mateo? Mr. Fitzsimmons."

"Let me say a few things first, Luz," the lawyer said, talking too slow for her taste.

"Did you find Eliseo?"

"USC Medical Center has a John Doe that fits your son's ethnicity and age."

"Is he hurt? Why don't they know if it's him or not?"

"The man is dead."

"Madre mía." Luz sat down at the kitchen table to avoid falling down. Nadia sat down across from her, poured a glass of wine, and slid it to Luz. She shook her head. Luz wanted to be sober.

"There's a strong chance that it's not your son," Fitzsimmons said. "We can't make assumptions. Take a breath. There are a lot of young Hispanic men in Los Angeles who fit your son's description. It doesn't mean it's him, but you have to go down there. Rule it out."

"It's him," Luz said. "I know it's him."

"Don't do that to yourself," the lawyer said. "I can meet you down there in a few hours. I have to be in court right now. Can you make it to the hospital around four o'clock?"

"How did he die?"

"I don't know."

Luz rose to her feet. "I'll be there in an hour."

"I understand your impatience," Fitzsimmons said, "but please wait for me. If it is your son, the police will want to talk to you. If the police want to talk to you, I should be there."

"If it's Eliseo, I'm not going to care about the police."

The bus left Luz at the bottom of the concrete steps leading up to the USC Medical Center. It was like climbing a Mayan pyramid, she assumed. Only tourists had the money to see pyramids in Mexico.

Nadia had offered to come with her, but Luz didn't want to put her at risk. Hospitals were notorious locations for ICE agents to pick up unauthorized migrants. If it didn't end up being Eliseo and Nadia got caught and deported, Luz wouldn't be able to take it. At the very least, she needed to protect the people who were still around her.

Besides, this was something that a mother needed to do alone.

The long climb took the wind out of her. She caught her breath, but didn't want to hesitate or delay the moment any longer. The more time she took, the more her brain imagined every conceivable outcome. The maybes hurt more than any definite answer.

The sliding glass doors opened to a cacophony that drowned out the city behind her. The chaos of the hospital drained whatever energy Luz had left from the climb. There were no empty seats to tempt her, though.

It reminded Luz of the Mexico City bus station. One hundred dramas playing out in multiple languages. Police officers, security guards, doctors, nurses, patients, and a few locos vied for the starring role on the mad stage of the tiled room. Everyone yelled. Nobody listened. And not a soul wanted to be there.

Luz stood in a long line waiting to speak to someone at the reception desk. In front of her, a young man with dreadlocks tried to impress an Asian girl by telling her a story about his bloody hand and how he was a DJ and there was a tooth embedded in the knuckle from some hater he hit. The Asian girl seemed unimpressed.

When Luz reached the front of the line, a tired Black woman at the counter stared at her. "*Yes?*"

"*They found a person. He is dead. I'm here to look at—to identify—to see if….Where do I go, please?*"

"*The morgue,*" the woman said. "*The elevators are around the corner. Take one down to LL-3. It's the lowest level.*"

"*Thank you.*"

"*You'll need this.*" The woman gave Luz a sticker that said "Visitor". Luz adhered it to her shirt. She walked to the elevators.

Behind her, the woman said, "*I'm sorry for your loss.*"

Luz stopped. She hadn't expected any acknowledgment from the woman, let alone sympathy. The common phrase, "*sorry for your loss,*" made the possibility of Eliseo's death more real.

At the bank of elevators, she pressed the down button. Everyone else was waiting to go up. An ICE officer held the arm of a handcuffed man. There was a bloody bandage on his head. When the officer turned in Luz's direction, she instinctively looked at the floor. The pair of men stepped into the next elevator. The bandaged man looked up at her, defeated but resolved.

The elevator doors opened onto the lower level. Without all the warm, yelling bodies of the reception area, the basement was colder by a season. Luz followed a yellow line and found the sign-in desk for the medical examiner.

"*My lawyer Mateo Fitzsimmons contacted me. I am here to view a person who died. He may be my son.*" Luz took out her small notebook. "*I was told to ask for John Doe 17-JD180919M.*"

"*Your name?*"

"*Luz Delgado.*"

The receptionist picked up the phone. "*Please take a seat. Someone will be with you shortly.*"

In the movies and on television shows, morgues glowed green-gray under hellish fluorescent light. Other than the cold, this area of the hospital didn't look any different than the rest of the place. The waiting room was cleaner than the one at the entrance. Empty and quiet. The fifteen minutes of peace helped to calm her. She simultaneously wanted this experience to be over and not have to do it.

"*Mrs. Delgado?*" The woman in the white doctor's smock was shorter than Luz. Movies and television were proving to be a poor reference point for many things. Morgue attendants were usually portrayed as either too fat or too thin, they always wore glasses, and inevitably seemed to be eating a sandwich while unaffected by the gore around them. This stocky, short-haired woman looked like Alma, the only female mechanic back home.

Luz followed the woman down a hall. They entered a narrow room. One wall was mostly a window that looked into an identical narrow room. No decoration, only function. Three chairs were lined against the wall behind them.

"The body will be brought to the room on the other side of the glass. The attendant will then remove the sheet from the face and shoulders. I have to warn you, while there are no injuries to the upper part of the body, the face will not look like he is sleeping. It can be off-putting. Please sit down if you are feeling at all lightheaded. I will be in the room with you. The police detective in charge of the case has requested to attend, as well. Do you have any questions?"

Luz shook her head.

The woman left the room. Luz stared into the empty space across the glass for five minutes. The woman returned with a man in short sleeves and a tie. He remained appropriately somber, holding out his hand.

"Thank you for coming down," the detective said. *"I know this cannot be easy. I am Detective Larios."*

Luz nodded. She didn't know what to say. She didn't want to say anything.

The three of them stood in silence until the door opened in the other room. Through the glass, they watched a Black woman with thick braids wheel in a body covered by a sheet. The woman looked through the glass waiting for some signal and then peeled the sheet down from the head and shoulders.

The world spun. It couldn't be, but it was. Luz fell back into the chair when she saw her dead son.

THE SOUTHLAND

PART FOUR

THE SOUTHLAND

THIRTY-SEVEN

Detective Larios brought Luz a paper cup of coffee. "*I didn't know if you took cream or sugar. I hope it's okay.*"

Luz took the cup from him and stared into the blackness of the liquid. Her distorted reflection looked back at her. She took a drink. The coffee was terrible, bitter and cold. The horrible taste in her mouth snapped her out of her daze and back to reality.

"*I am very sorry,*" Larios said.

"*The coffee is very bad,*" Luz said.

"*I meant—I am a parent myself. Two girls. I can't imagine what you're going through.*"

Luz nodded.

"*I know this is difficult, but I need to ask you a few questions about your son.*" There was no threat in his voice, but it wasn't a question.

"*Can I have a few more minutes?*" Luz asked.

"*Of course. Take some time,*" Larios said. "*When you're ready, I'll be in the next room to take your statement.*"

Luz nodded. Detective Larios left the room, closing the door behind him. The click of the latch sounded like a gunshot in the quiet space.

The room on the other side of the glass was empty now, but Luz could still see the outline of Eliseo on the gurney, like a fogged window fading into nothing. She would never be able to erase the picture of her son's lifeless body.

No matter how much Luz had prepared herself for the possibility, the grief of losing her only child drained her heart of life. Not only grief, but guilt eroded her resolve. She had brought her son to the United States only for him to be killed.

Luz had been a bad mother. Now she was no mother at all.

The small room with pea-green walls smelled like toilet bowl cleaner. A wood laminate table and two uncomfortable chairs were the only furnishings. There were no windows or decorations on the walls. Luz had brought the awful coffee with her. It sat unwanted on the table. She hadn't known why she had brought it. She had no intention of drinking any of it.

Detective Larios sat across from her, not smiling, but making his face as pleasantly neutral as possible. *"Thank you for speaking to me."*

The man across from Luz had been given the job of investigating her son's death. He may have given her friendliness and some coffee, but Luz reminded herself that he didn't care about her or Eliseo. Her son wasn't a person to him. He was an idea, the victim, a name on a folder.

"How did my son die?" Luz asked, trying to make it clear that the rest of the interview rested on him answering the question. *"Police would not be assigned if this was an accident. If no crime was committed."*

"Please understand that this is an ongoing investigation. I can only share limited information."

"I need to know how my son died."

"Your son was shot. A gunshot wound to the chest."

Luz nodded. As hard as it was to hear, she appreciated his bluntness. She had asked him and he had answered.

"I am going to begin the official interview," Larios said. *"If you would prefer the interview conducted in Spanish, let me know."*

"English is good."

Larios placed his cell phone on the center of the table. He hit a button to record the conversation. Larios stated his name and the location, date, and time.

"*Can you please state your name?*" he asked.

"*Luz Delgado.*"

"*Your address?*"

Luz didn't answer.

"*I don't care about your immigration status.*"

Luz shook her head.

"*Let's skip that for now,*" Larios said. "*Can you please state the full name of the deceased and his relationship to you?*"

"*Eliseo Luis Delgado. He is my son.*" Luz picked up the coffee, but set it down when she remembered it was disgusting.

"*When was the last time you saw Eliseo?*"

"*Where was he found? Who found him?*" Luz said. She had answered a few of his questions. It was Larios's turn to answer hers.

The detective pursed his lips in a rehearsed depiction of seriousness. "*I told you. I cannot reveal the details of an ongoing investigation.*"

"*What can you tell me?*"

"*There are rules. Laws,*" Larios said. "*We want the same thing.*"

"*No, we don't. I am his mother. This is your job. At night, you do not have to think about Eliseo. You can go home to your daughters. You can live your life. I cannot.*"

"*Of course. I'm sorry.*" The detective took a deep breath. "*Here's what I can tell you. This might be difficult to hear. The bodies of your son and an unidentified woman were found together in an abandoned warehouse in Bell Gardens. They were both victims of wounds we believe came from the same gun. A weapon was found at the scene. Your son's fingerprints were the only prints on the weapon. We believe his wound was self-inflicted.*"

"*My son would never do such a thing.*"

"*We haven't reached any conclusions in the investigation, but evidence suggests that your son shot the woman and then himself.*"

"*Who was the woman?*"

"*I was hoping you would give me some insight.*" Larios pulled out a folder and removed a photograph. He set it on the table and spun it to face Luz.

Luz examined the photograph of a young Mexican woman's face. The young girl's eyes were closed, but peaceful. Somehow her skin was simultaneously dark and pale, like ash.

"*I have seen this woman,*" Luz said.

"*You knew her?*"

"*No, but I saw a woman's drawing of her. The poor girl in the pictures, her name is Maite. That is all I know.*"

"*Go back a bit. Who did this drawing?*"

"*Her name is Ostelinda. I do not know her either. She is being held prisoner in a factory.*"

Larios didn't say anything for a moment. He took a long inhale. "*I'm confused. There is someone being held against their will? Where? What factory?*"

"*I don't know.*"

"*What does this have to do with your son? How did he know this Maite?*"

"*I don't know.*"

"*A woman gave you a drawing of the woman found dead with your son, but you don't know where that woman is or what her connection is to your son or the girl? When did she give you this drawing?*"

"*She didn't give it to me. I found it. You have to help Ostelinda.*"

"*Okay. How do I find her?*"

"*I don't know.*"

Detective Larios pulled a pack of tissues from his bag, set it on the table, and slid it to her.

Luz removed a tissue and wiped her face. "*I feel a little sick. Is there a bathroom?*"

"*The restrooms are down the hall on the right.*" Larios pointed toward the door. "*At the end by the elevators. When you get back, I'll take your full statement.*"

Luz stood and left the room. She walked down the hall, her stomach turning. When she rounded the corner, she saw the sign for the restrooms and the bank of elevators past them. She walked in their direction, but didn't stop at the restrooms. Instead, she pressed the "Up" button at the elevators.

She rode the elevator alone. When it opened on the ground floor, she walked through the still chaotic waiting room. She didn't stop when she got outside, walking down the steps.

She couldn't talk to the detective anymore. He could do nothing.

Luz entered her apartment, not remembering a single moment of the six-mile walk home. She had been deep within her thoughts.

Eliseo had not killed himself. She hated to admit that he might have been capable of killing a woman, but under the right circumstances, his mean streak might have gotten the best of him. However, Eliseo was far too self-absorbed to take his own life. Something else had happened and she had a good idea who would know.

Luz went to the kitchen drawer and took out Nadia's pistol. She had been waiting for Nadia to sober up to give it back to her, but that hadn't happened yet. It wasn't that she had forgotten about it. Guns were hard to forget.

The pistol was too big for her purse. She went to the closet and pulled down Eliseo's backpack from the top shelf. She emptied the contents onto the bed and stowed the gun inside. She picked up the compass that she had sent her son. The needle found north.

THIRTY-EIGHT

Nadia sat alone in the back row of the New Life Apostolic Church. She had found a spot as far from the rest of the congregation as possible. Nothing about the church reminded her of the ones that she had attended in her youth. It looked more like the location of a seminar on how to make millions through timeshares.

What the setting lacked in grandeur, the man at the front made up for in enthusiasm. Pacing the stage, Father Daniel spoke Spanish with only a hint of an Anglo accent, like he had lived in Mexico long enough to get the rhythm. It was a language learned from people, not from a textbook.

Nadia wasn't a hundred percent sure why she was there or what she expected to accomplish. She had felt useless in the apartment waiting to hear from Luz, who was going to identify a dead body that may or may not be her son. Attending the church service felt active, but harmless, better than the impotence of inactivity.

She had arrived in time for a Thursday night Spanish-language sermon. As she entered, the small group of men and women sang the hymn "Tú Estás Aquí." Then the sermon began. No fire or brimstone, but repackaged self-help optimism with Biblical scripture peppered in to keep it marginally religious. The pitch seemed to be that all you had to do was admit Jesus existed and you could get away with anything. According to Father Daniel, actions no longer had consequences. Nonbelievers, not sinners, would suffer. Believers were heaven bound, as long as they repented and had faith.

Nadia found it hard to believe that God would be more lenient than a court of law.

"Yes, judge, I did murder those nuns, but you are my best friend and I'm sorry."

"I understand, my son. You are free to go."

It didn't matter to her. She had no room for God in her life. He could burn in hell for all she cared.

When Father Daniel's spiel ended, Nadia had thought she was going to leave, but on her way to the exit, a squat woman marched over to her with a big smile and purpose. "I'm Marta. Welcome."

"Nadia." She held up her hand to shake, but Marta ducked under it and gave her a rib-crushing hug.

"I haven't seen you here before. Are you new to the church?"

"I was walking by." Nadia looked over her shoulder, as if to share a secret. "I heard the singing. I missed the hymns in Spanish. I am new to Los Angeles."

"You are safe here." Marta smiled. "Many are new to the country."

"It has been a hard journey."

"The church is here to help. There are baskets of food on Tuesday mornings for the needy and we offer other support."

"You are kind," Nadia said, "but it is work that I need. I should be looking now. I came in for a place to sit for ten minutes, but the spirit of the sermon took me over. He is very good."

"We love Father Daniel."

The prayer groups started. Nadia sat with a man and four other women. As each person took their turn, they all asked to pray for others, never themselves.

The man spoke about a neighbor who he didn't know, but saw

every day. The man thought he might be an alcoholic, but was afraid to approach him to offer help. He asked God to keep his neighbor safe until he could gather the courage to help this stranger.

Two of the women asked the group to pray for their children, one sick, the other young, pregnant, and in an abusive relationship.

As they prayed, Nadia sneaked peeks at Father Daniel walking among the groups, stopping to listen and then moving on. When it was her turn to make a prayer request, Father Daniel stopped at their group. She closed her eyes and bowed her head.

"Dear God, I would like to pray for three lost women. One I fear is lost for good, even if there are moments when I think she will return. And a second woman, searching for her family. I pray that she finds what she is looking for and that the pain of the situation doesn't overtake her along the way. Finally, I pray for a young girl, lost in the city, trapped between safety and danger. I pray that she finds her way to the home that she was promised. I pray for these three lost women. Thank you, Lord. Amen."

When everyone softly repeated "Amen," Nadia looked up at Father Daniel. He smiled at her and moved to the next group. Nadia didn't realize that she was crying until a woman handed her a tissue.

Nadia walked the long way back to Luz's apartment. She wanted to see the parking lot where Luz had met Ostelinda, maybe even ask around about the house with the young man in it. Surely, the neighbors couldn't be pleased with the occupants and maybe would be willing to talk.

The residential street in Boyle Heights reminded Nadia of some Mexican neighborhoods. Small houses with brown grass yards surrounded by chain link. The only difference was that, in Mexico, they were middle class homes, while in Los Angeles they were considered shacks for poor immigrants. No wonder so many immigrants stayed. In comparison, they lived like kings.

Two blocks up the street, Nadia spotted Luz walking in her direction. Nadia waved, but Luz's head was turned to the side. She called out, but Luz made no indication that she heard her. Something was wrong.

Luz opened a low chain link gate and walked with purpose over the lawn to the front door of the house. Without pausing, Luz turned the knob and walked inside.

"*Fuck.*" Nadia picked up her pace.

As she reached the gate, a gunshot rang out from inside the house. Nadia instinctively crouched, waiting for whatever was next.

"Luz!" she yelled.

A few seconds later, Luz walked out of the house. She held Gillies's gun at her side. Luz's eyes were wild, her head darting from side to side. She turned around to look back at the house then hurried down the walk toward Nadia.

"Luz?" Nadia said.

Luz drew the pistol, pointing it at Nadia.

Nadia raised her hands. "It's me. It's Nadia."

Luz stared for a moment, then lowered the pistol.

Without a word, she walked past Nadia onto the sidewalk. "Luz!" Nadia followed. "What happened? What's going on?"

"I have to go," Luz said.

"You can't walk down the street with a gun."

Luz looked down at the gun, as if realizing at that moment that she still held it in her hand. She handed it to Nadia. "Can you take it?"

Nadia took the gun from Luz. She had no bag, so she put it in her waistband and zipped up her jacket to hide it. It felt warm against her body. "What happened?"

"Eliseo is dead."

They fast-walked out of the residential neighborhood onto the main street. Constant looks over their shoulders revealed that no one followed them.

"I'm sorry, Luz." Nadia searched for something else to say, but found nothing. She repeated the same sentiment. "I'm sorry."

"They killed him."

"Who killed him?"

"He was shot. Someone shot him. Him and a woman. A girl. They're saying Eliseo killed her and then himself. That's not what happened. They killed him. They killed her."

"What girl? Who is the girl?" Nadia asked.

"The face in Ostelinda's drawing. Maite." Luz wandered forward in a daze. "The car and the girl. It has to be them."

"Luz!" Nadia grabbed her and made her stop. "Did you shoot someone in that house?"

Luz's eyes were wild. Her breathing unsteady. She shook off Nadia's hands and walked away, continuing down the street. Nadia caught up to her, but didn't try to stop her.

"Did you hurt someone?" Nadia asked.

"Not really," Luz said. "I only shot him in the foot."

THIRTY-NINE

"If that's what Corey said, I'm sure it's not what he meant to say. His Spanish is not very good," Sra. Moreland said.

Ostelinda had caught up with Sra. Moreland while on a break. She didn't want to argue, but she was terrified and couldn't stop shaking even a day later.

"His Spanish is very good, I think," Ostelinda said.

"He was trying to scare you. He's always been like that. A bully. It was cruel and stupid, but he's not a bad person. I'll convince him to go to church. Get him on the right path." Sra. Moreland didn't sound too sure of her own words.

"It sounded very real to me. I am scared, Sra. Moreland. I was not able to sleep. I don't want it to affect my work."

Sra. Moreland nodded.

Ostelinda put her head down, trying to show as much deference as she could. "I know I betrayed your trust. I have learned. I now know my place. I would not have told you if I didn't believe he was serious. I have made mistakes, but I have always felt safe here. You've always kept me safe."

"I do my best to take care of you and the other girls. I take that responsibility seriously."

"I have broken the rules in the past. When I have, I have accepted my punishment. You have been fair and forgiving. I have never been punished for doing nothing. This is different."

Sra. Moreland took her phone out of her pocket. She patted it in her hand like a blackjack.

"I am frightened," Ostelinda said.

"I see that," Sra. Moreland said. "Coming to me could not have been easy, considering your previous interactions with Corey. I understand that. I believe you. The boy has problems. I will talk to him. I will make sure that you are safe."

"Thank you, señora."

Sra. Moreland pressed a button on her phone and put it to her ear, maintaining eye contact with Ostelinda.

Ostelinda turned to walk away, but Sra. Moreland shook her head and motioned for her to stay. "I want you to hear this. I want to make sure you feel safe."

"Juanito? Where's Corey?" Sra. Moreland dropped her head. "I'm never going to call you Lobo, estúpido. Why do you have Corey's phone?" Sra. Moreland listened for a moment. "What do you mean? What hospital? What happened?"

Sra. Moreland walked a few steps away from Ostelinda.

"Shot? Is he okay? Is he hurt bad?" She listened for a moment. "Praise Jesus. He's not going to die from that. I need you to give me all the details. I'll come down right away."

Sra. Moreland walked a few more steps away. Ostelinda followed. She didn't understand what exactly was going on, but if Corey had been hurt, she wanted to hear about it. She needed some good news.

"A woman walked into the house and shot him in the foot. That's what he told you? The Boyle Heights house? What stupid thing did Corey do?" Sra. Moreland listened. "Doesn't matter. It's Corey. I'm sure she had her reasons."

Sra. Moreland turned around. Ostelinda stared back with a blank expression on her face.

"You can go back to work," Sra. Moreland said and returned to the phone.

Ostelinda walked a few steps away but stopped at a work cabinet. She opened a drawer for no reason, pretending to look for something. She fiddled with the scissors, thread, and pens inside, doing her best to eavesdrop.

"Wait. Cállate. Cállate. Did you say he was at the hospital? Where are you?" Sra. Moreland listened. "Why are you there? Are you a doctor? No, you're an idiot. It's a gunshot wound, estúpido. The police will ask questions. Cállate. Cállate. If he tells them it happened in the house, that's probable cause for them to search the house. Does that sound like a good thing?"

Sra. Moreland turned back to Ostelinda, who on cue held up a pair of fabric scissors, closed the drawer, and walked away slowly. Sra. Moreland was so distracted and angry that she didn't seem to even notice Ostelinda.

"Now the idiot understands. Make sure Corey knows to say it happened on the street. I don't care what street. One in a different neighborhood. A random act of violence. Then get to the house. How many girls are there?" Sra. Moreland pinched the bridge of her nose. "Bring them here. Anything else in the house, get rid of it. Clean the whole place. Burn it down if you have to. I've got to dig up our health insurance stuff." Sra. Moreland hung up the phone. She turned to Ostelinda. "What are you still doing here? Get back to work."

Back at her workstation, Ostelinda thought of her abuela, a true bruja. The woman loved to tell stories of spirits and spells and curses and animal gods. People came from all over to see her. Not just old women, but the young, as well. She commanded great respect for miles. Even Father Arturo, the town's Catholic priest, listened to her tales of the past gods with reverence.

When she had been sure of her impending death, Ostelinda's abuela had told her not to mourn. That death was the surest part of life. Not the end.

Not a beginning. But something closer to the center of life, a change with both ends open. Her grandmother told her that she would never be alone, as the spirits of her ancestors guided and protected her. And when her grandmother died, she would take her place among Ostelinda's protectors.

Ostelinda had smiled and nodded, not taking it as anything more than folk belief and stories of Old Mexico, tales of new saints and ancient monsters. She loved the stories, but they were make-believe to her. As time went on, the chance of her accepting the existence of the divine had worn to nothing.

But only the simple believed that they could plan their spiritual journey. Only the unimaginative trusted that what they believed as a child would hold true throughout their lives with no curiosity or discovery.

Revenge had a strange way of renewing hope. It had embedded itself inside her like a piece of shrapnel. Hearing that the cabrón, Corey, had been shot by someone felt like the moment you see a rare bird in the wild. It didn't balance out what he had done to Maite. He would have to feel pain and die for that, but it told Ostelinda that events might be turning. She had reached the bottom of the well, sure that was her fate, ready to quit, but she had been wrong. It was time to start the slow climb back to the surface.

Her grandmother had been right. Her ancestors hadn't abandoned her. They had been waiting to ensure justice was served.

The truth might have been that Sra. Moreland's evil son got shot because he was the kind of person who eventually got shot. A boy with his meanness made only enemies. She doubted that his friends trusted him. Violence opened the door for violence. Corey would die young.

He shared that fate with Ostelinda. She had died the moment that she walked into the factory, even if she hadn't known it until later. She had been removed from the world, haunting the third floor for the last year.

Her grandmother had taught her that death was neither the end nor the beginning, and that's where Ostelinda was trapped. Somewhere in the middle. A kind of death. In the United States, she had become a ghost.

And if a ghost couldn't understand vengeance, then no one could.

FORTY

Every two minutes, Nadia softly knocked on the door and said a few words. "Is there anything I can do?" "Are you hungry?" "I don't have to talk. I'll listen." Every two minutes, like she had it clocked.

Luz never responded, but she didn't want Nadia to stop. She needed to know she wasn't alone.

Two minutes passed. Nadia knocked again. "I still can't believe you shot someone in the foot."

"He isn't going to die," Luz said to the door.

"Do you want to talk?"

"No," Luz said. "Thank you. I will, but not now. Eliseo is dead, and I don't know what that means."

"Okay, I'm going to sit here in the hall. Just in case."

"You don't have to."

"I know."

Luz had so few good memories of her son that it only took fifteen minutes for her to flip through her mental scrapbook. The images of him stealing money from Rosa or pushing her to the ground quickly replaced his early Christmases.

Luz had brought Eliseo to stay with her in Los Angeles. She hadn't known him. When he arrived, she hadn't liked him. She didn't know what was to come, but she was still responsible for his death. While she couldn't have seen the future, she could have seen the possibility. It was her fault. She would have to live with that.

"Nadia?" Luz called out.

"I'm right here."

"Do we have wine?"

Luz drank three-quarters of the two-dollar bottle of wine in silence.

Nadia sat across the table with a finger of untouched wine in her glass. She remained silent, not pressuring Luz to talk.

Luz wiped invisible crumbs off the table with the back of her hand. "What do I do? What happens now?"

"I don't know," Nadia said. "I'm sorry. I'm probably the wrong person."

"You have a family. You're a mother. It's not something you can hide."

Nadia shook her head.

"But you were once?"

Nadia nodded.

"Will you tell me?" Luz asked.

A loud, insistent knock came from the door. They both turned.

Luz didn't think the police had any way to link the shooting to her apartment, but there was no way of knowing.

Nadia walked quietly to the door and looked through the peephole. "It's not the police."

"Who is it?" Luz asked.

A loud voice shouted from the other side of the door, answering the question. "*Luz. It is Farrokh. I know you're in there.*"

Luz stood up and stomped to the front door. Nadia moved to the side. Luz swung open the door fast enough to make Farrokh jump back. Not a tall man, he wore his dress shirt unbuttoned almost to the middle of his chest. He straightened his sunglasses.

"*What?*" she yelled. "*What do you want?*"

"*The rent is due at the beginning of the month,*" Farrokh said. "*Every month. It's the fifth. I know you struggle, but this is my business.*"

Luz walked back into the apartment, opened a kitchen drawer and pulled out the scattered money inside. Before she got back to the front door, Nadia stopped her and handed her a stack of bills.

"What's this?" Luz asked.

"Five hundred dollars," Nadia said. "It's the most I could get."

"How?" Luz looked at the money. Her eyes filled with tears. "What did you do?"

"I closed a door," Nadia said.

Luz walked back to Farrokh, clutching the money in her hands. She forced the bills into his hands. He took them, looking down almost ashamed.

"*It's not enough,*" Nadia said, "*but it's what I have. I'll get the rest. You have my word. Please do not push.*"

Farrokh straightened the bills in his hand and nodded. "*I will count it. Put a receipt in your mailbox. Have you heard anything about your son?*"

"*Yes, I have,*" Luz said and closed the door.

Luz stood for a moment with her hand on the knob. "He doesn't care. It's just the thing to ask." Luz sat on the ground, feeling all the energy drain from her body. The chair seemed too far away.

Nadia sat down next to her. She reached over and took her hand. They stared ahead in silence together until Nadia spoke, a whisper at first.

"My name—my real name—is Anabel. Anabel Garcés. Until about nine months ago, I worked as a journalist in Culiacán. I wrote stories that threatened powerful men. These men considered their wealth and power more important than the lives of other people. The lives of innocent people.

"I knew it was dangerous. I knew I should pull back. I knew how it would end. I had watched it play out tragically and violently for a few of my colleagues. But I couldn't stop. I kept going.

"My husband and son, Ignacio and Jaime—I can see them so

clearly—they wore white that day. When they left the house, I had joked that their suits made them look like two devils masquerading as angels.

"Outside the church, Jaime's short legs made each stone step look gigantic. I waited on the sidewalk for them. Ignacio had been adamant about raising Jaime Catholic, even if he didn't believe himself. I didn't fight him. The only times I went to church were christenings, weddings, and funerals. I slept in until eleven on Sundays.

"I heard the motorcycle before I saw it. Its engine roared over the sound of traffic. When it turned the corner, I knew. The men on the motorcycle wore black. For a moment, they looked like a single rider with two heads—a predator from another world. When the man in back leaned to the side, I saw his matte-black weapon.

"Ignacio and Jaime had reached the bottom of the stairs. My son ran toward me with his arms out. Ignacio followed behind, laughing.

"I ran.

"I didn't run from the men on the motorcycle. I couldn't outrun them. I ran from my family. I ran from my son. I ran from my husband. I ran to protect them. I didn't learn until later that you can't protect someone by running.

"I looked over my shoulder. Jaime still followed. Ignacio turned toward the motorcycle. When he looked back at me, his face broke my heart. He knew. He had warned me.

"I wanted to tell him how sorry I was. That he had been right. I wanted to do things again, create a different outcome. But that's not how things work. You get what you get.

"I tripped on the curb and stumbled onto the road. I never saw the taxi that hit me. I remember the squeal of the brakes and the impact against my hip. Then a brief calm. I flew through the air. I landed and hit my head. When I opened my eyes, the world spun in and out of focus. The sky above me pulsated, shifting from blue to yellow.

"Automatic weapon fire made the motorcycle engine sound like a bumblebee. Unnaturally loud, the gunfire lasted too long. People screamed. When it ended and the motorcycle receded in the distance, the sounds of the city returned, jarringly mundane.

"The first dead body I saw was a man I didn't recognize. Face down on the road a few feet away. I found out later his name was Israel Moreno. He had driven a taxi in the city for twenty-three years. He had tried to help me.

"My legs wouldn't respond. I searched for the white suits of my husband and son. There were more bodies. Others held bleeding wounds. When I finally found my family, Ignacio sat against a wall stained with his own blood. He held the lifeless body of our son in his arms. I watched the life drain from my husband's eyes. He died heartbroken.

"I tried to scream, but blood filled my mouth.

"I had killed my husband. I had killed my son. I could have stopped a hundred times. I could have quit. I could have admitted that it wasn't about a story, but about my pride. My ego. My stubbornness. Instead I traded all those things for their lives. I might as well have pulled the trigger myself.

"Anabel Garcés died that day, too."

FORTY-ONE

Nadia got off the bus at the underpass. Luz walked a step ahead of her. The buzz of freeway traffic vibrated overhead as they made their way toward the men. Nadia hadn't liked the idea of leaving Luz alone in the apartment, but she didn't know how she would react being back on the lot. Returning to the location couldn't have been easy on her.

Nadia caught up to Luz. "Are you going to be okay?"

"I don't know. Probably not," Luz said. "I hate this place, but it's better than an empty apartment."

"The only way you or I get through any of this is together."

"Everything awful happened here," Luz said. "How can an empty place, a dirt lot, have any importance? It looks like nothing."

"We won't be here long. I'll check in with Lupe. See if she's heard from—" Nadia froze when she saw Gillies among the men. A white bandage on his head, he looked like he was in the middle of telling a story. She screamed his name and ran toward him.

Gillies turned at the sound of his name. He showed nothing at first, squinting in her direction. The moment he spotted her, his face lit up. As she got closer, some of that light faded. His eyes looked cloudy and his skin gray to match his hair and beard.

Nadia considered giving him a hug, but neither of them were huggers. She punched his arm. He patted her shoulder. That was as intimate as their reunion would get.

"*It's good to see you,*" Nadia said. "*And alive, which is a pleasant surprise.*"

"*For you and me both,*" Gillies said, his speech a little slurred.

"*How's your head?*" Nadia asked, reaching up but not touching the bandage.

"*Got my bell rung, but it wasn't the first time. Still a little wonky.*"

"*Were you in the hospital this whole time?*"

"*Walked out of the VA last night. They wanted me to stay, but it felt like a prison. Only with worse food.*"

"*Wouldn't it be better if the doctors make that decision?*"

Nadia didn't like the distant look in Gillies's eyes. While it might be temporary, she worried that maybe there had been neurological damage. He looked ten years older and he had already looked like a warlock to begin with.

"*I can't stand all the rules,*" Gillies said. "*Got a line on a school bus that I can trick out. Where you sleeping?*"

"*I'm staying with Luz.*" Nadia turned to Luz, who had kept her distance. Luz waved. Nadia motioned for her to join them.

"I was sorry to hear you were hurt," Luz said. "It's my fault."

"No, it wasn't," Nadia said.

"I got both of you involved in something dangerous."

"*My memory's got gaps,*" Gillies said, "*and I ain't ever been that smart, but I don't remember you being the one hitting me with a bottle. Luz, I took your money. I knew what I was getting into. I'm all growed up.*"

"*Is it painful?*" Luz asked. "*Does it hurt?*"

"*Pain is a state of mind,*" Gillies said.

"I know he's okay," Nadia said to Luz, "because he's already back to talking bullshit."

"*When I was twelve years old,*" Gillies said, "*I got kicked in the head by an ox. No shit, a full-grown ox. I don't blame the ox. The ox was being an ox. I was being stupid, but that's what happens when you do something stupid. You get hurt. Luckily the young heal quickly.*"

Gillies paused for a moment. He repeated the word "*quickly*," looking for the next word.

"*You were saying you got kicked by an ox,*" Nadia said.

"*I know,*" Gilles said with a hint of frustration. "*I could've gotten kicked every day as a kid and survived. The young are good punching bags. But at my age, if I get kicked by one more ox, it's going to kill me. My days of stupid shit are over. I'm retired from stupid shit with a full pension.*"

"I doubt that," Nadia said.

"What I'm trying to say," Gillies said, "I'm sorry, Luz. I'll get your money back for you, but I can't help you look for your son anymore."

Luz nodded, her mouth moving but no words came out. Nadia put a hand on her shoulder.

"I can't be here anymore," Luz said. She turned and walked back toward the bus stop.

Gillies turned to Nadia. "*Shit. What did I do?*"

"Eliseo is dead," Nadia said. "Luz identified the body yesterday."

"*Aw, hell.*"

Gillies apologized multiple times on the bus back to Luz's apartment. He had felt bad, but Nadia wasn't sure if it was because he had forgotten that he had already done it. He wasn't the same.

Luz assured Gillies that she was not mad at him. "I'll be okay. It hits me when I'm not ready. I just need some time."

Back at Luz's apartment, Luz went into her bedroom. Nadia and Gillies sat down at the kitchen table to catch each other up. He appeared to nod off for a second or two. She hoped that he was just tired.

Nadia updated Gillies on everything that had happened, from Luz spotting the car in the church parking lot up to the last few hours. It took an hour and four cups of coffee, but she managed to tell it all without leaving anything out. Nadia only paused to check in on Luz, who "wanted to be alone, but not alone." Nadia understood exactly what that meant.

"*My brain isn't firing on all cylinders,*" Gillies said. "*So what you're saying is the woman who took the girl had something to do with Eliseo's death.*"

"*Same car. White boy was at the house by the church.*"

"*Then it's time you go to the police. Tell them everything.*"

"*We can't prove anything. Plus, they can put Luz in jail for shooting the kid.*"

"*Has Luz talked to her lawyer?*"

"*He's going to recommend the same thing,*" Nadia said. "*The police are not on our side. Luz's son might be dead, but there's a girl that we can still help. Luz and I are going to find Ostelinda. That's the girl's name.*"

"*That sounds like a bad idea.*"

"*It's a terrible idea,*" Nadia said, "*but that doesn't mean we aren't going to try. If we don't help her, nobody will. She's all alone.*"

"*If what you're saying is true, these folks killed Eliseo and another girl. That means they're willing to kill more people. You and Luz and anyone else. It's too dangerous.*"

"*You know better than to try and stop me.*"

"*It wasn't the beating I took that hurt the most,*" Gillies said. "*It was watching them hurt you and not being able to do anything about it. I couldn't protect you.*"

"*You could never protect me,*" Nadia said, "*but maybe together, we can protect this girl.*"

"*What are you going to do?*"

"*I'm going to pray.*"

"I'm glad you came back." Marta had immediately clocked Nadia walking into the New Life Apostolic Church. She marched over to Nadia like she was going to attack her, but gave her a big hug instead. Nadia was more prepared this time.

"I didn't know if I would see you again," Marta said, walking her to the refreshments table and handing her a glass of something pink.

"I almost didn't come, but I needed to renew my faith," Nadia said. "Until I find a job, all my time has to go into looking for work."

"It's hard when you don't have papers."

Nadia looked over her shoulder to make sure no one was listening.

Marta waved her off. "I told you. This is a safe place. In fact, when we talked before, it made me think." She looked around the room. Marta took Nadia's hand and walked her to a woman talking to Father Daniel.

"Sorry to interrupt," Marta said, obviously not sorry at all, and not open for debate. She was a force of nature.

"Marta," they both said simultaneously. Friendly, but exhausted. They had obviously experienced her particular brand of enthusiasm and tenacity.

"This is the woman I was telling you about," Marta said. "The one looking for work."

The woman extended her hand. "Teresa Moreland. Nice to meet you. I might be able to help."

FORTY-TWO

It had been one week since Ostelinda had spotted the woman with the map. Her savior. Her saint. Whenever Ostelinda walked by the windows on a bathroom break, she stopped and looked out at the industrial area below hoping to see the woman again, but the street was always empty. Not even Perrito.

It didn't stop Ostelinda from checking, but her expectations had become tempered. For a moment, she thought that a yellow plastic bag caught in a chain link fence might be some kind of signal, but it was nothing more than a piece of garbage that had been blown by the wind.

While washing her hands in the bathroom, the door swung open. It made her jump. She was surprised to see anyone in the bathroom, but more surprised that it was someone that she had never seen before. Not one of the third-floor workers. The woman in the baseball cap must have been a second-floor worker that had stumbled upstairs out of curiosity or for the same privacy that Ostelinda sought.

"There was a line downstairs," the woman said, answering her unasked question. She opened each of the stall doors one by one.

"I'm not supposed to talk to you," Ostelinda said.

"Why not?" the woman asked.

Ostelinda didn't answer. She walked toward the door. She had to assume that this was some kind of trick, a loyalty test from Sra. Moreland.

"You're Ostelinda?" the woman asked, closing the last stall door.

Ostelinda stopped with her hand on the door handle. She turned slowly. "How do you know my name?"

The woman held up the self-portrait that she had drawn. It had been in the Bible that she had dropped in the church parking lot. "Luz sent me. I'm here to help you."

Ostelinda's knees gave out for one second, buckling underneath her. The woman made a move to assist, but Ostelinda caught herself.

"Are you okay?" the woman said.

It felt like someone had used one of those machines that restarted a heart, one of those machines that shocked the body and made it jump. She had been revived. Her heart beat hard enough to make her ribs hurt.

"I'm okay," Ostelinda said, regaining her focus.

"I'm Nadia. We don't have much time. Luz and I are working to get you out of here."

"And Luz is the woman that—the one who tried to help?"

"Yes. She sent me."

"Are you the police?"

"No."

Once her shock settled, Ostelinda noticed this woman's discomfort. Her hands shook. Her armpits were wet with sweat. Her eyes darted from one corner to another. She looked unwell.

"How did you get inside?" Ostelinda asked.

"I got a job here. I don't have papers, either. They seem to like that power over their workers. I'm down on the loading dock."

"These are dangerous people. They killed my friend, Maite. They will catch you. You are risking too much."

"I know, which is why—"

The door opened and a third-floor worker who Ostelinda only knew as Chacha walked past them into one of the stalls. She didn't make eye contact or say a word to either of them. When she closed the stall door, Nadia mouthed the words "más tarde", pointed to the ground, and then held up two fingers.

Ostelinda nodded. They would meet back in the bathroom at two o'clock.

Before leaving the bathroom, Nadia reached out and squeezed Ostelinda's hands. She pulled her in for a hug. It was rigid and odd, like the woman had never hugged someone before, but it felt good to feel another body. It made Ostelinda feel protected, less alone.

Ostelinda's saint had a name. Luz. Light. The light that would lead her out of the darkness. And Nadia. Ostelinda didn't know what the name Nadia meant, but she wanted to believe that it meant hope or freedom or salvation.

She wondered why Luz and Nadia hadn't gone to the police or the army, but they must have had good reasons. She didn't know how things worked in America. If the police were anything like they were in Mexico, it could be more dangerous to involve them than to take their own chances with Sra. Moreland

Back at her workstation, Ostelinda stacked suit jackets on a wheeled trolley and wheeled the trolley next to two others in the back storage area. A hand tapped her shoulder.

"Nadia?" she asked, but when she turned, there was no one there until she spun all the way around.

Corey leaned on a single crutch, his foot wrapped in a bandage with a leg brace over it. His smile was terrifying. "Miss me?"

Ostelinda looked in the direction of her workstation, but it was out of view. She was in a blind spot. None of the other women could see her, and with the sound of the sewing machines and hum of the factory, she was outside of shouting distance.

"Does your foot hurt?" Ostelinda asked.

Corey stepped forward, but Ostelinda quickly skirted around him. He reached out a crutch, hitting her in the shin. It didn't slow her down.

When she got to her workstation, her breathing felt shaky. Sra. Moreland approached her.

"You don't look good. Is something wrong?"

Ostelinda looked up. Sra. Moreland followed her eyes and caught sight of Corey limping out of the back storage area. She shook her head and marched over to him. Leaning close, she said something into his ear. He shrugged. She smacked him on the head. Corey looked away from his mother, staring straight at Ostelinda. He hobbled to the landing and down the stairs.

Sra. Moreland returned to Ostelinda. "His injury has not brought out the best in him."

"It hasn't changed him."

"I suppose it hasn't. It might be time for him to become a missionary for the church. A new environment will do him good."

Ostelinda said nothing. The thought of Corey with the evangélicos in some small town in Mexico made her sick. He would turn it into a hunting ground for new prey.

"He won't bother you anymore," Sra. Moreland said and walked to the next workstation.

Ostelinda returned to work, rethreading the sewing machine. Even with people like Corey in the world, there would always be others like Luz and Nadia to make it right. She didn't know if they would succeed in getting her out of the factory, but she was grateful that people were more than just cruel and indecent and inhumane. It only took a hint of light to kill a world of darkness.

FORTY-THREE

Mateo Fitzsimmons called Luz every hour. Never on the hour, but ten minutes after the hour, the phone would ring eight times. After the eighth ring, he would give up, never letting it reach nine. She knew it was the lawyer because she had answered the first time but had hung up when she heard his voice.

Luz admired his stubbornness, but she had nothing to discuss with him. Eliseo was dead. The law no longer mattered. She appreciated the gesture. He must be busy with other clients, but still took the time to listen to eight rings on his phone.

Walking into the living room at ten minutes after the hour, she saw Gillies asleep on the couch. Not wanting the telephone to wake him, Luz picked up on the third ring intending to hang up. Something made her answer.

"Mr. Fitzsimmons."

"*Oh, damn*," the lawyer shouted, followed by muffled fumbling sounds.

"Hello?"

"*I'm here, Ms. Delgado.* I'm here. I wasn't expecting you to answer. Your voice startled me. I spilled my coffee in my lap."

Luz laughed. It wasn't funny, but she laughed. "I'm sorry."

"That's okay. I'm awake now."

"I'm sorry for not answering your calls, as well."

"I can't understand what you're going through." He shuffled some papers. "But there are a few things we need to talk about. Important things."

"Of course."

"You walked out on a police detective in the middle of an official interview," Fitzsimmons said. "Detective Larios would like to speak to you. He is not happy."

"I don't care about his happiness. He does not care about mine. Am I obligated to speak to him? Legally?"

Fitzsimmons coughed. "He isn't a threat to you. He's interested in finding out what happened to your son. You can help him in that regard."

"He does not care what happened to Eliseo. He wants an answer. Any answer. It doesn't matter to him if it is the right one. He is only interested in my son as a part of his job."

"More reason to speak to him. You can set him straight on the facts."

"Give me his number," Luz said. She no longer wanted to talk about Detective Larios.

Fitzsimmons read off the number. Luz wrote it down, writing "Larios—LAPD" underneath the number, followed by a question mark.

"One moment," Mateo Fitzsimmons said. He shuffled more papers. "My notes got mixed in with—here it is. There's one more thing. They are ready to release the body—I mean, remains—I mean, Eliseo. Are you ready to talk about this?"

"I have no money. What happens to him? What can I do?"

"It rules out any transport of the body, which leaves you with cremation."

Luz had not prepared herself for this conversation, a discussion that no parent wanted to consider having.

"If cremation is the only option..." Luz said. "Does that cost money?"

"The figure they gave me was five hundred dollars, but I should be able to get that waived. Give me until the end of the day."

"I can't even afford my son's death," Luz said. "What happens to his ashes?"

"I can take possession of them on your behalf."

"What would happen, if you did not take them?"

Fitzsimmons paused for long enough for Luz to wonder if he was still there. Then he said, "They would go into a landfill."

"The unclaimed get thrown away?"

"There are no more—I don't know the name in Spanish—*potter's fields*."

"What about the girl?"

"What girl?"

"The one they found with Eliseo. The dead girl. Maite."

"I don't know. I didn't ask."

"Please ask. I need you to ask. She cannot be thrown away."

"I will."

"I have no more money to pay you either," Luz said. "You are doing all this work, but I don't know when I'll have the money to pay you."

"To be honest, you haven't gotten the greatest results from me. I'll see what your choices are. It's the least I can do. Hospitals are often sympathetic in these cases."

Luz couldn't escape the image of Eliseo on a metal slab rolling into a flaming oven. She didn't just see it. She heard it. She smelled it. The smoke burned her eyes.

"Luz?"

She snapped out of it. "Is there anything else?"

"No. Call the detective. I'll figure out the remains for both your son and the girl."

"Thank you."

Luz hung up the phone. She kept her eyes on the table in front of her and the piece of paper with the police detective's phone number on it.

For the last six years, Luz had lived in constant fear of anyone in uniform. Even the security guard at the supermarket put her on edge. If she had been white or a citizen when Eliseo went missing, she would have immediately contacted the police. She would have demanded that they find her son. Life was different for the unwanted.

Luz felt hungover, but hadn't had a drop to drink. It was lack of sleep, her eyes burning in their sockets. The thought of taking the minute to make coffee and then the minute waiting for it to brew made her crave a Coca-Cola.

She glanced over her shoulder at Gillies sleeping on the couch. He had slept through her conversation with Mateo Fitzsimmons, but she still opened the refrigerator as quietly as she could.

Luz found a bottle in the back of the refrigerator, the glass cold to the touch. The moment it left the refrigerator, it clouded with condensation.

The bottle opener was nowhere to be found, but Luz had never owned a bottle opener growing up. Every hard surface was a bottle opener. She placed the lip of the bottle cap against the counter and gave the top a hard smack. The bottle opened, but the force knocked it out of her hand. It crashed to the ground, foamy Coke spilling everywhere. The bottle didn't break, but the bang combined with Luz's swearing made a racket.

She picked up the half-full bottle, set it on the counter, and wet a sponge. Getting on her knees to clean the sticky floor, she faced the couch. "Sorry, Mr. Gillies."

He hadn't moved.

She stopped cleaning. "Mr. Gillies?"

Leaving the sponge on the ground, she walked over the sticky linoleum and onto the carpet. She reached the couch and stood over Gillies. He was breathing. A really sound sleeper. She laughed.

One of Gillies's arms had fallen off the couch, a hand resting on the floor. A folded piece of paper sat on the ground next to his hand. Luz picked it up. Curious, she opened the note. It was from Nadia. Luz wouldn't have read it, but the first sentence made her read on. "Don't tell Luz." How could she not read it?

The note read, "Don't tell Luz. I went to the church. I talked to the woman Moreland. She gave me a job at the factory. The address is 418 Harding Ave. I'm going to make contact with the girl. Learn the situation.

Once I verify, we can call the police. If I'm not back by ten tonight, tell Luz, call the National Guard."

"Oh, Nadia," Luz said. "Mr. Gillies. Wake up. Nadia has done something incredibly stupid."

Gillies didn't respond. When she touched his arm, it was cold.

FORTY-FOUR

Nadia lowered the brim of her cap and tilted her head. She didn't know if the white boy on crutches would recognize her, but she didn't want to take any chances. She had known who he was right away.

Their eyes had only met for a moment as he gave the loading dock a bored glance. He hadn't looked back or lost stride as he hobbled forward on a crutch, but Nadia couldn't know for sure if he might get a delayed recognition. The context was so different from their last meeting, she could only wait and find out.

While Nadia worked, she made mental notes about the space and the people—workers and staff. She had no plan on how she would get Ostelinda out of there. She should have brought a camera. Nadia needed evidence. She didn't know if an anonymous phone call was enough probable cause for the police to enter the premises. The last thing Nadia wanted to do was tip off Moreland. That would put all the women in danger.

Moreland kept her movements to the upper two levels where the factory workers did all the sewing, packaging, and production. The second floor was devoted to the workers that made the place legit— or semi-legit as most of them were not documented. The workers on the third floor were the ones that everyone pretended didn't exist. She had directly been told not to talk to the women. They were none of her business.

The real problem was the men outside and on the loading dock. Usually, two or three of them sat outside and smoked near the truck entrance. Another one or two were visible on the loading dock. They never did any work. They only existed. They were all young, Mexican, bald, and tattooed. White America would have assumed they were gang members, but they looked more like wannabe tough guys to Nadia. Punks who craved respect, but didn't know the word's meaning. The young men played cards, joked, and made kissing sounds at the women when they came to work in the morning.

Nadia rolled the pallet jack from the far end of the loading area to the freight elevator. If the white boy had spotted her, she was in trouble. Hopefully, he was like most gringos and Mexican faces were all the same to him, even the face of a woman that had pulled a gun on him. The best she could do was stay away from the white boy for the rest of the day. The elevator doors opened onto the third floor.

The third floor stayed darker than the rest of the building. The fluorescent lights were sparser and many didn't work. The women hunched over their sewing machines didn't acknowledge her presence as she rolled the pallet jack past them. Even Ostelinda didn't seem to notice her, whether out of habit or a form of subterfuge.

Nadia rolled the pallet jack to the end of the building and left it next to the bathroom that no one used. She would wait it out there for a bit. Maybe the white boy was there to visit and would leave soon. If caught, she could tell Moreland that she had woman problems or had eaten some bad mariscos.

The moment she sat on the toilet, she got light-headed, cold sweat covering her body. Her hands shook and her breathing got short. Nadia placed one hand on the side of the stall, not sure if she was going to pass out. She felt trapped. She wanted to scream. It made no sense to her, but Nadia thought she might be dying.

It wasn't her first panic attack, but that didn't make it any less real or any less frightening. She couldn't logic her way past anxiety. All she could do was take even breaths and softly repeat, "I'm okay," until she eventually believed it.

It slowly dissipated. Five or ten minutes of steady breathing. Her skin crawled and her heart rate maintained its record pace, but her mind eased. Some of the dread was tempered with a form of excitement, something she used to feel when she was on the job. She missed the work. Not all of it, of course. Most jobs were primarily ditch digging, but those moments of discovery or the anticipation of a story about to break open were like a high. But like any addiction, it had taken everything from her. That didn't mean she didn't crave the feeling. A drunk didn't dump the bottle when she lost it all. A drunk got another bottle.

When Nadia heard someone enter the bathroom, she lifted her feet and peeked through the crack at the hinges of the stall door. Relieved to see Ostelinda, she opened the door a few inches and poked her head out.

"Ostelinda," Nadia whispered.

Ostelinda jumped and turned with a hand to her chest. "Ay, Nadia. You scared me. I almost screamed."

"I'm sorry."

"Are you hiding?" Ostelinda glanced at the closed door to the bathroom. "What is happening?"

Nadia stepped out of the stall. "There is a white man on crutches here today. Do you know him?"

"Yes," Ostelinda said with disdain. "Corey. He is Sra. Moreland's son. A cabrón. Be careful of him. He enjoys scaring people, hurting them."

"I know," Nadia said. "We've met before. He may have seen me."

"You must leave," Ostelinda said. "He is very dangerous. Do not put yourself at risk. Not for me. I cannot have more people hurt because of me."

"I'm going to get you out of here."

"The first time I tried to escape, I left without my friend Maite. Corey killed her. I am sure of it. He said she was already dead, but that was a lie. He killed her."

"The woman in the drawing."

Ostelinda nodded, then her eyes grew huge. She turned quickly. "Someone is coming."

The door opened. Nadia looked back at the stall, but it was too far. Instead, she walked to the sink, keeping her body pivoted away from the door. She turned on the faucet and washed her hands.

Out of the corner of her eye, Nadia watched the end of a crutch poke into the room. Corey walked into the bathroom.

"I thought I would find you here," Corey said.

Nadia was sure that she had been caught. She turned off the water and balled her hands into fists. No matter what he did to her, Nadia would hurt this sadist punk as much as she could.

"You at the sink," Corey said.

Nadia started to turn.

"Get out of here. I have to talk to my girlfriend."

Corey hadn't recognized her. That solved her problem, but she couldn't leave Corey alone with Ostelinda. Keeping her face hidden, she turned to Ostelinda.

"Do you want me to stay?" Nadia asked.

"I'm sorry," Corey said. "Who do you think you work for?"

"It is okay," Ostelinda said. "He would not dare hurt me. He fears his mother. I will be fine."

"Yes," Corey said. "She will be fine."

Nadia kept eye contact with Ostelinda, not wanting to look away, not wanting to leave.

"This is not new to me," Ostelinda said. "Please go."

Keeping her head down, Nadia walked past Corey and out the bathroom door. When the door closed behind her, she felt like a coward and a failure. She turned to go back in the bathroom, but stopped herself. It wasn't about this battle. She had to get out of there to win the war.

The only way to help Ostelinda was to get her out of the factory and she wasn't going to do that by losing a fight in the women's bathroom.

"*Fuck,*" she muttered, kicking a plastic bucket. It sailed across the room and bounced against the wall.

FORTY-FIVE

Corey locked the bathroom door behind him and took a step toward Ostelinda. "Did you miss me?"

"I have to go back to work." Ostelinda gave him a wide berth walking to the door. Corey's eyes followed. She took slow cautious steps, the way you would circle a coiled rattlesnake, the fear that any noise or sudden movement would shatter the tension and spark an attack.

Corey swept his arm and grabbed Ostelinda's bicep. She pulled away, but his grip was firm. Ostelinda stamped down with her heel, but missed his bandaged foot. He looked at her surprised, almost hurt that she would do such an underhanded thing. She stomped again. Corey shifted in time. He pushed her, throwing her back against the paper towel dispenser. The action made him lose his balance, the crutch sliding on the slick floor. Forced to put weight on his bad foot, he grimaced in pain.

"That hurt," he said. "You tried to hurt me."

"I want to leave," Ostelinda said. "I will tell your mother. She has told you to stop. She will send you away."

"Why do you think I'm mad at you? She has no business getting in the middle of what we have. This thing between us."

"We have nothing."

"There it is. That sexual tension," Corey said. "Why did you tell her lies? That I did things that I didn't do? Acting like it's not what you wanted. You told her I scared you when you're the one that keeps trying to screw me."

"That is not true. None of that is true. You make me want to throw up." Ostelinda looked around for anything she might use as a weapon. There was only a trashcan.

"That's your fiery Latin passion." His smile made her ill. "You can say 'no' a hundred times, but there's no way to hide that you want me. Your eyes say 'yes'. You love the fight. I get it. I do too."

Ostelinda took a few steps to the side, but Corey mirrored her movement blocking her angle to the door.

"Don't stop fighting completely. I like it rough." Corey smiled.

Ostelinda backed up, took the lid off the trashcan, and brandished it like a weapon. She held it over her head, ready to strike.

Corey looked hurt. He planted his feet and swung the crutch like a baseball bat. It struck the trashcan lid, making a loud bong.

The force knocked Ostelinda to the ground. In a desperate flurry, she kicked at Corey's legs. She felt her foot connect with Corey's kneecap.

Corey bent forward, dropping the crutch. He struck at her with one hand, while the other hand clutched his knee.

Ostelinda punched at his bandaged foot, feeling more wetness with each blow.

Corey screamed, falling backward. He had one hand on his knee, the other on his foot.

Frantic, Ostelinda scrambled to her feet and picked up the crutch. She didn't know what to do next. She knew nothing about fighting. The blood rushed to her head as she stood. She had to do something. She had to stop thinking.

She brought the rubber end of the crutch down on him. The first blow struck his chest. He barely reacted, if only to look at her briefly as if to ask, what do you think you're doing? The second blow hit him in the neck, knocking the rubber tip off the crutch. A frightening whistle and wheeze formed in his breathing. He squirmed underneath her. She hadn't meant to strike his face, but the third blow hit him in the eye. Without the rubber tip, the metal pipe at the end the crutch sank deep into the socket. When she pulled up the crutch, it made a sucking sound. Corey's eye was no longer there, a red emptiness in its place.

Corey flailed and slid across the bathroom floor. He bled profusely from his eye socket, his body mopping the blood along the ground. His hands were at his throat, gasping for breath. Blood streaked the filthy tile floor as he kicked. It looked like he was drowning. He propped himself against the wall.

"Help me," Corey said, a barely audible rasp.

Still holding the crutch, Ostelinda stood over him.

"Please," Corey pled. "I'll do anything. I'm hurt."

"I will help you." Ostelinda crouched down and stared into his good eye. "Tell me what you did to Maite. The truth."

"You'll get help?"

Ostelinda nodded. "What happened to Maite?"

"I—we—thought she was dead," Corey said. He spit blood onto the ground. "We found a spot on the LA River to dump her body. Out where it gets kind of wild. Not like in the city. That's all it was about, getting rid of her body."

"You dumped her like garbage."

"Then she moved and took a breath. Not like a healthy breath, but a loud, ugly one. Scared the shit out of all three of us. We freaked out. Lobo wanted to leave, figured she would die anyway. The wetback kid we brought along kept saying he had to take her to the hospital. Lobo doesn't like to be told what to do."

"You were going to let her die."

"Never had to make that call," Corey said. "My neck really feels wrong. Like I'm bleeding inside."

"Finish."

"Fuck," Corey said. "I was strictly on the sidelines. Lobo and the kid went at it. Throwing punches. Then Lobo dropped his gun. The kid picked it up. His hands were shaking. It wasn't the first time someone pointed a gun at Lobo. He charged the kid. The kid fired. Shot your friend instead. An accident."

"You might as well have killed her yourself."

"Did you hear any of what I just said?" Corey coughed. "I had nothing to do with it."

"You blame others. It was you. You were their leader."

"Now get me some help."

Ostelinda rose and walked out of the bathroom. She shut the door behind her. Corey's constricted cries were lost in the sounds of the sewing machines. She heard a lot of faint swearing in Spanish and a few bad words she knew in English. A loaded pallet jack sat next to the bathroom door. She rolled it in front of the door and stacked more boxes on it until the door was concealed.

She returned to her workstation. She never once considered going for help.

A year ago, the idea of inflicting that kind of violence would have been unthinkable, but Sra. Moreland and her son had made her brutal. They had worn her down to an animal. She could still feel the crutch sink into his eye socket. She hoped it hurt.

Threading the sewing machine, she saw a patch of blood on her bare wrist. She found a rag and wiped at it, leaving only a pink stain. She checked her hands and clothes, as best she could. Her shoes were red with blood.

"Is everything okay?" Sra. Moreland said.

Ostelinda jumped, pushing her feet as far under her workstation as she could. She gave a half turn and nodded. She sewed a label to the inside of a jacket hoping the vibrations of the sewing machine would hide her shaking hands. For a brief moment, she thought she could hear Corey's desperate, gurgling pleas. She thought she could smell his blood.

"Have you seen my no-good son?" Sra. Moreland asked. "He seems to have disappeared."

Ostelinda shook her head. She bit the inside of her cheek.

"That's good news," Sra. Moreland said. "I'm glad he's leaving you alone. Probably just left without saying goodbye."

FORTY-SIX

It took an hour for the ambulance to get there. Some neighborhoods didn't rate as a priority.

Luz watched from across the street. She had left the door open for them and a note on the table that gave Gillies's name and recent medical issues. It was the best that she could do for him. She couldn't be there. She couldn't answer any questions.

When she had found Gillies unconscious, his breathing and pulse had been steady, but she could not wake him. She was ashamed that she had hesitated before calling 9-1-1. Fear had driven so many of her past decisions that it had become instinct to let it dictate her choices.

After Luz made the call, she filled Eliseo's backpack with everything that she needed and walked out of her apartment, quite possibly for the last time.

The ambulance's arrival brought Farrokh out of his office. The other residents remained in their apartments, looking out their windows. A police car accompanied the ambulance. Its presence did not go unnoticed. While Farrokh spoke to one of the police officers, he spotted Luz across the street. Other than a slight shake of his head, he didn't give her away. She owed him for that.

The EMTs wheeled Gillies on a stretcher and into the ambulance. He had a clear mask on his face and tubes attached to his arm. A woman hovered over him while two men carried him down the stairs. From what she could tell from the distance, he remained unconscious.

There was nothing more to do or see at her apartment building. Luz gave the chipped stucco and dying palm trees one last look and walked down the sidewalk. She threw the backpack over her shoulder, feeling the weight of Gillies's gun at the bottom. It uncomfortably poked her back, but she liked knowing it was there.

Turning the corner into the industrial neighborhood, Luz spotted the small group of teenage boys in the middle of the block. They were all about fifteen. Children who probably thought they were men. They smoked cigarettes and drank from big bottles in brown paper bags, passing them around and laughing at unheard jokes. One of them leaned on a bicycle. The others sat on the steps of an abandoned building. One of the crew slapped another and gave a head nod toward Luz as she approached.

Luz could have turned around and gone down a different street. She could have avoided them easily. She chose to walk straight toward them. She had purpose. She needed to be somewhere. Ostelinda didn't have time for distractions or childish nonsense.

"How you doing today, beautiful lady?" one of the kids said.

The boy on the bicycle slowly circled around behind her, seemingly to give her room but in doing so preventing her escape.

Luz smiled. "I'm in a hurry, children."

"You don't want to hang out with us?" He held out the bottle.

"Please move."

The boy turned to his friends and smiled.

Before he could say something else stupid, Luz stepped up to him, her face inches from his. "Who are you looking at, little boy? You're talking to me."

He tried to step back but tripped over one of the other boy's feet. He stumbled, but Luz stayed close.

"I shot the last boy that messed with me."

"Hey, I was playing around," the boy said, turning and walking away from her and his friends. "You're crazy."

Luz turned to the others. "I do not play. Do you understand?"

They stared at her, not knowing what to do.

"Do you understand?" she shouted, spit flying from her mouth.

They nodded.

Luz continued on her way, expecting one of them to make a snide comment once she put some distance between them, the coward's goodbye. It never came. She thought she heard a muttered apology.

They were boys. No different than Eliseo had been. Dumb and impetuous. Wanting so bad to be men that it made them act more like children. It was a wonder that any men survived that age.

Then Luz remembered some of them didn't.

Luz found the address and immediately recognized the intersection. She had stood in the street with a map in her hand and stared up at the billboards across from it. The idea that she had stood a few yards from where Ostelinda had been held prisoner and had been unable to do anything about it made her angry.

The outer gate of the factory fence was open a few feet. A man stood just inside the gate. It was still early. They hadn't quit for the day.

Luz found a comfortable spot outside the abandoned warehouse across the street. She sat next to an empty dumpster. If anyone spotted her, they would just assume she was homeless.

A dog wandered into the alley and put its nose to her face. Luz smiled without even realizing she had. Dogs had that ability. The dog licked her face. His job complete, he strolled further down the street, stopping to sniff at corners and posts.

After an hour, the man opened the gate to the facility all the way. A group of two dozen women filtered out, talking to each other in Spanish. They looked tired, but no different than any other group after a long day at work.

Luz rose, threw the backpack over her shoulder, and walked across the street. The man at the gate looked at his phone. While he might have been a guard of sorts, his function seemed to be mostly ornamental. There didn't appear to be any real fear of a threat. He was probably there to deter theft and to keep the girls inside.

Luz walked onto the grounds of the factory past the other women, patting her pockets as if she had forgotten something. The ruse hadn't been necessary. The man never looked up from his phone.

The only entrance into the building appeared to be the loading dock. Luz walked toward the door. Ten feet away, Nadia walked out of the same door. They made eye contact. Nadia fast-walked to her.

"What are you doing here?" Nadia said, pulling her around the corner and out of view from the man at the gate.

"There's no more time," Luz said.

"What are you talking about?"

"Is Ostelinda inside? Did you see her?"

"Yes, she's here. On the third floor."

"I have to do this. I have to do it right now."

"What's going on?"

"They don't get to win."

"What does that mean? You're not making sense."

Luz set the backpack on the ground and pulled Gillies's pistol out of the bag. The weight felt comfortable in her hand. "It has to end."

PART FIVE

FORTY-SEVEN

Luz took Nadia's hand and pulled her away from the factory wall toward the shadows of the yard. Five cars, one on blocks, were parked haphazardly among the abandoned machinery, twisted metal, and wood crates. A rusted popcorn machine had become an urban sculpture in one corner. A makeshift fútbol goal was visible behind a panel truck parked against the factory wall.

Moreland's car, the Chevrolet with the primered front quarter panel, sat in the center of the parked cars. Luz pulled Nadia between Moreland's car and the tall metal fence. They crouched down, out of view of the front gate.

"How did you end up with my gun again?" Nadia asked.

"I found it."

"Gillies told you I was here."

Luz shook her head. "Mr. Gillies is in the hospital."

"What? No." Nadia reacted like Luz had struck her. "He just got out."

"He was on the couch. He wouldn't wake up. He was breathing, but he wouldn't wake up."

"What did the doctor say?"

"I don't know." Luz shook her head. "I called the ambulance. I had to leave. USC is the closest. They'll take him there."

"You left him to come here with a gun?"

"I had to."

A man walked out of the factory and lit a cigarette. He paced around the open yard only twenty feet from where they crouched.

Nadia stared at Luz. The two of them remained silent. Luz couldn't determine if Nadia's expression was anger or concern. When the man finished his cigarette and went back in the factory, they both relaxed.

"I knew Ostelinda was here."

"It's like we thought." Nadia half-stood. "Her and about ten others. We have to go. Call the police. They can't hide it."

Luz shook her head, holding up the gun. "I'm going to get Ostelinda. Right now. I'm going to get her out of there."

Nadia laughed without humor. "You're going to get killed."

"This isn't a military installation. These aren't soldiers," Luz said. "They're a bunch of matones. Idiots and bullies who don't expect a fight."

"You don't have to do this, Luz. Not now. One anonymous call and it's all over."

"Okay," Luz said. "Make the call. But I'm not going anywhere. You go. You call the police. I'll wait here. I need to make sure that woman doesn't go anywhere. I'm not going to let her get away with this."

"Luz. This is crazy."

"Tell the police there's a crazy woman with a gun at this address. They're more likely to show up than if you tell them that a group of migrants is in trouble."

"Please, don't do this," Nadia said.

"They killed my son."

"I know, Luz." Nadia looked down at the ground.

"I can't afford to cremate him," Luz said.

"*Fuck.*" Nadia reached forward and squeezed Luz's hand. "I'm going to call. You stay here. Do not move or do anything stupid."

"Thank you," Luz said.

Nadia stayed low until she reached the factory wall. She took a moment, stood straight, and walked out of the gate, giving the man on the phone a nod.

Luz didn't care if Nadia called the police. She didn't care if they showed up. Luz was relieved that Nadia was out of harm's way. Luz wanted her far away. She no longer cared about herself, but there was no reason to drag anyone else with her. She sat on the ground against the front tire of the Chevrolet Caprice. When Luz heard the gate closing, she dared to take a peek. The guard, his eyes never leaving his phone, walked into the loading dock door.

Luz looked at the pistol in her hand. She could see the appeal after spending so much of her life feeling powerless. The simple tool gave her power in the moment that she had never felt before.

Fifteen minutes later, the guard walked out of the factory with two other men. He opened the gate while the two men got in their cars.

Luz dropped as low as she could, halfway underneath Moreland's car. They drove out of the driveway and onto the street. The man left the yard, closing and locking the gate behind him.

There couldn't be many more people inside. There were only a few cars and once the factory was locked, how many people would it take to keep a group of frightened women in line?

It was another ten minutes before Teresa Moreland exited the factory. As she dug in her purse, Luz stood and took two steps toward her. She held the gun in both hands, pointing it at Moreland's head.

"Move very slowly," Luz said, trying to sound confident and keep the flutter out of her voice.

Moreland jumped at Luz's voice and dropped her purse, her keys still in her hand. When she saw Luz and the gun, she kicked the purse toward Luz. "Take it. It's all yours."

"Turn around."

"Wait a minute." Moreland squinted at Luz. "I know you."

"We've met," Luz said, "but you do not know me."

"Church parking lot." Moreland looked over Luz's head for a moment, as if trying to figure out how Luz had gotten from there to here, what series of events made sense.

"Turn around," Luz repeated.

Moreland looked at her car door, then at the door to the factory. She thought better of whatever plans passed through her mind but remained facing Luz, defiance growing on her face.

"I shot your son," Luz said. "I will shoot you."

"That was you?" Moreland said. "I don't understand any of this."

Luz looked around, worried that someone might see them. "Turn around. Now."

"I've never done anything to you."

Luz cocked the pistol and stepped forward. "I will not ask again."

"Okay, okay." Moreland turned around and faced the factory. "I don't know what you want, but you're welcome to it."

"I'm here for Ostelinda," Luz said. "She's leaving tonight."

"Who?" Moreland said, unconvincingly.

"Don't."

"Is that what this about? You're saving her? You're an illegal. How are you going to keep her safe?"

"Walk." Luz stepped forward and pushed the barrel of the gun into Moreland's back. They stepped into the factory.

The guard was definitely not expecting a strange Mexican woman with a gun to walk into the factory. He didn't look like he was expecting anything other than a nap. He was unarmed and immediately threw up his hands.

"Stand next to him," Luz said, pushing Moreland forward with the gun barrel. "I want to always see your hands."

"Great job, Lou," Moreland said.

The guard shrugged.

"Who else is here?" Luz asked.

Moreland didn't say a word.

Luz pointed the gun at Lou. *"Who else is here?"*

"Other than the girls locked up on the third floor, this is it. It's just me at night."

"Those keys." Luz pointed to Moreland's hand still holding her keys.

"Throw them here."

Moreland threw the keys, a weak toss that landed between the two of them.

"Why are you doing this?" Moreland said. "Some kind of hero?"

"You killed my son."

"I don't know what you're talking about." Those were the words Moreland said, but her face gave everything away. She saw a connection that made Luz more than a random good Samaritan. For the first time, Moreland looked scared. "I've never hurt anyone in my life. I'm a Christian."

"I watched you drag a young girl into a car. You have made prisoners of other human beings. Of children. You are stupid, weak, and cruel."

"I am a businesswoman. You know nothing about business."

"All of this for money?"

"Of course for money," Moreland said.

Luz didn't see the man walk in the open door behind her, but she felt the metal bar come down on her arm. The gun fired before it slipped from her hand and slid away. Moreland twisted, holding the side of her head. Luz saw blood. Before Luz could turn, she got hit again.

FORTY-EIGHT

Nadia walked away from the factory. She needed to find a payphone or a stranger with a cell phone, but the industrial area was devoid of life.

It took her fifteen minutes and fifteen blocks before she found a payphone in front of a bodega. She dialed 9-1-1.

"9-1-1. What is your emergency?"

In her calmest voice and most articulate language, Nadia gave the woman the address of the factory and explained as concisely as she could that there was a group of women being held against their will. The woman asked questions. Nadia did her best to answer, but she had started to get the sense that the woman on the other end of the telephone wasn't entirely convinced that the situation was an emergency.

She had become so frustrated with all the questions that she almost didn't recognize the man walking past her on the sidewalk. It was the man on the cell phone who had guarded the factory gate. He was heading back in the direction of the factory.

As the operator asked her another question, Nadia dropped the receiver and followed.

She knew where he was going, so she could follow at a distance. There was no sense of urgency in his stride. It was doubtful he would notice her. There was nothing threatening about a Mexican woman walking down the street in Los Angeles.

Staying a block back in the shadows, she watched the man unlock the gate and enter the yard.

Nadia counted to ten and then slipped inside the gap in the gate, just in time to see the man stop at the loading dock door, pick up a long piece of metal, and then rush into the building. Nadia was halfway to the door when the gunshot tore through the silence.

She didn't know what she would see when she entered the building. She didn't know what she would do. All she knew was that Luz needed help.

On the loading dock, the man with the pipe stood over Luz who was trying to stand. Moreland held her bleeding head. The air smelled like gunpowder. Nobody noticed Nadia. Gillies's gun sat on the ground in between her and the man with the pipe. It took four quick steps. As the man reeled back to take another swing with the pipe, Nadia pointed the gun in his direction.

"Stop!" she yelled.

The man froze, slowly turning. He saw the gun before he saw Nadia.

"Drop it!"

He complied, setting the pipe on the ground slowly, one hand held open in her direction.

"Help her up!" Nadia heard the shake in her voice. The gun trembled in her hand. She must have looked both terrified and terrifying.

"I can do it myself," Luz said, getting up on her own. She held her arm, a red mark forming where she had been struck. She walked to Nadia. "You came back."

"I called the police, but they won't come. Even if they did it would take hours in this neighborhood."

"It doesn't matter," Luz said.

"It's time to end this." Nadia handed the gun to Luz.

Nadia was accustomed to the third floor being filled with the sound of a dozen workers hunched over their sewing machines or rolling merchandise from one place to the other. When she stepped onto the landing, the quiet gave her chills.

Nadia had left Luz with the gun. Their three captives sat in chairs in the middle of the loading dock. The top of Teresa Moreland's ear was gone, the wound bleeding down her neck and onto her shoulder. The guard and the other man appeared disappointed by the events, but did not look ready to try anything stupid. Luz had everything under control.

The wildcard was Corey. She didn't know where he was or if he had left. Armed with the metal pipe, Nadia took cautious steps farther out onto the top floor.

She tried the knob of the first storeroom door, but it was locked. She gave the door a light knock.

"Hola," Nadia said. "I'm here to help. To get you out."

Nadia should have demanded the keys from the guard or Moreland, but this was a moment better suited for destruction. She swung the pipe down on the knob. It dented slightly, but held. Someone screamed inside the room.

"Be calm. I'm here to help," Nadia yelled. Someone yelled something back, but it wasn't in a language she understood.

Nadia took three more swings until the knob broke off and the door opened.

Three small Indio women sat on the floor of the storeroom, holding each other in the corner. Nadia didn't pause to explain. She moved to the next door. The knob came off in one blow. She was getting better at this.

Nadia didn't reach Ostelinda's room until the third door. In all, eleven women stood around, wide-eyed and scared. They talked softly to each other, asking questions, looking for answers.
They waited to be told what to do.

"Are you here to get all of us out?" Ostelinda asked.

Nadia and Luz had come for Ostelinda. They had never discussed the fate of the other women. Seeing all their frightened faces, Nadia didn't have a choice. "We're getting everyone out of here. Right now. Let's go."

Ostelinda pulled Nadia into a hug. She held her so tight that it hurt her ribs and shoulders.

"Are there more?" Nadia asked.

Ostelinda glanced behind her. "No, this is all of us."

"Downstairs," Nadia said.

"We—none of us—have been out of the factory. Me, only twice."

"Okay. Tell everyone to grab their things, whatever they want to keep. They are never coming back here."

Ostelinda spread the word to the other Mexican women and to the Guatemalans through the one girl that spoke both Spanish and K'iche'. The women scattered back into their rooms and grabbed the one or two important possessions they still had: photographs, jewelry, pieces of clothing.

While the women got their things, Nadia walked to the railing to check on Luz down on the loading dock. She calmly held the gun on Moreland and the two men. It looked like she was giving them a lecture, but Nadia couldn't hear what she was saying.

Nadia turned back to watch the women reemerge from their small rooms. Seeing them together gave her a shock of panic. She had no idea there would be so many. Nadia started to worry that all they had managed to do was make their situation different. Not worse, but not that much better.

"I am sorry," Ostelinda said, "but there is something I have to show you."

Ostelinda moved the boxes and pallet jack. She opened the bathroom door and cautiously entered.

"*Fuck,*" Nadia said.

Blood painted the floor in wide, bold strokes. Abstract expressionism by way of Jack el Destripador.

Corey had propped himself in the corner. His left eye was a bloody void. His clothes were saturated red. His throat, lips, and eyes were swollen. He looked like a bullfrog. He wasn't moving, and they were too far away to detect any breathing.

Nadia approached Corey. Her feet stuck to the half-dried blood like walking on caramel, leaving footsteps in the gore. With one hand, she reached to take his pulse.

"Is he dead?" Ostelinda asked from the doorway. "Did I kill him?"

Corey moved, his head jerking to the side. Ostelinda screamed. Nadia jumped back.

"*Help me*," he said, his voice damaged and soft. "*You said you would help me.*"

Nadia leaned in. Corey moved quickly, grabbing her wrist. She wrested her wrist from his grasp and fell backward onto the bloody floor. She pushed herself by her heels, sliding away from Corey.

"Dumb bitch," he said, trying to stand. He pointed at Ostelinda. "I'm going to kill you."

He got halfway up the wall before sliding back down and slumping to the side.

Nadia rose to her feet, her entire backside covered in blood. She looked at her palms, painted red. She remembered the night when Corey hurt Gillies.

"Is he going to die?" Ostelinda asked, her voice just above a whisper.

"I really don't care."

FORTY-NINE

Ostelinda was not a violent person. The sight of the injured Corey made her both numb and confused. A part of her wanted to help him. Another part wanted to hurt him more, hoping that he was suffering. Corey had brought nothing but pain and cruelty to people she cared about.

Before attacking Corey the night he took Maite—which only resulted in Ostelinda getting beaten—the last violent act that she could remember was back in school when she had pushed Abril Nuñez for teasing her. Ostelinda had been seven and Abril was unhurt, albeit angry enough to kick her in the shin.

The sight of the blood and Corey's empty socket flashed in her mind. Ostelinda found it difficult to believe that she had been the one to inflict that much damage. She was surprised that there was any blood left in his body.

She had known boys like him her whole life. He was no different than the young men she had encountered in Mexico. Boys who thought physical strength was enough to get them what they wanted. Men who thought they could take something because they were entitled to it. She had assumed that was the way things were, unchanging and universal. They were that way because they had always been that way.

She had been wrong. She could fight back.

Ostelinda guided the women down the stairs to the loading dock. Many of them hadn't left the third floor in months.

On the second floor, she saw Nadia talking to the woman from the parking lot—her savior, Luz. Ostelinda instructed the women to wait for them on the loading dock, that they would be leaving soon. She didn't want to interrupt Nadia and Luz, so she approached quietly, listening to the tail end of their conversation.

"I don't see any other way," Nadia said. "You can't take them all. It won't work."

"Are you sure about this?" Luz asked.

"I've thought it through. It's not perfect, but at least they'll have an advocate."

"You're risking too much. You could be sent back."

"It has to be me," Nadia said. "You shot Moreland in the ear and her son in the foot. The girl is responsible for everything else that's happened to that kid. He might not make it."

Luz looked up at the ceiling as if looking for the answer.

"Just promise me," Nadia said, "that you'll make sure Gillies is okay. That you'll take care of him, if necessary."

"Of course." Luz nodded. "I hate this."

Ostelinda felt uncomfortable, eavesdropping on an intimate moment. She coughed to get their attention. They both turned to her.

"Ostelinda," Nadia said, waving her over. "This is Luz."

Ostelinda walked to Luz and gave her a big hug. She didn't want to let go, whispering "gracias" in her ear. It wasn't just for the rescue, but the shreds of hope that hurt but kept her going. When she let go of Luz, she couldn't stop smiling at the face of the woman who saved her.

"It's nice to meet you too," Luz said. "You're going to come with me. I'm going to take you out of here. You'll stay with me for a while."

"What about the others?"

"There are too many. We can't."

"What will happen to them?"

"I don't know," Luz said. "They—you—are the victims of a crime. Nadia will help."

"I cannot leave Marisol and Anita."

"They will be safe," Nadia said. "I will look after them."

"I'm sorry," Ostelinda said. "I won't leave them."

Before Nadia could present her counterargument, Luz stepped in. "I can take two more."

"Okay." Nadia turned to Ostelinda. "As quick as you can, I need you to write down—You can write, yes?"

Ostelinda nodded, a bit insulted. She had known illiterate people, so it was a fair question, but it made her feel like she looked illiterate, whatever that looked like.

"I need you to write down everything about your arrival here. How they contacted you in México, the journey north, everything you remember, details, names, places. Everything you know about this place. Conditions in the factory. Everything that you've seen here. You understand? Everything. I have to tell your story for you."

"I understand." Ostelinda walked into Sra. Moreland's office, and sat at her desk. The chair was very uncomfortable. She wondered if that was the reason Sra. Moreland was so mean, but then scolded herself for making an excuse for such a cruel and heartless opportunist. Ostelinda opened the top drawer, looking for paper. It was filled with bills and invoices. All the documents were in the names of Daniel and Teresa Moreland.

Underneath the business papers were stacks of passports and identification cards. There were so many passports, more than the dozen women downstairs. She took out each one, looking at the photos. She recognized some of the women. The others must have been from before, women who no longer worked at the factory, faces she didn't recognize.

A stack of Voter Identification Cards sat underneath the passports. She found her own and put it in her back pocket. Then she found Maite's, her photograph looking up at her. Young and pretty and how she wanted to remember her best friend. She kissed a finger and pressed it against Maite's face.

"I'm so sorry."

Ostelinda returned the passports to the drawer and closed it. She opened the second drawer and found some paper. She continued to search, curious about what else was there. In the bottom drawer, under a few ledgers were four thick envelopes. Three envelopes were stuffed with American bills in different denominations. The other envelope filled with pesos.

The lack of security or concern showed Ostelinda just how confident Sra. Moreland had been in her power over her prisoners. Ostelinda didn't hesitate. She took one of the envelopes and shoved it down the front of her pants. She knew it was wrong and that it wasn't hers, but those weren't good reasons not to take it.

She closed the drawer and wrote everything that she could remember. Her journey to the factory, starting with the evangélicos who had come to her town and the promises that had turned out to be lies. She wrote about the last year. About Maite. About Corey. About Sra. Moreland. About Father Daniel and the church. It felt good to put it on paper. It was no longer only in her head. Other people would know what happened.

Ostelinda didn't know how long she had been writing. She set down the pen, stood, and stretched her back. It really was an uncomfortable chair. In the trashcan, she saw a paper cup with a plastic lid and straw. She pulled it out of the trash.

She gave the papers to Nadia and told her about the passports and the three envelopes of money.

"Luz is waiting for you downstairs," Nadia said.

"Thank you," Ostelinda said. "I thought I would die here."

"It was Luz," Nadia said. "Thank her."

Ostelinda didn't argue. She grabbed Nadia in an awkward hug, released her, and walked down to the first floor.

Luz spoke to the women who waited patiently. "It's your decision. You are free women. You can walk out of that door right now if you like. But if you have nowhere to go, no relatives, your best option is with Nadia."

A few women shouted questions. One spoke in K'iche', needing a translation. Three of the women held each other and cried together.

Ostelinda walked to the industrial sink and filled the paper cup with water. She walked to the lockers and knocked on the first one.

"My legs hurt," Sra. Moreland shouted from inside the locker. "Please let me out."

Ostelinda moved to the next locker without responding. She pushed the end of the straw into the small vent at the top.

"Thank you," the guard said.

"You better keep your mouth shut, Lou," Sra. Moreland said.

The guard didn't respond. He was too busy drinking the water that Sra. Moreland wouldn't get to enjoy.

Walking out of the factory with Luz, Marisol, and Anita, Ostelinda felt like she had woken up from a long sleep. The nightmare of the last year would become a bad memory, but it would be with her forever. So would the present moment—the moment when she walked outside. She made an effort to remember every detail. There was nothing remarkable about the walk through the yard to Sra. Moreland's car, but each step was another step closer to freedom.

"You ready?" Luz asked.

"What about the checkpoints?" Ostelinda asked. "The immigration patrols?"

"It's bad, but not that bad. Yet."

Driving off the property felt like the beginning of something new. Not a fluid start. The car stalled and lurched forward when Luz pulled into the street, forcing her to restart the engine.

"It's been a while," Luz said, gripping the wheel tightly.

"We are in no hurry," Ostelinda said. "You are doing very well."

Luz focused on the windshield straight ahead.

Pulling onto the empty street, Ostelinda turned around and watched the factory shrink in the distance. They turned a corner and it was gone.

"How long have you been in the United States?" Ostelinda asked Luz.

"Seven years," Luz said.

"I feel like I just arrived."

FIFTY

Luz concentrated on the road. She hadn't been behind the wheel of a car for almost ten years and had never had a license. For the first six blocks, she had forgotten to turn on the headlights. Her left leg shook uncontrollably.

The three girls in the car were so young. Luz watched them stare out the windows at the passing lights of the city. It must have looked like a different planet. Or maybe they were in their heads, reliving every moment of their captivity. How much of the excitement of their freedom was offset by the horrors of the past?

Luz didn't know what was going to happen. To them or to her. To the women back at the factory or to Nadia. She did know that she would defend these three girls with all her heart and body. They were in her care now and she would protect them. Nobody was going to hurt them anymore. They had gone through barbaric and unnecessary hardships for stupid reasons.

She had been both bold and stupid to enter the factory. Not something that she thought herself capable of, but a gun and an unbending will had a way of setting events in motion. Sometimes all it took were a couple of broken Mexican women to make things right.

Taking responsibility for Ostelinda and the two girls—Luz was embarrassed she had already forgotten their names—would never bring

Eliseo back or come close to balancing the scales, but a simple act of kindness and compassion helped shift the scales toward balanced.

"Once we're close to my place, we'll dump the car," Luz said. "Are you hungry?"

Ostelinda and the older girl shook their heads, but she caught a nod from the youngest girl.

"Have you ever had Chinese food?" Luz asked, catching the young girl's eyes in the rearview mirror.

She shook her head.

"You're going to like it."

Luz let a red-faced Farrokh yell at her. She took the abuse. She understood his anger. It was justified. Picking up the phone and calling 9-1-1 had put him and the other residents of the apartment building at risk.

"*I can't have the police coming around,*" Farrokh said.

Luz nodded, her eyes to the ground.

"*Do you know the trouble I can get in? None of you people care. You will get sent back to Mexico or Honduras or wherever. That's how it ends anyway. Nobody comes here thinking it's permanent. But me? I live here. I could go to prison. They already look at me like I'm a terrorist.*"

"*I'm sorry,*" Luz said. "*I didn't know what to do. Mr. Gillies needed an ambulance.*"

"*All it takes is one Trump-supporting cop. And that's most of them. Even the Mexican cops hate illegals. That cop calls ICE. They love to raid immigrant buildings. Idiots that think they're cowboys, ridding the Old West of Indians. They act like police, but they're assholes.*"

Luz turned and looked back at Ostelinda who stood only a few steps away. The two younger girls stood behind her, peeking out with wide eyes.

"*They are victims of human trafficking,*" Luz said.

"*None of my business,*" Farrokh said. "*And remember, you still owe me two hundred and sixty-three dollars for rent.*"

"*I'm tired, Farrokh. I'm going home. Our dinner is getting cold.*"

"*You can't live here for free.*"

Ostelinda stepped forward and nudged Luz, who turned and smiled. "It's okay. We'll be inside soon."

"Yo necesito mi dinero." Farrokh enunciated each syllable, mocking the language.

"*I understood.*"

Ostelinda nudged Luz again.

Luz turned. "It'll be okay. Don't worry."

"Will this help?" Ostelinda asked, handing Luz a thick envelope.

Luz opened the envelope, shocked to find it full of money. She thumbed through the different denominations of bills: ones, fives, tens, some twenties, a fifty, and a few hundreds.

"Yes, Ostelinda. This will help." She leaned in and whispered. "We'll talk about where this came from later."

Luz counted out three hundred dollars and paid Farrokh. "*Rent, plus interest.*"

Marisol and Anita sat at the kitchen table. She had asked Ostelinda their names and then repeated them in her head until they stuck. Marisol wolfed down the sweet and sour chicken, but Anita picked at her plate, mostly eating the white rice.

Luz showed Ostelinda around the small apartment. The poor girl never strayed farther than a few feet from her.

"Treat the whole apartment like it's your own," Luz said, walking into the bedroom. "This will be your room. Yours with Anita and Marisol. Is it okay for the three of you to share?"

Ostelinda nodded. "What's going to happen to your friend and the others?"

"I don't know, but I trust Nadia."

"Why did you help me? You don't know me."

"I'm not a hero," Luz said. "My son got mixed up with those people. They had something to do with his death. I am still looking for answers."

"Do you have a picture?"

Luz found the only photograph she had of her son as an adult. The one that she had used when she had first started asking around.

Ostelinda nodded as soon as she saw his face. "This is your son? I saw him. He was at the factory."

Chills ran from Luz's shoulders into her fingers. Sweat dripped down the middle of her back. She sat down on the bed, her legs shaky. "Can you please tell me what you know? What you saw?"

Ostelinda told her about the night that Corey and the others had taken her friend Maite, the girl that the police had found with her son. How they had carried the sick girl out of the factory. She told Luz that her son had been there when they beat her, but he had not participated.

"I'm sorry," Luz said. "I'm so sorry."

"I don't think he could have stopped it," Ostelinda said, "but according to Corey, your son shot Maite."

"That can't be true," Luz said. "You can't trust him."

But Luz knew that it might be true. The police had said that the gun had his fingerprints on it. She felt tears in her eyes.

"Corey maybe lied," Ostelinda said.

"My son could never kill a defenseless girl."

"No, no," Ostelinda said. "It was not on purpose. He was trying to stop the other man. They fought. Your son had tried but could not save her."

"Or himself."

FIFTY-ONE

Nadia had expected something more dramatic. She had expected an assault of police entering the factory in formation, guns a-blazing, ready for anything. The reality was far more lazy and uninspired.

Twenty minutes after Luz and the three girls left the factory, two curious uniformed police officers—guns drawn—poked their heads through the loading dock door. The announced themselves loudly, voices shaking.

Nadia stood in the center of the room with her hands in the air. The eight women in her care sat on the ground behind her. Moreland and the two men remained in the lockers. Nadia did her best to remain calm, but the police officers' guns made her shake.

"*I called 9-1-1,*" Nadia said. "*I was the caller.*"

The police officers' eyes darted to the upper landings, looking for an ambush. They were scared. Nadia was used to the arrogance of Mexican police. These two men looked as if they had been thrust behind enemy lines.

"*We—myself and these women—have been held prisoner in this factory for over a year. We freed ourselves. We need your help.*"

The police officers huddled together in conversation. One of the officers walked out of the factory while the other one remained.

"We're calling it in. We'll get someone down here that can assess the situation. Have a seat. It'll be awhile." The man did not holster his weapon.

Moreland screamed for help from the locker. The police officer bristled.

"Who is that?" the officer said.

Nadia pointed at the lockers. *"We placed one woman and two men in the employee lockers for our safety. They have abused and held us here. We were worried for our lives."*

The police officer pointed to the ground. *"I don't know what's going on, but I need you to sit with the others until our backup arrives. Where are the keys to the lockers?"*

Backup arrived in the form of three ICE vans carrying ten ICE agents in full tactical gear. They ran into the building past the two police officers like they had the element of surprise. The only thing that surprised anyone in the building after waiting over an hour was why they were playing soldier for victims of human trafficking.

A dozen LAPD officers showed up as well, but they remained outside as support and crowd control for a crowd that never arrived.

When Nadia tried to explain to one of the ICE agents that this was a criminal matter, she was told to stay with the others and that they would take her statement shortly. She had thought it would play out differently. She realized that while the women were no longer in danger, they weren't free, either. Nadia felt bad for the women, but the alternative would have been to let them run into the Los Angeles night and that had seemed like a more dangerous option.

She had expected more reason from someone in law enforcement, but had forgotten to factor in that American authority worked with imbedded narratives. Immigration and Customs Enforcement agents had the resources to protect the exploitation of immigrants, but they only saw themselves as wranglers and detainers. They were part of Homeland Security and this wasn't Nadia or the other women's homeland.

The police officers had released Moreland and the two men from the lockers. While Moreland pointed at her ear and screamed her side of the story, the officers found the three of them chairs and coffee and separated them from the group. They had their statements taken first.

Nobody tried to talk to the women. Nobody offered them anywhere to sit other than the floor. Forget about coffee. They might as well have been stray dogs, but then someone would have at least patted their heads.

While the police officers had seen no threat from the women, the ICE agents bound all of the women's hands—including Nadia's—in front of them with plastic restraints. If you see brown, clamp it down. If you see white, they're all right. The confused women cried and talked among themselves. A few pled to the stone-faced ICE agents. They asked Nadia what was going on. She tried to calm them. They were safe from harm and would be fed and given water. They would still be leaving the factory.

Nadia scooted on her butt to the nearest ICE officer, a paunchy man with a mustache. If not for the word ICE printed large on the back of his bulletproof vest, she would have thought he was a mall cop.

"*Excuse me,*" she said. "*Sir?*"

The ICE agent turned and pointed his Tazer at Nadia.

"*I am the person that called the police. I can explain the situation. The people they are talking to, they are dangerous. I can show you evidence. These women are not criminals. They are victims of human trafficking. They have been kidnapped and abused. The people in that office, they are guilty of many crimes, including murder.*"

"You talk real good English," the ICE agent said, not lowering the Tazer.

"*Did you hear what I said? These women are not undocumented workers, they were kidnapped in Mexico, brought over the border by that woman and her organization, and kept in this factory for over a year.*"

"*You might not be lying, but there's no way to be sure. We get a lot of illegals blaming real Americans for their problems. All sorts of sob stories. You wouldn't believe it. Wouldn't be a problem if they stayed in Mexico.*"

"These women didn't have a choice."

"You might be telling the truth. We'll find out. Don't worry. We're professionals. Once we get everyone processed, we'll sort it out."

"This should be a criminal investigation," Nadia said. *"From what I can see, you appear to be treating it like an immigration raid."*

"Lady, I'm just the guy with the Tazer. And right now, I need you to be patient." He turned the Tazer a little in his hand to indicate the unspoken "or else."

While the ICE agents congratulated themselves on a successful raid, the two police officers were left with the task of clearing the rest of the facility. The ICE personnel seemed to honestly think that they had done more than just show up. Heroes on the front line.

Interrupting all the high fives and chest bumps, one of the police officers yelled down from the third floor, urgency in his voice. *"Has the ambulance arrived? We've got an injured man up here."*

They had found Corey. Unfortunately, he was still alive.

While Corey and the other three "victims"—Moreland, the guard, and the other man—were given medical attention and taken away in two ambulances, Nadia and the eight women were walked into the back of two separate vans. No doctors, EMTS, counselors, no support of any kind.

Sitting in the back of the van, Nadia could at least be happy that Ostelinda and the two girls had gotten away. These other women's lives would continue as they had for the last year, with unsympathetic strangers treating them like numbers and determining their fate based on nothing human or decent.

The detention center was not built for comfort. It wasn't even built to house the number of people that currently resided in it. Twenty people and eight places to sit. Even with all the body heat, the room was freezing cold.

Nadia scanned the room, looking at the faces of the other women. She had brought them from one prison to another, but none of them looked angry. They looked accepting of whatever was next. If the wind blows you in every direction, there's a point you accept it and wait to see where you land.

It wasn't until six hours later that any official spoke to Nadia. She had taken a risk and it hadn't worked out as planned. She had known that she only had equal rights on paper, but she hadn't figured that law enforcement could screw up such an easy bust. Apparently, nine illegals were even easier.

If she was going to help these women, she needed to take a bigger risk. She needed to do something bold. She might not have much power, but even the merciless feared bad publicity. Or at least they used to, when people still had shame.

The bored man across the table didn't seem particularly interested, staring down at the form in front of him. Each woman reduced to little more than fifteen bubbles to fill in with letters and numbers.

"Your name?" he said in decent Spanish, pen at the ready, his mind on the dinner he wasn't eating.

"*My name is Anabel Garcés,*" Nadia replied in English. "*Up until recently, I was a Mexican journalist in Sinaloa.*"

The man stopped writing. He wasn't used to speaking to Mexican women who spoke English without a hint of an accent.

"*After an attempt on my life from members of the Mexican government and the cartels, I was forced to leave the country. On my journey to the United States to legally request asylum, Daniel, known as Father Daniel, and Teresa Moreland, along with their compatriots, imprisoned me, transported me over the border, and brought me to work in their clothing factory. Along with the eight other women I was incarcerated with, we have not left this building since our arrival. We are not unauthorized. We are victims of human trafficking along with countless others who have moved through their factory.*"

Sometimes a person had to tell a few lies to ultimately reveal a truth.

The man set down the pen. "*Did anyone take your statement at the scene?*"

"No. They did not. In fact, they hostilely refused to."

"I work with fucking idiots." He looked at his watch and then the form with only the name Anabel Garcés written on it. *"I'm going to be here for fucking hours now."*

He never came back to the room. Ten minutes later, another man entered and sat across from her. He didn't bother to identify himself.

"You are a journalist seeking asylum?"

"Yes. I am seeking asylum and protection for myself and the eight other victims of human trafficking who I arrived with."

"And your name is—" He read the form. *"Anabel Garcés. Do you have a passport or any identification?"*

"They took all our paperwork. Your agents were so lax at the scene, our captors may have had a chance to hide evidence. If not, there were passports and IDs in a drawer in an office on the second floor of the factory. I saw them once."

The man made a note on the inside of the folder.

"You can Google my name. My picture will show up. I know it's not official, but I'm telling the truth. I am who I say I am. At some point, I will be writing a story—multiple stories—about this event and your department's handling of the investigation. Hopefully, I will be writing from the safety of the United States. Can I please have your name with the correct spelling? You are required by law to identify yourself, which you did not. And then I would like to speak to a lawyer."

FIFTY-TWO

Ostelinda sat on the couch reading the American children's book. Luz told her that she had bought it for her son to help with his English. The vocabulary wasn't particularly practical, but Ostelinda smiled when she covered the words at the bottom and was able to name the animals. It was hard to remember the English words for vaca, caballo, and cerdo, but the big cats were easy. *Tiger*, *panther*, and *lion* were words she liked to say.

With Marisol and Anita asleep in the bedroom, Luz sat at the kitchen table making phone call after phone call. She spoke mostly in English, often raising her voice. Ostelinda didn't know what she was saying, but she knew that Luz was trying to help Nadia and the other women. There was also something about a man named Gillies, but Ostelinda didn't know anything about him.

Ostelinda knew her struggle wasn't over. She had escaped the walls of the factory, but she was still in a country where she didn't belong, where she wasn't wanted.

She tried to remember the girl she had been when she left Mexico. She and Maite looking at the clothes in el centro, holding dresses up to each other until the shop owner chased them away. They never bought anything. All her clothes had been found, hand-me-downs, or made by her or her relatives.

Ostelinda had never had much and had always wanted more, but sitting on a stranger's couch in Los Angeles, America, she only wanted one thing. Something she couldn't have. She wanted her best friend back. She could hear Maite's laugh, even if her face was fading at the edges of Ostelinda's memories. She would miss her friend forever.

She considered going back to Mexico, but that life was ancient history. If she returned to Mexico, it would be a wasted year, a defeat. Ostelinda had struggled and fought. She had been abused and exploited. Now her choices were her own. Everyone she met, aside from Luz and Nadia, had kept her from the simple dream she had when she had set out for Los Angeles. Unlike the blonde women that came to be movie stars or hairdressers, all she had wanted was to live in a small apartment with her best friend, get a job in a factory—a regular one where you could leave—and save a little money to walk into a store and buy a new dress, one nicer than the ones in el centro. She hadn't wanted anything more than a simple life.

Ostelinda had only been in Luz's apartment for a day and her saint had made her feel welcome, but nothing there was hers. Without family or firm ground, she had to hold home in her heart until she found a place to put it. She didn't know if it was possible to create a real home in a land where she wasn't wanted. She wanted to tell the white Americans that she hadn't done anything wrong except want a simple life. She wasn't trying to take it from someone else.

Luz slammed the receiver down, snapping Ostelinda out of her thoughts. Luz stood slowly like she carried weight on her shoulders. She walked to the refrigerator, pulled out a beer, and put it back. She poured herself some water instead. She drank a little, looked like she was contemplating throwing the glass against the wall, but set it down on the counter.

"Is everything okay?" Ostelinda asked.

Luz smiled, but it held no light. "Police and immigration and lawyers. They are frustrating. I talk to one, they tell me to talk to the other one, who tells me to talk to someone else. I end up back where I started. Like a bad joke. I never know if I'm doing things wrong or if they are making it more difficult for me. It is complicated on purpose. I will outlast them. I am patient."

"Any news about Nadia?" Ostelinda asked.

"Good news there," Luz said. "It looks like Nadia is going to be released with a date for her asylum request. She raised enough of a stink to make them want her out of there. Nothing the law hates more than someone who knows the rules. They consider it cheating."

"Would it be okay for me to go outside?"

"Of course." Luz ran her fingers through her hair. "It would be good to get out of the apartment. Do you want to go for a walk?"

Ostelinda stood up. "I will tell Marisol that we are going out. I don't want them to be scared if they wake up alone."

The ducks in Hollenbeck Park made Ostelinda giggle. Sitting on a hill and feeling the grass between her fingers and the wetness through her clothes, Ostelinda couldn't have been calmer. Cool sensations that were natural and clean. Maybe she would look for a job where she could work outdoors.

Two elderly white women walked by talking and laughing. When they saw Ostelinda on the grass, they gave her a wave. She waved back. It was the nicest thing that had ever happened to her. She didn't think she was crying, but she felt the tears roll down her cheeks.

The park felt like a dream that she would soon wake from, going from the bright sunshine and beautiful greens and blues of the day to a stark, gray reality. If she closed her eyes for too long, she might open them and be back in the factory, beaten and broken and lost.

Luz sat down next to her and handed her a Coke. Ostelinda took a sip. The sweetness hurt her teeth.

"Is it over?" Ostelinda asked. "Is it really over?"

"The worst parts," Luz said.

"As long as I can feel the grass, it will be okay."

"I will do everything I can to make that happen."

There was nothing else to say. Ostelinda and Luz watched the ducks until the sun got low in the sky.

On the walk back to the apartment, Ostelinda felt lighter. Even on the busiest streets with the honking, swearing, and the buzz of tires on asphalt, the city looked fresher and newer. The smell of exhaust might as well have been hyacinths.

When they rounded the corner onto Luz's street, Luz stopped Ostelinda with a hand across her chest. She pulled her back, retreating a couple steps.

"What is it?" Ostelinda asked, able to hear the ugliness of the city again.

"I'm not sure." Luz pointed to a young Mexican man sitting on the steps across the street from Luz's apartment building.

Ostelinda recognized him right away. It was the one that called himself Lobo. "He is with them. He works for Corey. He is a bad person."

"They know where I live."

Ostelinda looked down. Her hands shook. "They're never going to leave me alone."

FIFTY-THREE

It was Luz's fault that they had found her apartment. When she had told Teresa Moreland that she was Eliseo's mother, she had given herself away. Corey must have driven Eliseo home at some point. The connection was simple arithmetic.

The more immediate question was whether or not this man was the only one. He could be the lookout for others waiting in the apartment.

"Marisol and Anita," Ostelinda said, reading her mind.

"I know," Luz said.

Luz wished she had the gun, but she had left it in the apartment. Before a few weeks ago, she had never even held a gun. It was alarming how quickly she had become attached to it. She now understood the security that it gave, even if she knew that its presence could only make things worse.

"What are we going to do?" Ostelinda asked.

The girl was visibly shaking, but she showed no urge to run. It looked like she was ready to fight, more anger than fear. She had been through so much, but was ready to protect her friends.

"We're going to use racism to our advantage," Luz said.

It took Luz a half hour to find a payphone and another forty-five minutes for the patrol car to arrive. She took particular joy in watching both police officers approach the young man with their hands on the top of their sidearms. Luz had told the 9-1-1 operator that a man fitting the young man's description had been waving a gun around in the neighborhood.

Luz and Ostelinda walked to her apartment complex. Across the street, the man spoke to the officers, moving slow and keeping his hands visible. Luz knew it was childish, but when she made eye contact with the young man, she gave him a wink.

"What if there are more men inside?" Ostelinda asked.

"The police are across the street," Luz said. "Be ready to scream."

At her apartment, Luz unlocked the door as slowly and quietly as she could. She took a deep breath and turned the knob. A silent count of three. She threw the door open and rushed inside, ready for anything.

Marisol and Anita sat on the couch looking at the children's book that Luz had bought for Eliseo. Anita dropped the book, startled by Luz's sudden entrance.

"Are you two okay?" Luz asked.

The girls nodded.

"Did anyone come to the apartment."

"Someone knocked," Marisol said, "but we didn't answer."

"Thank God," Luz said, waving Ostelinda inside. "Gather everything you need or think you may need. We aren't coming back here."

If Fernando and Rosa were put out by the presence of four more people in their new home, it never showed on their faces or in their hospitality. Even their teenage sons, recent arrivals to the United States, seemed more than happy to give up their room and sleep in the living room. The oldest confessed that it was because the television was in the living room. As far as he was concerned, they could stay forever.

"It will only be a few days," Luz said, sitting on a lawn chair across from Rosa in the small backyard.

The grass was brown and the chain link fence was rusted, but the idea of a backyard seemed so luxurious compared to the apartment living that Luz had experienced since her arrival. If it was hers, she would have planted tomatoes and peppers against the far wall.

"Stay as long as you need," Rosa said. "And the girls are welcome, of course."

"Thank you, Rosa. I'm so lost right now."

"Fernando and I never meant to leave the way we did. With the apartment and no one to take our place. And with Eliseo missing. I'm sorry. We couldn't see past our own family."

"We're all trying to survive."

"It had been so long since I'd seen my children. It was all that I could see. All that mattered to me. I was wrong."

"I would have done the same thing."

"You wouldn't have, but thank you." Rosa waved over Ostelinda, who was in the corner of the yard trying to pet an uninterested cat. "That puta will scratch you."

"It's just scared," Ostelinda said, giving up and sitting with the two women. "Some things have never been shown tenderness."

"You're a sweet girl,' Rosa said. "If you need anything, you let me know. My sons haven't been around girls as pretty as the three of you in a long time. If they act like fools, you have my permission to give them a kick."

Ostelinda smiled and blushed. At that moment, Luz saw the young girl who Ostelinda should have been allowed to be.

"I've got good news and bad news," Mateo Fitzsimmons said on the other end of the phone.

Luz sat on the floor in Rosa's kitchen below the wall-mounted telephone. "Tell me the bad news in English and the good news in Spanish. It'll feel right that way."

"The bad news is that ICE wanted a win on paper and treated everything that happened at the factory as an immigration bust. They will file criminal charges against Teresa and Daniel Moreland, but only

for immigration violations, illegal hiring. They've already been released on bail. They'll be fined and maybe, put probably not, get some probation or house arrest. They are not pursuing charges for false imprisonment, kidnapping, or assault. The awful part is that the Morelands will probably have the factory back open in a few months."

"How can that be?"

"*It just is. ICE has no interest in the welfare or rights of the immigrant population. They see themselves as soldiers, when in fact, they're political pawns. And dipshits. America first and all that garbage.*"

"*What about the detective? Larios?*" Luz asked. "*Did you contact him? Did you tell him what we know about Eliseo's murder. About Maite and what happened?*"

"*I talked to Detective Larios. He told me that if you had not walked out on his interview, maybe he could have done something back then. But as of now, there's no evidence that connects the Morelands to the deaths. Eliseo will be listed as the suspected offender. He is closing the case.*"

"*They had the girl's identification card. That connects them.*"

"*That's not enough. It's not like a detective novel. You can't spin a story that makes sense and points at the bad guy. Without hard evidence, Larios can't make a case. Besides, he doesn't need to. He's cleared this one.*"

"Tell me the good news. Please."

"*The good news is...*"

"In Spanish."

"*Of course,*" Fitzsimmons said. "The good news is that Nadia will definitely be released. Between her journalist contacts—one of them is writing a piece about her—and the petition they started, there's a lot of heat. Bureaucrats are all about the path of least resistance. Her asylum application is strong, on top of that. Still working on the cases for the other women, but I think I can wear them down."

"Thank you for your hard work," Luz said.

"You're going to get your money's worth."

Luz smiled. She loved the thought that Teresa Moreland's money was being used to pay for the women's lawyer. Luz only wished that Ostelinda had taken all of it.

FIFTY-FOUR

Nadia had spent most of her newspaper career convincing herself that her work as a journalist had been about taking a stand for the people. Defending the public against the corrupt and the powerful that dictated the rules that the public were forced to live by. Fighting for the powerless, the poor, the uneducated, and the weak. Shining a light on the truth to balance the scales of unfairness tipped against most of us.

While she had done her job well, she had not accomplished any of that. Few of the people she had exposed had been held accountable. Regular citizens continued to be robbed and killed at the whim of those in power. Her family had been murdered and her life had been destroyed. The romantic notion of a hopeless cause was undermined by its hopelessness.

This wasn't the same. This wasn't a pointless quest to save society from itself or whatever she thought she had been doing. This was about eight living, breathing people standing in front of her. Eight women who had been lied to and mistreated. Nadia saw in them her chance to do some actual good.

After the ICE agent had confirmed her identity and given her access to a lawyer, she had been able to relay messages to all the contacts she could remember in the United States and Mexico. Many of her former colleagues in Mexico had either retired or were dead.

She didn't know what the fate of the women from the factory would be, but the men in charge were listening to her. They saw a potential problem and were ready to do what they could to make it go away. It had nothing to do with law or justice or rights. The lazy and the unimaginative preferred the path of least resistance. Nadia would be released from detention first. Once outside, she could do even more to help the women. For as long as she could stay alive.

Somehow Luz had found some money to pay Mateo Fitzsimmons to take all the women's cases. Nadia admired his adorable, not-yet-jaded youthful belief that he could make a difference. It was dented at the corners, but still intact. Maybe a victory here could stave off the inevitable cynicism that came from the futility of too many losing battles.

The Guatemalan women had strong asylum cases. Because economic oppression was not grounds for granting asylum, country of origin mattered. A few of the Mexican women might get sent back, if they could not prove they had been taken against their will. That would be disappointing, but at least they were free. No matter what happened, there was triumph in the fact that Ostelinda and the other two girls had avoided the system.

Nadia had given her real name—a dead woman's name—because if she hadn't tried everything to help those women—if she had only gone half in—she would have never forgiven herself, and she had learned a lot about not forgiving herself. She could stand failing, but she couldn't live with not trying hard enough.

Anabel Garcés.

The moment she had said the name aloud, she had become paranoid, looking for her assassin at every turn. Isolated in ICE detainment, there was no danger from the other detainees. They had come in with her and had little contact with the outside. The guards were the only potential threat, but they appeared too unambitious to be killers. Negligent and incompetent, but not a direct threat. She could only hope that her name

259

hadn't hit the radar of the men who wanted her dead. Nadia figured that if she could survive her incarceration, she could disappear again. A new name, a new city. Her and Gillies on the road.

The day before her release from the third ICE facility that she had been transferred to, Nadia got a message from Luz through Fitzsimmons. She had tracked down Gillies. He had been released from the VA hospital and would convalesce at Luz's friend's house in Montebello until they figured out something else. There had been some internal bleeding and swelling in his head, which had caused his coma. He suffered a stroke during the six-hour operation, but the doctors had been able to stabilize him and he was recovering. It would be a matter of time before they saw the extent of the damage to his brain and body. He was forgetful and struggled to regain the use of the left side of his body.

It was the best bad news she had heard. Even better than the acceptance of her asylum application and upcoming release. Nadia had convinced herself that Gillies had died. Despite the horror show of medical issues, Nadia knew that if anyone could brush off a coma and a stroke, it was Gillies. He was too dumb to know he couldn't. At the same time, it made her angry that the people that had hurt him would never be properly punished. Ostelinda had managed to take Corey's eye and Luz had shot him in the foot, but that didn't seem like an even trade. Especially considering everything else those pendejos had done.

The time spent in custody had not been easy. Nadia sat on the floor, tired, forced sober, and losing weight. Her shakes had abated, but she sweat more than the water she drank and it gave her a constant headache. She needed to sleep for fifteen hours in a room with only her in it. The physical toll of detention wasn't inhumane by any legal standard, but that didn't mean that it was not cruel. Dogs were treated better than immigrants.

To get her mind off her withdrawals, she wrote for the first time in almost a year. At first, it was interviews with the eight women to get their stories. With that information, she compiled a laundry list of all the crimes committed against the detained women, including as much detail as possible. She linked the church and factory to the imprisonment of migrant women and the murders of Eliseo Delgado and Maite De La Cruz. She had no interest in publishing the story under her name—many of the details and facts would need to be independently confirmed—but a good journalist could use the data as a starting point to expose the Morelands' operation. With the right story, she might be able to shame the justice system into doing their job.

At some point during the process, she began to write notes about her own story. About Ignacio and Jaime. About her role in their deaths. Her guilt. Her pain. Her inability to fix the unfixable and the grief that came with past mistakes.

She didn't know if she would let anyone read it, but she needed to get it down on paper.

"My husband and son wore white. The men on the motorcycle wore black..."

FIFTY-FIVE

Ostelinda did her best to help Gillies into the front seat of Sr. Fitzsimmons's car. They had only met the day before when Luz had picked him up at the VA hospital, but they had become fast friends. Gillies couldn't speak, but he made expressive grunts and was always making jokes and rolling his eyes. No matter the occasion, he had a smile for Ostelinda, even when she accidentally bumped his head on the top of the car door.

From the driver seat, Sr. Fitzsimmons helped with the seat belt. "There are bottles of water in the back," the young lawyer said. "It gets hot out in the desert. It's supposed to get up to ninety-five today."

Ostelinda and Luz looked at each other in the back seat and laughed. They had crossed the desert for days. They were from Mexico. They had known heat. It didn't count as hot until it was in triple digits.

Sr. Fitzsimmons's car gave him directions in English and he translated what the computer lady told him. The drive out to Adelanto to pick up Nadia would take a few hours. He said that it was close to Victorville as if that would mean something to her. While Ostelinda appreciated his effort, the only information she gained was the travel time and the name of the town. Adelanto meant *advancement*, which was a dumb name for a town of prisons.

"When this is done," Luz said, "I have to leave Los Angeles. I'm looking at Oregon. You and Marisol and Anita are welcome to come with me. And so are Nadia and Mr. Gillies."

"Is Oregon like Los Angeles?"

"It is farther north. Closer to Canada than México. It rains a lot, but that makes it green. All the pictures I've seen are big trees and rivers and mountains."

"That sounds nice," Ostelinda said. She did not know what to do, but she did know that Luz had been kind to her and she didn't want to be on her own. Marisol and Anita, too. She didn't think that she could take care of them herself. "We can go together? We can all be in Oregon?"

"Yes," Luz said. "All of us, if that's what Nadia wants, too. She would come later, as she has to stay for her court appearance. Isn't that right?"

"Yes," Fitzsimmons said, concentrating on the road. "Although the backlog is so big, it will be over a year before she gets a hearing date. It's a broken system. Don't get me started. The important thing is that she is being released today."

"But after the hearings, Nadia will come to Oregon with us. We will all be together," Ostelinda said.

"I hope so," Luz said. "You can ask her yourself in a few hours."

One step out of the car and Ostelinda felt the asphalt through the sole of her shoe. She had been overconfident about the heat. Fitzsimmons had pulled the car into the Adelanto Detention Facility parking lot five minutes early. Even with the windows down, the car had quickly become an oven.

The town of Adelanto had reminded her of places she had been in Mexico. A small downtown with few local businesses, more boarded-up than open. Graffiti and trash everywhere. It looked like someone had started to build a town but realized that it was an awful location and had given up before the project was complete.

Fitzsimmons gave them strict instructions before entering the building. "This is an Immigrations and Customs Enforcement processing and detention center. As you have no US identification, it is not a good idea for you to come inside with me. Hopefully, this won't take long, but past experience has taught me that these facilities aren't operated by the smartest, most organized folks. It is the government, after all. Nobody should bother you or even talk to you, but if someone does—in uniform or not—you do not have to speak to them or give them an ID. No matter how demanding or sure of themselves they are. Be polite, say *lawyer* in English and point inside. Nothing will happen to you. You are safe with me."

The young lawyer gave Ostelinda's arm a squeeze that made her feel safe. She sat in the backseat and repeated the word *lawyer* in English— "loller, loller, loller"—until it got too hot. Luz had tried to get her to stay in the car, but after a while she couldn't take it either and joined her outside.

Ostelinda took a drink of water and watched a woman and her two small children get out of a car and walk into the detention center. There were twenty cars in the lot. It was an odd mix. There were older cars that looked like they had never been washed, but also newer looking SUVs and pickup trucks, all spotless. She assumed the cleaner cars were owned by employees, guards, or lawyers.

She knocked on the window and opened the front passenger door. Gillies turned his head as best he could.

"Do you want to get out of the car? Find some shade? I can help you. It is very hot."

Gillies shook his head and flashed his crooked smile, the left side of his mouth mostly paralyzed from the stroke.

Ostelinda held up the bottle of water.

He nodded.

She carefully poured water into his mouth, some of it dribbling down one side of his face and neck. He gave a thumb's up with his right hand. She lifted the bottle from his mouth. There was no need to dry the water that had spilled. Nature would accomplish that in less than a minute.

"If you need anything else, let me know," Ostelinda said.

Gillies nodded.

She stood back up and stretched. She had adjusted to the heat. She could adjust to anything, as long as she was outside and free. Maybe she would like the rain in Oregon.

When Ostelinda saw the van pull into the parking lot, she didn't think anything of it. She didn't recognize the name on the side, *New Life Apostolic Church*. The words in English meant nothing to her. It wasn't until she saw Luz's reaction that she knew something was wrong.

"I knew it wasn't over," Luz said. "It's them."

Ostelinda didn't need more of an explanation. She knew who "them" was. "Why are they here?"

"I don't know," Luz said.

"Why won't they leave us alone?"

"Because that's not who they are. The small need to feel big."

"What should we do?" The sight of Sra. Moreland stepping out of the van made Ostelinda's stomach turn.

"They won't do anything here," Luz said, not sounding confident.

Sra. Moreland and Corey took a couple steps toward Luz and Ostelinda, still forty meters between them. Father Daniel stayed by the van. Sra. Moreland had a bandage over her ear. Gauze had been taped over Corey's eye. He walked using two crutches. He didn't look like he was in much pain, which was disappointing.

"What a nice surprise," Sra. Moreland said. "I didn't know you two would be here. I was only expecting the other one."

"You owe me for my eye, bitch," Corey said, trying to hobble forward menacingly. Sra. Moreland put a hand on his shoulder, stopping him.

"Not here," Sra. Moreland said. "You women have cost me a lot of money."

They stood in the parking lot like one of the old Western movies that Ostelinda's Tío Ricardo loved so much. Two gunfighters on each side of the lot, the tension building in the empty space between them.

"It's over," Luz said. "You won. You got away with murder."

"You don't get to tell me when my business is done," Sra Moreland said. "You don't get to tell me anything. I'm an American. You aren't. You will never be. You're Mexican. Trash."

"You have no power over me or Ostelinda," Luz said, a quaver in her voice. "You can't hurt us anymore."

"Of course, we can. We can hurt you. We can hurt your friends. We can hurt your family in México. We can do whatever we want. You can't stop us. I'm going to make sure you regret ever meeting us."

"I already do," Luz said.

Nadia and Fitzsimmons walked out of the detention facility.

FIFTY-SIX

The minute after Nadia exited the detention facility would be a moment that Luz would relive for the rest of her life. She would replay it in her head. She would see it in her worst sleep. Her brain would fill in the gaps lost in each blink, the details lost when she dived to the ground, shutting her eyes and clapping her hands over her ears. No matter how she remembered it, nothing would change the impact of the event.

The aftermath was easier for Luz to dissect than the actual moment. Too much happened in too short a time to fully absorb the events until they were over. Luz could only see what she saw, experienced from one angle and one perspective.

Nadia's wide smile greeted Luz, as she exited the detention facility. She wasn't prone to smiling, so it appeared that much bigger, reflecting bright white in the desert sun. It grew wider when she spotted Gillies in the passenger seat of Fitzsimmons's car. He gave her a lazy wink and a grin. Tears reflected light off her still-smiling face, as she walked toward him.

Then Nadia saw the church van and the Morelands. She stopped. Her smile disappeared. She wiped the tears from her face with the length of her forearm. Her eyes scanned the parking lot. "How did you know I was here?"

"*The internet, bitch*," Corey said.

"One of your reporter friends came to talk to me," Teresa Moreland said. "I declined, knowing she would only write lies. I was right. The fake news reported a witch hunt hatchet job claiming we're bad people. It was on some Mexican website. It mentioned your upcoming release from this shithole."

Fitzsimmons caught up to Nadia. He seemed to be trying to measure and understand the tension between everyone in the lot. He leaned toward Nadia, keeping his voice down. "Who are these people?"

"The factory people," Nadia said. "The ones who held Ostelinda and the others."

Ostelinda stepped toward the group, but Luz held her arm. It didn't take much force. Ostelinda stopped. Luz thought she heard her growl.

"*This is harassment*," Fitzsimmons said. "*I am going to file for a restraining order. You are in enough legal jeopardy. Leave my clients alone.*"

"*Whatever, Grisham*," Corey said. "*They're not legal people. We can do what we want. They don't have rights.*"

"This is unacceptable," Fitzsimmons said. "I'm getting security. You have no business here." He stormed back into the detention center.

"*Hey, girl*," Corey said, giving Ostelinda a wave. "We got unfinished business."

"Leave me alone," Ostelinda shouted.

"He can't hurt you," Luz said. She put an arm around her and tried to move her back toward the car.

"Pinche puta," Corey shouted at their backs

When Luz turned around, Nadia was no longer looking at the Morelands. Her attention was locked onto something in the parking lot behind Luz. Nadia nodded to herself, as if she had just received the answer to a question someone asked long ago.

"I should have listened to you, Gillies," Nadia yelled. "I love you."

Something was wrong. Luz turned to see what Nadia was looking at. The parking lot looked exactly how it had been. Nothing extraordinary. Cars and pickups, the light refracting from the heat coming off the metal. Then she noticed the white SUV creeping forward. She turned back to Nadia.

Nadia made eye contact with Luz. She mouthed the word, "Corre."

Luz pulled Ostelinda faster toward Fitzsimmons's car.

"What's happening?" Ostelinda asked. "What are you doing?"

Luz ducked down behind the car, pulling Ostelinda down with her. She waved toward Nadia. "Quick, Nadia! Run!"

Teresa Moreland and her son looked at each other confused. They took a few steps back toward the van, but mostly they watched the strange Mexicans do strange things.

Nadia did not run. She walked. Not toward Luz and Ostelinda. Not toward Gillies and the car. She took slow and deliberate steps toward Teresa Moreland and Corey. A glance at the van and she picked up the pace, but not to a run. Nadia was done running.

"What are you doing?" Moreland asked, maybe seeing something in Nadia's expression. She looked frightened. "Get away from us."

In an effort to protect his wife, Father Daniel stepped away from the van to get in between Nadia and Moreland.

Luz screamed out again for Nadia to run.

Ostelinda asked again what was happening.

Gillies, eyes focused on the SUV, groaned a deep guttural noise, the cry of a wounded animal. He knew.

When Nadia reached Moreland, the bigger woman pushed her away, but Nadia persisted. Rather than attack, Nadia pulled Teresa Moreland into an embrace, latching her fingers together behind her back. Father Daniel and Corey grabbed at Nadia's arms and clothes, attempting to detach Nadia from Moreland.

"*Let go of her!*" Corey shouted, punching Nadia's back.

Ostelinda rose to help Nadia, but Luz pulled her back down. When Ostelinda turned to protest, Luz shook her head and said, "No."

Gillies rocked in the seat. He tipped his body out of the car onto the asphalt, landing on his side. He squirmed and crawled a foot or two in Nadia's direction. He roared from deep within his body, all pain and impotence.

The white SUV's tires screeched and the vehicle sped up in the direction of the church van. It stopped as suddenly, skidding to a halt. Both the driver and passenger jumped out. They were both armed. The assassins wore black hoodies.

The sound of their rifles tore through the desert air and echoed as far as the mountains. A sound that Luz would hear for the remainder of her life.

Luz covered Ostelinda's eyes and put her own head down. She could control none of what was happening, but she didn't have to see her friend murdered.

By the time Fitzsimmons and two guards emerged from the detention center, it was over. The SUV had become a cloud of dust in the distance.

Luz ran to Nadia. She fell to her knees and clutched her friend close. Her hands pointlessly tried to stop the flow of blood from the numerous wounds on her chest and stomach. Nadia gasped and coughed blood. Her eyes stared into the unknown.

"Nadia," Luz said. There was too much blood.

"My name is Anabel." She grimaced "Are they dead?"

On the sidewalk near her were the bloody bodies of Daniel and Corey Moreland. Father Daniel Moreland's eyes were wide open, a round wound above his left eye.

Teresa Moreland crawled toward the van, dragging her damaged legs behind her. After a few feet, her body bucked, then crumpled. The only movement left was her right hand which opened and closed, reaching for something she would never attain.

"Yes," Luz said.

"Take care of Gillies. He'll need you." Her voice lost volume.

"I will, Anabel."

"Thank you, Luz." She smiled and with a final effort, she said her last words. "Ignacio. Jaime."

Anabel Garcés died with her son's name on her breath.

Luz set down her body gently. She stood and walked, lost in a daze, to Ostelinda who immediately embraced her. Luz held her hands out to the side to avoid getting more blood on the girl.

"Why?" Ostelinda asked.

"Later," Luz said. "Mr. Gillies needs us. He needs us."

Luz and Ostelinda rushed to Gillies and helped him back into the passenger seat. His cries shook his body. His face was red with anger and pain.

Luz collapsed against the side of the car, an arm around Ostelinda. She tried to stay strong for the girl, but felt the pain rise from her stomach.

When twenty armed men in full tactical gear exited the detention center a few minutes later, running around like idiots in formation and disrupting the silence with military commands, Luz finally stopped crying. Her laughter held just as much pain.

FIFTY-SEVEN

The madman on the bus hated Mexicans. Among others. He hated Muslims and gay people, too. He had barked nonsense from the moment he boarded on Burnside Avenue in downtown Portland.

He sat five seats back, but turned his attention to Luz, spitting hate in her direction.

Luz appeared to be the only one who wasn't shocked by the poor chiflado's statements. She had heard so much worse that all she could feel was pity for the poor soul. She did her best to ignore him.

After a half-minute of earsplitting shouting, two young white men—one with dreadlocked hair and a tie-dyed shirt, the other in a suit and tie—approached the madman and informed him that what he was saying was racist. They suggested that he keep his voice down, as he was disturbing the other passengers.

The madman protested with a few loud barks but remained silent until he got out at the next stop. The bus passengers clapped when he was on the sidewalk.

Right before the doors closed, he yelled his final salvo. "*If a country has no borders, it is not a country. America is doomed because of social justice warriors like you. Free speech is dead! Political correctness gone mad!*"

A few people shook the hands of the white men that had confronted the madman. Nobody asked if Luz was okay. No one on the bus spoke to her or even looked her way. It didn't bother her. She had always preferred her Mexican invisibility. Only the mad could see her.

The working class neighborhood in the suburb of Gresham had many Latin American immigrants. Similar to her old neighborhood in Boyle Heights, except it was greener with more trees and space, and the air didn't smell like petrol. A growing number of young white people had started moving to the neighborhood. Not the same white people that flew their rebel flags outside their houses or lived in the methamphetamine shacks at the edges, but college students with wispy mustaches and guitars. Having moved a few times due to the changing migration of gentrification, she knew how that story ended. She had a few years in the neighborhood before prices rose and she'd move to where the kitchen workers and landscapers lived.

As far as the landlord was concerned, Gillies and Luz were married and Ostelinda, Marisol and Anita were their daughters. It made for a plausible enough story, even if the girls looked nothing like either of them. Nobody questioned it. The lease for the small house was in Gillies's name, so for the first time Luz didn't have to pay the usual "illegal tax."

In their small suburban home, she no longer felt like an outlaw on the run. She knew she lived in a country where she was unwanted, but within those walls she was safe. Gillies had even offered to marry her for real—"*without any obligation for a round of tube snake boogie*"—but because she had entered the country illegally, it wouldn't have helped any residency request. It was a kind gesture, but things worked the way they were.

Ostelinda found a job taking care of a young couple's twins. They lived in a big house in the Columbia River Gorge. She took the bus out there every day and got a ride home every night. She studied English on her commute and at night. Gillies taught her all the swear words, even some that Luz had never heard. When Ostelinda gained more confidence in her English, she planned to take the GED and eventually attend college.

Marisol and Anita were both enrolled at the local high school. It wasn't easy for them, but there were enough other Spanish-speaking students that they had made friends and had people to help them. They lived in fear of being called out as undocumented, but found pockets in the day when they could be teenagers.

Luz got off the bus at her stop. A light rain created a shroud of gray mist. She had an umbrella in Eliseo's freshly repaired and waterproofed backpack, but she wanted to feel the rain. The water on her face felt clean and fresh.

Nadia—Luz knew her name was Anabel, but she would always be Nadia to her—was buried in Mexico next to her husband and son, graves Nadia had never seen. The newspaper where she had worked for over a decade paid for the cost with help from a couple of organizations dedicated to the awareness of the threats to journalists around the world.

Nadia's death made the national news. Twenty-five seconds on two of the networks, but it was reported as a drive-by shooting that took four lives. The headline in the Los Angeles Times read, *"Christian Preacher And Three Other Victims Gunned Down At ICE Facility."* It mostly described the gory aftermath, thin on actual details.

Luz kept in touch with Mateo Fitzsimmons. He was able to secure asylum appointments or temporary permission to stay for all but one of the women from the factory. While no one was charged with their imprisonment, with the alleged perpetrators dead, it was easier for ICE to accept the events as described. In other words, it reduced their paperwork. Mateo Fitzsimmons offered to file paperwork for Luz, Ostelinda, and the girls now that the assaults on Corey and Teresa Moreland were moot, but none of them trusted the system enough to expose themselves to it.

The death of Eliseo Delgado and Maite De La Cruz was officially designated as a murder/suicide and the case was closed by the LAPD's Detective Larios. It didn't matter to Luz. She knew the truth. The correction on a piece of paper would be nothing more than empty ceremony. Every immigrant was accustomed to government documents that supplied their own presupposed narrative. Luz had come as close to justice as an unauthorized immigrant could expect.

The essay that Nadia had written while in detention—the final piece of writing by Anabel Garcés—was published online by a number of different groups. It probably wouldn't change anything, but Luz was satisfied that a version of the truth existed. There were so many people claiming truths. All that Luz could hope for was that the truest version of the truth was available to those who sought it out.

Walking to the front door, Luz pulled a dandelion from between a crack in the concrete walk. She held it for a moment. The flower wasn't any less beautiful than any of the others in her yard. She walked with the dandelion to the edge of the yard and replanted it in the dirt under the magnolia tree.

Luz set her backpack down by the front door. She smelled tomatoes, onions, and garlic.

"I made dinner," Gillies said, walking out of the kitchen with the help of his walker. He was getting around better and his speech was improving, but he still had a long way to go. He didn't let it stop him though.

"Really?" Luz smiled, walking with him into the small dining area.

Gillies motioned with a sweep of his arm toward the dining room table. Two pizza boxes and a stack of plates sat on the table.

"You said you were going to start eating healthier," Luz said. "I was standing right next to you when you promised the doctor."

"*One of them is veggie,*" Gillies said. "*Baby steps. Although full disclosure, that one has extra cheese on it. I'm comfortable in my failings.*" He looked at his watch. "*Oh, shit. Got to go.*"

He made his way to the front door, grabbing his scarf and jacket off the hook.

"I thought we were having the delicious dinner you made."

"I have a meeting," Gillies said. "That's for you and the girls."

"Take an umbrella. It's raining a little."

"Hate the things. I prefer getting wet." Gillies gave her a wave and left, the door closely softly behind him.

Luz put the pizzas in the refrigerator. She would heat them up when the girls were all home. They could have dinner together. Luz parked herself on the couch.

On the mantel in front of her sat two copper boxes. The one on the left held Eliseo's ashes. The other, Maite's. Luz had meant to buy proper urns, but never got around to it. She now appreciated the simplicity of the containers that had come in the mail from the hospital.

Luz stood and walked to the mantel. She picked up the box with her son's ashes inside. Luz wanted to feel its weight, lighter than her expectation. She hadn't held Eliseo since he was a small boy. Once he had turned seven, he outright refused. Now she could hold him whenever she wanted without any argument. She set the copper box back down, her reflection staring back at her on the shiny surface.

The door opened behind her. Luz turned. Ostelinda walked in the front door and set down her bag. Luz smiled at her oldest daughter. "You're home."

Acknowledgments

Money might have its function, but it's not important. The pursuit of money is unimaginative and uninspired. When it comes to money, I have never been a rich man nor strived to become one. Instead, I've always measured my wealth by the number of interesting people in my life. By that standard, I am a very wealthy man.

I have been very fortunate to have so many incredible people in my life. While I did all the writing on this book, there are so many people to thank for it getting ready for publication and making it into the world. I won't have nearly enough room for everyone, but I'll do my best. If you know me and your name isn't on the list, it probably should be. I'll write it in myself the next time I see you.

To begin with, a huge thank you to Chantelle Aimée Osman & Jason Pinter at Polis/Agora for believing in this book and for all the hard work they put into the publication and promotion. As with any new publisher, I didn't know what to expect, but I am ecstatic with the process so far. And to be included in such a strong catalogue with so many other fantastic writers is an honor.

Next up is a big, fat list of names. These are people who gave the book an early read, writers who gave me advice or a recommendation to an agent (even if I still remain agentless), or who just listened to me complain at just the right time. I am blessed to have every single one of these people my life. They probably don't even know how much of an impact they've had, but this book might not exist without Jacque Ben-Zekry, Renato Bratkovič, Steve Cavanagh, Angel Luis Colón, Jose

Corona, Hilary Davidson, Christa Faust, Matthew FitzSimmons, Barry Graham, Chris Holm, Gabino Iglesias, Bart Lessard, Jess Lourey, Erica Ruth Neubauer, Sheila Redling, Todd Robinson, Marcus Sakey, Helen Smith, and Jay Stringer.

Not many people would throw everything in a storage unit and hit the road with me. There is constant uncertainty in how I choose to live my life, but there's one thing I can count on. I'm the luckiest man in the world to have spent the last twenty-six years with a woman of amazing courage, creativity, humor, intelligence, beauty, and just the correct amount of insanity. I love our ongoing adventure together, and I love you, Roxanne.

And finally, thank you to everyone who has ever supported my work. To the readers and booksellers and event organizers and librarians. When my first book came out nine years ago, I couldn't imagine making a career out of doing something that I enjoy so much. I do the work, but the readers make a career happen. I will always do my best to never take that for granted.

My first six books were all written in the Portland, Oregon pub, Beulahland. This book was written in no single place. It was written on strangers' dining room tables, makeshift desks, and in bars, cafes, and libraries around the world. Through all that madness, the bulk of the writing and my best work got done at the Coffee Pod in Glasgow, Scotland; Kavana Lav in Zagreb, Croatia; and the Ramon Llull Library in Palma de Mallorca, Spain.

I support the Florence Immigrant and Refugee Rights Project, a nonprofit organization that provides free legal and social services to adults and unaccompanied children in immigration custody in Arizona. You can learn more and donate to the Florence Project at www.firrp.org.

About the Author

Johnny Shaw was born and raised on the Calexico/Mexicali border in the stifling heat of the California desert. He is the author of seven novels including the Jimmy Veeder Fiasco border novels: *Dove Season*, *Plaster City*, and *Imperial Valley*.

Johnny has been nominated for the Anthony Award three times, winning for Best Paperback Original in 2013 for the comedic adventure novel *Big Maria*. He has been shortlisted for a number of awards and has won the Spotted Owl Award twice. His short fiction has appeared in *Thuglit, Plots with Guns, Crime Factory, Shotgun Honey*, and numerous anthologies.

He was the Grand Marshal of the Holtville Carrot Festival Parade in 2016, which means nothing to you, but everything to him. You can find Johnny on Twitter at @BloodandTacos.

He Said, She Said

Journal

....
....
....
....
....
....
....
....
....
....
....
....
....
....
....
....
....
....
....
....
....
....
....
....
....
....
....
....
....
....
....
....
....
....
....